36 183
£2.50

The Chestermark Instinct

By
J.S. Fletcher

We are pleased to present this easier-to-read, specially formatted Classic Mystery Story, The Chestermark Instinct, by J.S. Fletcher For your Reading Pleasure

Copyright © 2022
All Rights Reserved

Originally Published in 1919
This Edition Published in 2022

ISBN: 9798371754431

Chapter 1

Every Monday morning, when the clock of the old parish church in Scarnham Market-Place struck eight, Wallington Neale asked himself why on earth he had chosen to be a bank clerk. On all the other mornings of the week this question never occurred to him. On Sunday he never allowed a thought of the bank to cross his mind. From Sunday to Saturday he was firmly settled in the usual rut, and never dreamed of tearing himself out of it. But Sunday's break was unsettling. There was always an effort in starting afresh on Monday.

The striking of St. Alkmund's clock at eight on Monday morning invariably found him sitting down to his breakfast in his rooms, overlooking the quaint old Market-Place, once more faced by the fact a week of dull, uninteresting work lay before him. He would go to the bank at nine, and at the bank he would remain, more or less, until five. He would do it again on Tuesday, and on Wednesday, and on Thursday and on Friday, and on Saturday. One afternoon, strolling in the adjacent country, he had seen a horse walking round and round and round in a small paddock, turning a crank which worked some machine or other in an adjoining shed. On this particular Monday morning, Neale, happening to catch sight of his reflection in the mirror which stood on his parlor mantelpiece, propounded the usual question with added force. There were reasons. It was a beautiful morning. It was early spring.

There was a blue sky, and the rooks and jackdaws were circling in a clear air about the church tower and over the old Market-Cross. He could hear thrushes singing in the trees in the Vicarage garden, close by. Everything was young. And he was young. It would have been affectation on his part to deny either his youth or his good looks. He glanced at his mirrored self without pride, but with due recognition of his good figure, his strong muscles, his handsome, boyish face, with its cluster of chestnut hair and steady grey eyes. All he knew, wanted life, animation, movement. At twenty-three he was longing for something to take him out of the treadmill round in which he had been fixed for five years. He had no taste for handing out money in exchange for checks, in posting up ledgers, in writing dull, formal letters. He would have been much happier with an old flannel shirt, open at the throat, a pick in his hands, making a new road in a new country, or in driving a path through some primeval wood. There would have been liberty in either occupation. He could have flung down the pick at any moment and taken up the hunter's gun. He could have turned right or left at his own will in the unexplored forest. But there at the bank it was just doing the same thing over and over again. What he had done last week he would do again this week. What had happened last year would happen again this year. It was all pure, unadulterated, dismal monotony. Like most things, it had come about without design.

He had just drifted into it. His father and mother had both died when he was a boy and inherited a small property which brought in precisely one hundred and fifty pounds a year. It was tied up to him in such a fashion he would have his three pounds a week as long as ever he lived. But as his guardian, John Horbury, the manager of Chestermarke's Bank at Scarnham, pointed out to him when he left school, he needed more than three pounds a week if he wished to live comfortably and like a gentleman. Still, a hundred and fifty a year of sure and settled income was a fine thing, an uncommonly fine thing. All that was necessary was to supplement it.

Therefore a nice, quiet, genteel profession...banking, to wit. Light work, an honorable calling, an eminently respectable one. In a few years he would have another hundred and fifty a year. A few years more, and he would be a manager, with at least six hundred. He might, well before he was a middle-aged man, be commanding a salary of a thousand a year. Banking, by all means, counseled John Horbury and offered him a vacancy which had just then arisen at Chestermarke's. And Neale, willing to be guided by a man for whom he had much respect, took the post, and settled down in the old bank in the quiet, sleepy market-town, where one day was precisely like another day and every year his dislike for his work increased, and sometimes grew unbearably keen, especially when spring skies and spring air set up a sudden stirring in his blood. On this Monday morning that stirring amounted to something very like a physical ache.

"Hang the old bank!" he muttered. "I'd rather be a ploughman!"

Nevertheless, the bank must be attended, and, at ten minutes to nine, Neale lighted a cigarette, put on his hat, and strolled slowly across the Market-Place. Although he knew every single one of its cobblestones, every shop window, every landmark in it, that queer old square always fascinated him. It was a bit of old England. The ancient church and equally ancient Moot Hall spread along one side of it; the other three sides were filled with gabled and half-timbered houses; the Market-Cross which stood in the middle of the open space had been erected there in Henry the Seventh's time.

A midst all the change and development of the nineteenth century, Scarnham had been left untouched. Even the bank itself was a time-worn building, and the manager's house which flanked it was still older. Underneath all these ancient structures were queer nooks and corners, secret passages and stairs, hiding-places, cellars going far beneath the gardens at the backs of the houses. Neale, as a boy, had made many an exploration in them, especially beneath the bank-house, which was a veritable treasury of concealed stairways and cunningly contrived doors in the black oak of the paneling. But on this occasion Neale did not stare admiringly at the old church, nor at the plastered Moot Hall, nor at the toppling gables.

His eyes were fixed on something else, something unusual. As soon as he walked out of the door of the house in which he lodged he saw his two fellow-clerks, Shirley and Patten, standing on the steps of the hall by which entrance was joined to the bank and to the bank-house. They stood there looking about them. Now they looked towards Finkleway, a narrow street which led to the railway station at the far end of the town. Now they looked towards Middlegate, a street which led into the open country, in the direction of Ellersdeane, where Gabriel Chestermarke, senior proprietor of the bank, resided. All that was unusual. If Patten, a mere boy, had been lounging there, Neale would not have noticed it. But it was Shirley's first duty, on arriving every morning, to get the keys at the house door, and to let himself into the bank by the adjoining private entrance. It was Patten's duty, on arrival, to take the letter-bag to the post-office and bring the bank's correspondence back in it. Never, in all his experience, had Neale seen any of Chestermarke's clerks lounging on the steps at nine o'clock in the morning, and he quickened his pace. Shirley, turning from a prolonged stare towards Finkleway, caught sight of him.

"Can't get in," he observed laconically, in answer to Neale's inquiring look. "Mr. Horbury isn't there, and he's got the keys."

"What do you mean...isn't there!" asked Neale, mounting the steps. "Not in the house?"

"Mean just what I say," replied Shirley. "Mrs. Carswell says she hasn't seen him since Saturday. She thinks he's been week-ending. I've been looking out for him coming along from the station. But if he came in by the 8.30, he's a long time getting up here. And if he hasn't come by that, there's no other train till the 10.45."

Neale made no answer. He, too, glanced towards Finkleway, and then at the church clock. It was just going to strike nine and the station was only eight minutes away at the most. He passed the two junior clerks, went down the hall to the door of the bank-house, and entered. And just within he came face to face with the housekeeper, Mrs. Carswell. Mrs. Carswell had kept house for John Horbury for some years. Neale remembered her from boyhood.

He had always been puzzled about her age. Of late, since he knew more of grown-up folk, he had been still more puzzled. Sometimes he thought she was forty, sometimes he was sure she could not be more than thirty-two or three. Anyway, she was a fine, handsome woman, tall, perfectly shaped, with glossy black hair and dark eyes, and a firm, resolute mouth. It was rarely that Mrs. Carswell went out, when she did, she was easily the best-looking woman in Scarnham. Few Scarnham people, however, had the chance of cultivating her acquaintance. Mrs. Carswell kept herself to herself and seemed content to keep up her reputation as a model housekeeper. She ordered Mr. Horbury's domestic affairs in perfect fashion, and it had come upon Neale as a surprise to hear Shirley say Mrs. Carswell did not know where the manager was.

"What's all this?" he demanded, as he met her within the hall. "Shirley says Mr. Horbury isn't at home? Where is he, then?"

"But I don't know, Mr. Neale," replied the housekeeper. "I know no more than you do. I've been expecting him to come in by that 8.30 train, but he can't have done that, or he'd have been up here by now."

"Perhaps it's late," suggested Neale.

"No...it's in," she said. "I saw it come in from my window, at the back. It was on time. So I don't know what's become of him."

"But what about Saturday?" asked Neale. "Shirley says you said Mr. Horbury went off on Saturday. Didn't he leave any word...didn't he say where he was going?"

"Mr. Horbury went out on Saturday evening," answered Mrs. Carswell. "He didn't say a word about where he was going. He went out just before dusk, as if for a walk. I'd no idea he wasn't at home until Sunday morning. You see, the servants and I went to bed at our usual time on Saturday night, and though he wasn't in then, I thought nothing of it, because, of course, he'd his latch-key. He was often out late at night, as you know, Mr. Neale. And when I found he hadn't come back, as I did find out before breakfast yesterday, I thought nothing of that either. I thought he'd gone to see some friend or other, and had been persuaded to stay the night. Then, when he didn't come home yesterday at all, I thought he was staying the week-end somewhere. So I wasn't anxious, nor surprised. But I am surprised he's not back here first thing this morning."

"So am I," agreed Neale. "And more than surprised." He stood for a moment, running over the list of the manager's friends and acquaintances in the neighborhood, and shook his head as he came to the end of his mental reckoning of it. "It's very odd," he remarked. "Very surprising, Mrs. Carswell."

"It's all the more surprising," remarked the housekeeper, "because of his going off for his holiday tomorrow. And Miss Fosdyke's coming down from London today to go with him."

Neale pricked his ears. Miss Fosdyke was the manager's niece, a young lady whom Neale remembered as a mere slip of a girl he had met years before and never seen since.

"I didn't know that," he remarked.

"Neither did Mr. Horbury until Saturday afternoon... that is, for certain," said Mrs. Carswell. "He'd asked her to go with him to Scotland on this holiday, but it wasn't settled. However, he got a wire from her, about tea-time on Saturday, to say she'd go, and would be down here today. They're to start tomorrow morning."

Neale turned to the door. He was distinctly puzzled and uneasy. He had known John since his own childhood, and always regarded him as the personification of everything that was precise, systematic, and regular. All things considered, it was most remarkable he should not be at the bank at opening hours. And already a vague suspicion something had happened began to steal into his mind.

"Did you happen to notice which way he went, Mrs. Carswell?" he asked. "Was it towards the station?"

"He went out down the garden and through the orchard," replied the housekeeper. "He could have got to the station that way, of course. But I do know he never said a word about going anywhere by train, and he'd no bag or anything with him...he'd nothing but that old oak stick he generally carried when he went out for his walks."

Neale pushed open the house door and went into the outer hall to the junior clerks. Little as he cared about banking as a calling, he was punctilious about rules and observances, and it seemed to him somewhat indecorous the staff of a bank should hang about its front door, as if they were workshop assistants awaiting the arrival of a belated foreman.

"Better come inside the house, Shirley," he said. "Patten, you go to the post-office and get the letters."

"No good without the bag," answered Patten, a calm youth of seventeen. "Tried that once before. Don't you know! They've one key and we've the other."

"Well, come inside, then," commanded Neale. "It doesn't look well to hang about those steps."

"Might just as well go away," muttered Shirley, stepping into the hall. "If Horbury's got to come back by train from wherever he's gone to, he can't get here till the 10.45, and then he's got to walk up. Might as well go home for an hour."

"The partners will be here before an hour's over," said Neale. "One of them is always here by ten."

Shirley, a somewhat grumpy-countenanced young man,

made no answer. He began to pace the hall with looks of eminent dissatisfaction. But he had only taken a turn or two when a quietly appointed one-horse coupé brougham came up to the open door, and a well-known face was seen at its window. Gabriel Chestermarke, senior proprietor, had come an hour before his time.

Chapter 2

Had the three young men waiting in the hall not been so familiar with him by reason of daily and hourly acquaintance, the least observant among them would surely have paused in whatever task he was busied with, if Gabriel had crossed his path for the first time. The senior partner of Chestermarke's Bank was a noticeable person. Wallington Neale, who possessed some small gift of imagination, always felt his principal suggested something more than was accounted for by his mere presence. He was a little, broadly built man, somewhat inclined to stoutness, who carried himself in very upright fashion, and habitually wore the look of a man engaged in operations of serious and far-reaching importance, further heightened by an air of reserve and a trick of sparing in speech.

But more noticeable than anything else in Gabriel was his head, a member of his body which was much out of proportion to the rest of it. It was a very big, well-shaped head, on which, out of doors, invariably rested the latest-styled and glossiest of silk hats. No man had ever seen Gabriel in any other form of head-gear, unless it was in a railway carriage, there he condescended to assume a checked cap. Underneath the brim of the silk hat looked out a countenance as remarkable as the head of which it was a part.

A broad, smooth forehead, a pair of large, deep-set eyes, the pupils of which were black as coal, a prominent, slightly hooked nose, a firm, thin-lipped mouth, a square, resolute jaw. These features were thrown into prominence by the extraordinary pallor of his face, and the dark shade of the hair which framed it. The black hair, those black eyes, burning always with a strange, slumbering fire, the colorless cheeks, the vigorous set of the lips, these made an effect on all who came in contact with the banker which was of a not wholly comfortable nature. It was as if you were talking to a statue rather than to a fellow-creature. Mr. Chestermarke stepped quietly from his brougham and walked up the steps. He was one of those men who are never taken aback and never show surprise, and as his eyes ran over the three young men, there was no sign from him that he saw anything out of the common. But he turned to Neale, as senior clerk, with one word.

"Well?"

Neale glanced uncomfortably at the house door. "Mr. Horbury is not at home," he answered. "He has the keys."

Mr. Chestermarke made no reply. His hand went to his waistcoat pocket, his feet moved lower down the hall to a side-door sacred to the partners. He produced a key, opened the door, and motioned the clerks to enter. Once within, he turned into the partners room. Five minutes passed before his voice was heard.

"Neale!"

Neale hurried in and found the banker standing on the hearth-rug, beneath the portrait of a former Chestermarke, founder of the bank in a bygone age. He was suddenly struck by the curious resemblance between the dead Chestermarke and the living one, and he wondered he had never seen it before. But Mr. Chestermarke gave him no time for speculation.

"Where is Mr. Horbury?" he asked.

Neale told all he knew. The banker listened in his usual fashion, keeping his eyes steadily fixed on his informant. When Neale had finished, Mr. Chestermarke shook his head.

"If Horbury had meant to come into town by the 8.30 train and had missed it," he remarked, "he would have wired or telephoned by this. Telephoned, of course, there are telephones at every station on that branch line. Very well, let things go on."

Neale went out and set his fellow-clerks to the usual routine. Patten went for the letters. Neale carried them into the partners room. At ten o'clock the street door was opened. A customer or two began to drop in. The business of the day had begun. It went on just as it would have gone on if Mr. Horbury had been away on holiday. And at half-past ten in walked the junior partner, Joseph Chestermarke. Joseph was the exact opposite of his uncle. He was so much his opposite it was difficult to believe, seeing them together, they were related to each other. Joseph, a man of apparently thirty years of age, was tall and loose of figure, easy of demeanor, and a little untidy in his dress.

He wore a not over well-fitting tweed suit, a slouch hat, a flannel shirt. His brown beard usually needed trimming. He affected loose, flowing neckties, more suited to an artist than to a banker. His face was amiable in expression, a little weak, a little speculative. All these characteristics came out most strongly when he and his uncle were seen in company. Nothing could be more in contrast to the precise severity of Gabriel than the somewhat slovenly carelessness of Joseph. Joseph, indeed, was the last man in the world any one would ever have expected to see in charge and direction of a bank, and there were people in Scarnham who said he was no more than a lay-figure, and Gabriel did all the business. The junior partner passed through the outer room, nodding affably to the clerks and went into the private parlor. Several minutes elapsed, then a bell rang. Neale answered it, and Shirley and Patten glanced at each other and shook their heads: already they scented an odor of suspicion and uncertainty.

"What's up?" whispered Patten, leaning forward over his desk to Shirley, who stood between it and the counter. "Something wrong?"

"Something Gabriel doesn't like, anyhow," muttered Shirley. "Did you see his eyes when Neale said Horbury wasn't here? If Horbury doesn't turn up by this next train...ah!"

"Think he's sloped?" asked Patten, already seething with boyish desire of excitement. "Done a bunk with the money?"

But Shirley shook his head at the closed door through which Neale had vanished.

"They're carpeting Neale about it, anyhow," he answered. "Gabriel will want to know the whys and wherefores, you bet. But Neale won't tell us anything, he's too thick with Horbury."

Neale, entering the partners room, found them in characteristic attitudes. The senior partner sat at his desk, stern, upright, his eyes burning a little more fiercely than usual. The junior, his slouch hat still on his head, his hands thrust in his pockets, lounged against the mantelpiece, staring at his uncle.

"Now, Neale," said Gabriel. "What do you know about this? Have you any idea where Mr. Horbury is?"

"None," replied Neale. "None whatever!"

"When did you see him last?" demanded Gabriel. "You often see him out of bank hours, I know."

"I last saw him here at two o'clock on Saturday," replied Neale. "I have not seen him since."

"And you never heard him mention he was thinking of going away for the weekend?" asked Gabriel.

"No," replied Neale.

He made his answer tersely and definitely, having an idea the senior partner looked at him as if he thought something was being kept back. And Gabriel, after a moment's pause, shifted some of the papers on his desk, with an impatient movement.

"Ask Mr. Horbury's housekeeper to step in here for a few minutes," he said.

Neale went out by the private door, and presently returned with Mrs. Carswell. By this time Joseph had lounged over to his own desk and seated himself, and when the housekeeper came in tilted his chair back and sat idly swaying in it while he watched her and his uncle. But Gabriel, waving Mrs. Carswell to a seat, remained upright as ever, and as he turned to the housekeeper, he motioned Neale to stay in the room.

"Just tell us all you know about Mr. Horbury's movements on Saturday afternoon and evening, Mrs. Carswell," he said. "This is a most extraordinary business altogether, and I want to account for it. You say he went out just about dusk."

Mrs. Carswell repeated the story which she had told to Neale. The two partners listened. Gabriel keenly attentive; Joseph as if he were no more than mildly interested.

"Odd," remarked Gabriel, when the story had come to an end. "Most strange! Very well, thank you, Mrs. Carswell. Neale," he added, when the housekeeper had gone away, "Mr. Horbury always carried the more important keys on him, didn't he?"

"Always," responded Neale.

"Very good! Let things go on," said Gabriel. "But don't come bothering me or Mr. Joseph Chestermarke unless you're obliged to. Of course, Mr. Horbury may come in by the next train. That'll do, Neale."

Neale went back to the outer room. Things went on, but the missing manager did not come in by the 10.45, and nothing had been heard or seen of him at noon, when Patten went to get his dinner. Nor had anything been seen or heard at one o'clock, when Patten came back, and it became Shirley and Neale's turn to go out. And thereupon arose a difficulty. In the ordinary course the two elder clerks would have left for an hour and the manager would have been on duty until they returned. But now the manager was not there.

"You go," said Neale to Shirley. "I'll wait. Perhaps Mr. Joseph will come out."

Shirley went, but neither of the partners emerged from the private room. As a rule they both went across to the Scarnham Arms Hotel at half-past one for lunch. A private room had been kept for them at the old-world hostelry from time immemorial. But now they remained within their parlor, apparently interned from their usual business world. And Neale had a very good idea of what they were doing.

The bank's strong room was entered from that parlor. Gabriel and Joseph were examining and checking its contents. The knowledge distressed Neale beyond measure, and it was only by a resolute effort he could give his mind to his duties. Two o'clock had gone, and Shirley had come back, before the bell rang again. Neale went into the private room and knew at once something had happened. Gabriel stood by his desk, which was loaded with papers and documents. Joseph leaned against a sideboard, where a decanter of sherry and a box of biscuits laid. He had a glass of wine in one hand, and a half-nibbled biscuit in the other. The smell of the sherry, fine old brown stuff, which the clerks were permitted to taste now and then, on such occasions as the partners birthdays filled the room.

"Neale," said Gabriel, "have you been out to lunch? No? Take a glass of wine and eat a biscuit, we shall all have to put off our lunches for an hour or so."

Neale obeyed, more because he was under order than because he was hungry. He was too much bothered, too full of vague fears, to think of his midday dinner. He took the glass which Joseph handed to him, and picked a couple of biscuits out of the box. And at the first sip Gabriel spoke again.

"Neale!" he said. "You've been here five years, so one

can speak confidentially. There's something wrong...seriously wrong. Securities are missing. Securities representing...a lot!"

Neale's face flushed as if he had been charged with abstracting those securities. His hand shook as he set down his glass, and he looked helplessly from one partner to another. Joseph merely shook his head, and poured out another glass of sherry for himself. Gabriel shook his head, too, but with a different expression.

"We don't know exactly how things are," he continued. "But there's the fact, on a superficial examination. And Horbury! Of all men in the world, Horbury!"

"I can't believe it, Mr. Chestermarke!" exclaimed Neale. "Surely, sir, there's some mistake!"

Joseph brushed crumbs of biscuit off his beard and wagged his head.

"No mistake!" he said softly. "None! The thing is... what's best to do? Because he'd have laid his plans. It'll all have been thought out carefully."

"I'm afraid so," assented Gabriel. "That's the worst of it. Everything points to premeditation. And when a man has been so fully trusted..."

A knock at the door prefaced the introduction of Shirley's head. He glanced into the room with an obvious desire to see what was going on, but somehow contrived to fix his eyes on the senior partner.

"Lord Ellersdeane, sir," he announced. "Can he see you?"

The two partners looked at each other in evident surprise. Then Gabriel moved to the door and bowed solemnly to some person outside.

"Will your lordship come in?" he said politely.

Lord Ellersdeane, a big, bustling, country-squire type of man, came into the room, nodding cheerily to its occupants.

"Sorry to disturb you, Mr. Chestermarke," he said. "I understand Horbury isn't at home, but of course you'll do just as well. The Countess and I only got back from abroad night before last. She wants her jewels, so I'll take them with me, if you please."

Gabriel, who was drawing forward a chair, took his hand off it and stared at his visitor.

"The Countess's jewels!" he said. "Does your lordship

mean..."

"Deposited them with Horbury, you know, some weeks ago when we went abroad," replied Lord Ellersdeane. "Safe keeping, you know, said he'd lock them up."

Gabriel turned slowly to Joseph. But Joseph shook his head and Neale, glancing from one partner to the other, felt himself turning sick with apprehension.

Chapter 3

Gabriel, after the one look at his nephew, turned again to the Earl, politely motioning him to the chair which he had already drawn forward. And the Earl, whose eyes had been wandering over the pile of documents on the senior partner's desk, glancing curiously at the open door of the strong room, and generally taking in a sense of some unusual occurrence, dropped into it and looked expectantly at the banker.

"There's nothing wrong?" he asked suddenly. "You look...surprised."

Gabriel stiffened his already upright figure.

"Surprised, yes!" he answered. "And something more than surprised...I am astonished! Your lordship left the Countess's jewels with our manager? May I ask when and under what circumstances?"

"About six weeks ago," replied the Earl promptly. "As a rule the jewels are kept at my bankers in London. The Countess wanted them to wear at the Hunt Ball, so I fetched them from London myself. Then, as we were going off to the Continent two days after the ball, and sailing direct from Kingsport to Hamburg, I didn't want the bother of going up to town with them, and I thought of Horbury. So I drove in here with them one evening, the night before we sailed, as a matter of fact and asked him to lock them up until our return. And as I said just now, we only got home the night before last, and we're going up to town tomorrow, and the Countess wants them to take with her. Of course, you've got them all right?"

Gabriel spread out his hands.

"I know nothing whatever about them!" he said. "I never heard of them being here."

"Nor I," affirmed Joseph. "Not a word!"

Gabriel looked at Neale, and drew Lord Ellersdeane's attention to him.

"Our senior clerk, Mr. Neale," he said. "Neale, have you

heard of this transaction?"

"Never!" replied Neale. "Mr. Horbury never mentioned it to me."

Gabriel waved his hand towards the open door of the strong room. "Any valuables of that sort would have been in there," he remarked. "There is nothing of that sort there beyond what I and my nephew know of. I am sure your lordship's jewels are not there."

"But...Horbury?" exclaimed the Earl. "Where is he? He would tell you!"

"We don't know where Mr. Horbury is," answered Gabriel "The truth may as well be told, he's missing. And so are some of our most valuable securities."

The Earl slowly looked from one partner to another. His face flushed, almost as hotly as if he had been accused of theft.

"Oh, come!" he said. "Horbury, now, of all men! Come...come! You don't mean to tell me Horbury's been playing games of that sort? There must be some mistake."

"I shall be glad to be assured I am making it," said Gabriel coolly. "But it will be more to the purpose if your lordship will tell us all about the deposit of these jewels. And there's an important matter which I must first mention. We have not the honor of reckoning your lordship among our customers. Therefore, whatever you handed to Horbury was handed to him privately, not to us."

Joseph nodded his head at that, and the Earl stirred a little uneasily in his chair.

"Oh, well!" he said. "I...to tell you the truth, I didn't think about that, Mr. Chestermarke. It's true I don't keep any account with you...it's never seemed...er, necessary, you know. But, of course, I knew Horbury so well, he's a member of our golf club and our archaeological society...that..."

"Precisely," interrupted Gabriel, with a bow. "You came to Mr. Horbury privately. Not to the firm."

"I came to him knowing he was your manager, and a man to be thoroughly trusted, and he'd have safes and things in which he could deposit valuables in perfect safety," answered the Earl. "I never reflected for a moment on the niceties of the matter. I just explained to him that I wanted those jewels taken care of, and handed them over. That's all!"

"And their precise nature?" asked Gabriel.

"And their value?" added Joseph.

"As to their nature," replied the Earl, "there was my wife's coronet, her diamond necklace, and the Ellersdeane butterfly, of which I suppose all the world's heard...heirloom, you know. It's a thing that can be worn in a lady's hair or as a pendant...diamonds, of course. As to their value....well, I had them valued some years ago. They're worth about a hundred thousand pounds."

Gabriel turned to his desk and began to arrange some papers on it, and Neale, who was watching everything with close attention, saw his fingers trembled a little. He made no remark, and the silence was next broken by Joseph's soft accents.

"Did Horbury give your lordship any receipt, or acknowledgment he had received these jewels on deposit?" he asked. "I mean, of course, in our name?"

The Earl twisted sharply in his chair, and Neale fancied he saw a shade of annoyance pass over his good-natured face.

"Certainly not!" he answered. "I should never have dreamed of asking for a receipt from a man whom I knew as well as I knew or thought I knew Horbury. The whole thing was just as if...well, as if I should ask any friend to take care of something for me for a while."

"Did Horbury know what you were giving him?" asked Joseph.

"Of course!" replied the Earl. "As a matter of fact, he'd never seen these things, and I took them out of their case and showed them to him."

"And he said he would lock them up in our strong room?" suggested the soft voice.

"He said nothing about your strong room," answered the Earl. "Nor about where he'd put them. That was understood. It was understood...a tacit understanding he'd take care of them until our return."

"Did your lordship give him the date of your return?" persisted Joseph, with the thorough-going air of a cross-examiner.

"Yes, I told him exactly when we should be back," replied the Earl. "The twelfth of May...day before yesterday."

Joseph moved away from the sideboard towards the hearth, and leaning against the mantelpiece threw a glance at the strong room.

"The jewels are not in our possession," he said, half indolently. "There is nothing of that sort in there. There are two safes in the outer room of the bank. I should say Mr. Neale here knows everything that is in them. Do you know anything of these jewels, Neale?"

"Nothing!" said Neale. "I never heard of them."

Gabriel looked up from his papers.

"None of us have heard of them," he remarked. "Horbury could not have put them in this strong room without my knowledge. They are certainly not there. The safes my nephew mentioned just now are used only for books and papers. Your lordship's casket is not in either."

The Earl rose slowly from his chair. It was evident to Neale he was more surprised than angry. He looked around him as a man looks whose understanding is suddenly brought up against something unexplained.

"All I know is I handed that casket to Mr. Horbury in his own dining-room one evening some weeks ago," he said. "That's certain! So I naturally expect to find it here."

"And it is not here, that is equally certain," observed Gabriel. "What is also certain is our manager...trusted in more than he should have been, is missing, and many of our valuable securities with him. Therefore..."

He spread his hands again with an expressive gesture and once more bent over his papers. Once more there was silence. Then the Earl started as if a thought had suddenly occurred to him.

"I say!" he exclaimed, "don't you think Horbury may have put those jewels away in his own house?"

Joseph smiled a little derisively.

"A hundred thousand pounds worth!" he said softly. "Not very likely!"

"But he may have a safe there," urged the Earl. "Most people have a safe in their houses nowadays. They're so handy, you know, and so cheap. Don't you think maybe it?"

"I am not familiar with Horbury's domestic arrangements," said Gabriel. "I have not been in his house for some years. But as we are desirous of giving your lordship what assistance we can, we will go into the house and see if there is anything of the sort. Just tell the housekeeper we are coming in, Neale."

The Earl nodded to Mrs. Carswell as she received him and the two partners in the adjacent hall.

"This lady will remember my calling on Mr. Horbury one evening a few weeks ago," he said. "She saw me with him in that room."

"Certainly!" assented Mrs. Carswell, readily enough. "I remember your lordship calling on Mr. Horbury very well. One night after dinner, your lordship was here an hour or so."

Gabriel opened the door of the dining-room, an old-fashioned apartment which looked out on a garden and orchard at the rear of the house.

"Mrs. Carswell," he said, as they all went in, "has Mr. Horbury a safe in this room, or in any other room? You know what I mean."

But the housekeeper shook her head. There was no safe in the house. There was a plate-chest, there it was, standing in a recess by the sideboard, she had the key of it.

"Open that, at any rate," commanded Gabriel. "It's about as unlikely as anything could be, but we'll leave nothing undone."

There was nothing in the plate-chest but what Gabriel expected to find there. He turned again to the housekeeper.

"Is there anything in this house...cupboard, chest, trunk, anything in which Mr. Horbury kept valuables?" he asked. "Any place in which he was in the habit of locking up papers, for instance?"

Mrs. Carswell again shook her head. No, she knew of no such place or receptacle. There was Mr. Horbury's desk, but she believed all its drawers were open. Her belief proved to be correct. Gabriel opened drawer after drawer, and revealed nothing of consequence. He turned to the Earl with another expressive spreading out of his hands.

"I don't see what more we can do to assist your lordship," he said. "I don't know what more can be done."

"The question is...so it seems to me...what is to be done," replied the Earl, whose face had been gradually growing graver. "What, for instance, are you going to do, Mr. Chestermarke? Let us be plain with each other. You disclaim all liability in connection with my affair?"

"Most certainly!" exclaimed Gabriel. "We know nothing

of that transaction. As I have already said, if Horbury took charge of your lordship's property, he did so as a private individual, not on our behalf, not in his capacity as our manager. If your lordship had been a customer of ours..."

"That would have been a very different matter," said Joseph. "But as we have never had any dealings with your lordship..."

"We have, of course, no liability to you," concluded Gabriel. "The true position of the case is your lordship handed your property to Horbury as a friend, not as manager of Chestermarke's Bank."

"Then let me ask you, what are you going to do?" said the Earl. "I mean, not about my affair, but about finding your manager?"

Gabriel looked at his nephew. Joseph shook his head.

"So far," said Joseph, "we have not quite considered that. We are not yet fully aware of how things stand. We have a pretty good idea, but it will take another day."

"You don't mean to tell me you're going to let another day elapse before doing something?" exclaimed the Earl. "Bless my soul! I'd have had the hue and cry out before noon today, if I'd been you!"

"If you'd been Chestermarke's Bank, my lord," remarked Joseph, in his softest manner, "that's precisely what you would not have done. We don't want it noised all over the town and neighborhood our trusted manager has suddenly run away with our money and your jewels in his pocket."

There was a curious note...half-sneering, half-sinister in the junior partner's quiet voice which made the Earl turn and look at him with a sudden new interest. Before either could speak, Neale ventured to say what he had been wanting to say for half an hour.

"May I suggest something, sir?" he said, turning to Gabriel.

"Speak...speak!" assented Gabriel hastily. "Anything you like!"

"Mr. Horbury may have met with an accident," said Neale. "He was fond of taking his walks in lonely places...there are plenty outside the town. He may be lying somewhere even now...helpless."

"Capital suggestion! Much obliged to you," exclaimed

the Earl. "Gad! I wonder we never thought of that before! Much the most likely thing. I can't believe Horbury..."

Before he could say more, the door of the dining-room was thrown open, a clear, strong voice was heard speaking to someone and in walked a handsome young woman, who pulled herself up on the threshold to stare out of a pair of frank gray eyes at the four startled men.

Chapter 4

Mrs. Carswell, who had left the gentlemen to themselves after opening the plate-chest, followed the new-comer into the room and looked appealingly at the senior partner.

'This is Miss Fosdyke, sir," she said, as if accounting for the unceremonious entrance. "Mr. Horbury's..."

But Miss Fosdyke, having looked round her, entered the arena of discussion as abruptly as she had entered the room.

"You're Mr. Chestermarke!" she said, turning to Gabriel. "I remember you. What's all this, Mr. Chestermarke? I come down from London to meet my uncle, and to go on with him to Scotland for a holiday, and I learn he's disappeared! What is it? What has happened? Why are you all looking so mysterious? Is something wrong? Where is my uncle?"

Gabriel, who had assumed his stereotyped expression of calm attention under this tornado of questions, motioned Joseph to place a chair for the young lady. But Miss Fosdyke shook her head and returned to the attack.

"Please don't keep anything back!" she said. "I am not of the fainting-to-order type of young woman. Just say what is the matter, if you please. Mrs. Carswell knows no more..."

"Than what we do," interrupted Joseph, with one of his peculiar smiles. "Hadn't you better sit down?"

"Not until I know what has happened," retorted the visitor. "Because if anything has happened there will be something for me to do, and it's foolish to sit down when one's got to get up again immediately. Mr. Chestermarke, are you going to answer my questions?"

Gabriel bowed stiffly.

"I have the honor of addressing..." he began.

"You have the honor, if you like to put it so of addressing Miss Betty Fosdyke, who is Mr. John Horbury's niece," replied the young lady impatiently. "Mrs. Carswell has told you that already. Besides you saw me, more than once, when I was a little girl. And that's not so very long ago. Now, Mr. Chestermarke, where is my uncle?"

"I do not know where your uncle is," replied Gabriel suddenly, and losing his starchiness. "I wish to Heaven I did!"

"None of us know where Mr. John Horbury is," repeated Joseph, in his suave tones. "We all wish to Heaven we did!"

The girl turned and gave the junior partner a look which took in every inch of him. It was a look which began with a swift speculation and ended in something very like distaste. But Joseph met it with his usual quiet smile.

"It would make such a lot of difference if we knew!" he murmured. "As it is things are unpleasant."

Miss Fosdyke finished her reflection and turned away.

"I remember you now," she said calmly. "You're Joseph Chestermarke. Now I will sit down. And I insist on being told everything!"

"My dear young lady!" exclaimed Gabriel, "there is next to nothing to tell. If you will have the unpleasant truth, here it is. Your uncle, whom we have trusted for more years than I care to mention, disappeared on Saturday evening, and nobody knows where he is, nor where he went. All we know is we find some of our property missing...valuable securities. And this gentleman, Lord Ellersdeane tells us six weeks ago he entrusted jewels worth a hundred thousand pounds to your uncle's keeping, they, too, are missing. What can we think?"

The girl's face had flushed, and her brows had drawn together in an angry frown by the time Gabriel had finished, and Neale, silently watching her from the background, saw her fingers clench themselves. She gave a swift glance at the Earl, and then fixed her eyes steadily on Gabriel.

"Are you telling me that my uncle is a thief?" she demanded. "Are you, Mr. Chestermarke?"

"I'm not, anyhow!" exclaimed the Earl. "I...I...so far as I'm concerned, I say there's some mistake."

"Thank you!" she answered quietly. "But you, Mr. Chestermarke? Come, I'm entitled to an answer."

Gabriel showed signs of deep annoyance. He had the reputation of being a confirmed woman-hater, and it was plain he was ill at ease in presence of this plain-spoken young person.

"You appear to be a lady of much common sense!" he

said. "Therefore..."

"I have some common sense," interrupted Miss Fosdyke coolly. "And what amount I possess tells me that I never heard anything more ridiculous in my life than the suggestion my uncle should steal anything from anybody! Why, he was, and is, I hope, a fairly well-to-do man! And if he wanted money, he'd only to come to me. It so happens I'm one of the wealthiest young women in England. If my uncle had wanted a few thousands or tens of thousands to play ducks and drakes with, he'd only to ring me up on the telephone, and he'd have had whatever he asked for in a few hours. That's not boasting, Mr. Chestermarke...that's just plain truth. My uncle a thief! Mr. Chestermarke! There's only one word for your suggestion. Don't think me rude if I tell you what it is. It's...bosh!"

Gabriel's colorless face twitched a little, and he drew himself up.

"I have no acquaintance with modern young ladies," he remarked icily. "I daresay they have their own way of looking at things and of expressing themselves. I, too, have mine. Also I have my own conclusions, and..."

"I say, Mr. Chestermarke!" said the Earl, hastening to intervene in what seemed likely to develop into a passage-at-arms. "We're forgetting the suggestion made just before this lady, Miss Fosdyke, I think? Entered. Don't let's forget it...it's a good one."

Miss Fosdyke turned eagerly to the Earl.

"What suggestion was it?" she asked. "Do tell me? I'm sure you agree with me. I can see you do. Thank you, again!"

"This gentleman," said the Earl, pointing to Neale, who had retreated into a corner and was staring out of the window, "suggests that Horbury may have met with an accident, you know, and be lying helpless somewhere. I sincerely hope he isn't but..."

Miss Fosdyke jumped from her chair. She turned an indignant look on Gabriel and let it go on to Joseph.

"You don't mean to tell me that you have not done anything to find my uncle?" she exclaimed with fiery emphasis. "You've surely had some search made? Surely!"

"We knew nothing of his disappearance until ten o'clock this morning," replied Gabriel, half-angrily.

"But since then? Why, you've had five hours!" she said.

"Has nothing been done? Haven't you even told the police?"

"Certainly not!" answered Gabriel. "It is not our policy."

Miss Fosdyke made one step to the door and flung it open.

"Then I shall!" she exclaimed. "Policy, indeed! High time I came down here, I think! Thank you, Lord Ellersdeane and the other gentleman for the suggestion. Now I'll go and act on it. And when I act, Mr. Chestermarke, I do it thoroughly!"

The next moment she had slammed the door, and Gabriel glanced at his partner.

"Annoying!" he said. "A most unpleasant young woman! I should have preferred not to tell the police until...well, at any rate, tomorrow. We really do not know to what extent we are... but then, what's the use of talking of that now? We can't prevent her going to the police-station."

"Why, really, Mr. Chestermarke," observed the Earl, "don't you think it's the best thing to do? To tell you the truth, considering I'm concerned, I was going to do the very same thing myself."

Gabriel bowed stiffly.

"We could not have prevented your lordship either," he said, with another wave of the white hands which seemed to go so well with the habitual pallor of his face. "All that is within your lordship's jurisdiction not in ours. But, especially since this young lady seems determined to do things in her way, I will tell your lordship why we are slow to move. It is purely a business reason. It was, as I said, ten o'clock when we heard Horbury was missing. That in itself was such a very strange and unusual thing my partner and I at once began to examine the contents of our strong room. We had been so occupied five hours when your lordship called. Do you think we could examine everything in five hours? No...nor in ten, nor in twenty! Our task is not one quarter complete! And why we don't wish publicity at once in here? We hold a vast number of securities and valuables belonging to customers. Title-deeds, mortgages, all sorts of things. We have valuables deposited with us. Up to now we don't know what is safe and what isn't. We do know this, certain securities of our own, easily convertible on the market, are gone! Now if we had allowed it to be known before, say, noon today, our manager had disappeared, and these securities with him, what would have been the result? The bank would have been besieged! Before we let the public know, we ourselves want to know exactly where we are. We want to be in a position to say to Smith, 'Your property is safe!' to Jones, 'Your deeds are here!' Does your lordship see that? But now, of course," concluded Gabriel, "as this Miss Fosdyke can and will spread the news all over the town...why, we must face things."

The Earl, who had listened to all this with an evident desire to comprehend and to sympathize, nodded his head.

"I see...I see, Mr. Chestermarke," he said. "But I say! I've got another notion, I'm not a very quick thinker, and I daresay my idea came out of Mr. Neale's suggestion. Anyway, it's this, for whatever it's worth. I told you that we only got home night before last...early on Saturday evening, as a matter of fact. Now, it was known in the town here we'd returned, we drove through the Market-Place. Mayn't it be Horbury saw us, or heard of our return, and when he went out that evening he had the casket in his pocket and was on his way to Ellersdeane, to return it to me? And on his way he met with some mishap? Worth considering, you know."

"I daresay a great many theories might and will be raised, my lord," replied Gabriel. "But..."

"Does your lordship also think or suggest Horbury also carried our missing securities in his pocket?" asked Joseph quietly. "Because we, at any rate, know they're gone!"

"Oh, well!" said the Earl, "I...I merely suggest it, you know. The country between here and Ellersdeane is a bit rough and wild. There's Ellersdeane Hollow, you know, a queer place on a dark night. And if a man took a short cut, as many people do through the Hollow, there are places he could fall into. But, as I say, I merely suggest as a reasonable theory."

"What does your lordship propose to do?" asked Gabriel.

"I certainly think inquiry should be set going," answered the Earl.

"Already done," remarked Joseph drily. "Miss Fosdyke has been with the police five minutes."

"I mean it should be done by us," said the Earl.

"Very well," said Gabriel suddenly, "it shall be done, then. No doubt your lordship would like to give the police your own story. Mr. Neale, will you go with Lord Ellersdeane to

Superintendent Polke? Your duty will be to give him the mere information Mr. Horbury left his house at a quarter to eight on Saturday evening and has not been heard of since. No more, Neale. And now," he concluded, with a bow to the Earl, "your lordship will excuse my partner and myself if we return to a singularly unpleasant task."

Lord Ellersdeane and Neale left the bank-house and walked towards the police-station. They crossed the Market-Place in silence, but as they turned the corner of the Moot Hall, the elder man spoke, touching his companion's shoulder with a confidential gesture.

"I don't believe a word of all that, Mr. Neale!" he said. "Not one word!"

Neale started and glanced at the Earl's moody face.

"Your lordship doesn't believe...?" he began, and checked himself.

"I don't believe Horbury's done what those two accuse him of," affirmed the Earl. "Not for one moment! I can't account for those missing securities they talk about, but I'll stake my honor Horbury hasn't got them! Nor my wife's jewels either. You heard and saw how astounded that girl was. By the by who is she!"

"Mr. Horbury's niece, Miss Fosdyke from London," replied Neale.

"She spoke of her wealth," remarked the Earl.

"Yes," said Neale. "She must be wealthy, too. She's the sole proprietor of Fosdyke's Brewery."

"Ho-ho!" laughed the Earl. "That's it, eh? Fosdyke's Entire! Of course I've seen the name on no end of public-houses in London. Sole proprietor? Dear me! Why, I have some recollection Fosdyke, of that brewery, was at one time a member of Parliament."

"Yes," assented Neale. "He married Mr. Horbury's sister. Miss Fosdyke is their only child. Mr. Fosdyke died a few years ago, and she came into the property last year when she was twenty-one."

"Lucky young woman!" muttered the Earl. "Fine thing to own a big brewery. Um! A very modern and up-to-date young lady, too. I liked the way she stood up to your principals. Of course, she'll have told Polke all the story by this time. As for ourselves...what had we better do?"

Neale had considered the question as he came along.

"There's only one thing to do, my lord," he answered. "We want the solution of a problem. What became of Mr. Horbury last Saturday night?"

Chapter 5

Polke, superintendent of the Scarnham police force, a little, round, cheery-faced man, whose mutton-chop whiskers suggested much business-like capacity and an equal amount of common sense, rose from his desk and bowed as the Earl of Ellersdeane entered his office.

"I know what your lordship's come for!" he said, with a twinkle of the eye which betokened infinite comprehension. "The young lady's been here."

"And has no doubt told you everything?" remarked the Earl, as he dropped into the chair which the superintendent drew forward. "Has she?"

"Pretty well, my lord," replied Polke, with a chuckle. "She's not one to let much grass grow under her feet, I think."

"Given you the facts, I suppose?" asked the Earl.

Polke motioned to Neale to seat himself, and resumed his own seat. He put his fingers together over his desk and looked from one to the other of his visitors.

"I'll give the young lady this much credit," he said. "She can tell one what she wants in about as few words as could possibly be used! Yes, my lord, she told me the facts in a couple of sentences. Her uncle disappeared...nobody knows where he is...suspected already of running away with your lordship's jewels and Chestermarke's securities. A very nice business indeed!"

"What do you think of it?" asked the Earl.

"As a policeman, nothing, so far," answered Polke, with another twinkle. "As a man, I don't believe it!"

"Nor do I!" said the Earl. "That is, I don't believe Horbury's appropriated anything. There's some mistake and some mystery."

"We can't get away from the fact Mr. Horbury has disappeared," remarked Neale, looking at the superintendent. "That's all I'm sent here to tell you, Mr. Polke."

"That's an accepted fact," agreed Polke. "But he's not the first man who's disappeared under mysterious circumstances. Some men, as your lordship knows, disappear and reappear with good reasons for their absence. Some never reappear. Some men aren't wanted to reappear. When a man disappears and he's wanted...why, the job is to find him."

"What does Miss Fosdyke wish?" asked the Earl, nodding assent to these philosophies. "She would say, of course."

"Miss Fosdyke's way, my lord, so far as I could gather from ten minutes talk with her, is to tell people what to do," answered Polke drily. "She doesn't ask, she commands! We're to find her uncle quick. At once. No pains to be spared. Money no object. A hundred pounds, spot cash, to the first man, woman, child, who brings her the least fragment of news of him. That's Miss Fosdyke's method. It's not a bad one...it's only rich young ladies who can follow it. So I've already put things in train. Handbills and posters, of course and the town-crier. I suggested to her by tonight, or tomorrow morning, there might be news of Mr. Horbury without doing all that. No good! Miss Fosdyke, she can tell you a lot inside a minute, informed me since she was seventeen she had only had one motto in life. It's...do it now!"

"Good!" laughed the Earl. "But where are you going to begin?"

"That's the difficulty," agreed Polke. "A gentleman walks out of his back garden into the dusk and he's never seen again. I don't know. We must wait and see if anybody comes forward to say he, she, or it saw Mr. Horbury after he left his house on Saturday night. That's all."

"Somebody must have seen him," said the Earl.

"Well, you'd think so, my lord," replied Polke, "but he could get away from the back of his orchard into the open country without being seen. The geographical position of our town's a bit curious, so your lordship knows. Here we are on a ridge. Horbury's garden and orchard run down to the foot of that ridge. At that foot is the river. There's a foot-bridge over the river, immediately opposite his orchard gate. He could cross the foot-bridge, and be in the wood on the other side in two minutes from leaving his house. That wood extends for a good mile into the country. Oh, yes! He could get away without being seen, and once in that country, why, he could make his way to one or other of half a dozen small railway stations. We shall telephone to all of them. That's all in the routine. But then, that's all supposing he left the town. Perhaps he didn't leave the town."

The Earl started, and Neale looked quickly up from a brown study.

"Eh?" said the Earl. "Didn't leave the town?"

"Speaking as a policeman," answered Polke, with a knowing smile, "I don't know he even left his house. I only know his housekeeper says he did. That's a very different matter. For anything we know…absolutely know! Mr. Horbury may have been murdered in his own house, and buried in his own cellar."

"You're not joking?" said Neale. "Or you are!"

"Far from it, Mr. Neale," answered Polke. "That may seem a very, very outrageous thing to say, but, I assure you, one never knows what may not have happened in these cases. However, Mrs. Carswell says he did leave the house, so we must take her word to begin with, and see if we can find out where he went. And as your lordship is here, there's just a question or two I should like to have answered. How many people know your lordship handed over these valuables to Mr. Horbury?"

"So far as I know, no one but the Countess and myself," replied the Earl. "I never mentioned the matter to any one, and I don't think my wife would either. There was no need to mention it."

"Well, I don't know," remarked Polke. "One's got to consider all sorts of little things in these affairs, or else I wouldn't ask another question. Does your lordship think it possible the Countess mentioned it to her maid?"

The Earl started in his chair. "Ah!" he said. "That may be! She may have done that, of course. I hadn't thought of it."

"Is the maid a trustworthy woman?" inquired Polke.

"She's been in our service twelve or fourteen years," replied the Earl. "We've always found her quite trustworthy. So much so I've more than once sent her to my bankers with those very jewels."

"You took her with you to the Continent, of course, my lord?" asked Polke.

"No, we didn't," replied the Earl. "The fact is we wanted to have, for once in our lives, a thoroughly unconventional holiday. You know the Countess and I are both very fond of walking. Well, we had always had a great desire to have a walking tour, alone, in the Ardennes district, in early spring. We decided some time ago to have it this year. So when we set off, six weeks ago, we took no servants and precious little luggage and we enjoyed it all the more. Therefore, of course, my wife's maid was not with us. She remained at Ellersdeane with the rest of the servants."

Polke seemed to ponder over this last statement. Then he rose from his chair.

"Um!" he said. "Well, I'm doing what I can. There's something your lordship might do."

"Yes?" asked the Earl. "What, now! It shall be done."

"Let some of your men take a look round your neighborhood," answered the superintendent. "Gamekeepers, now they're the fellows! Just now we're having some grand moonlight nights. If your men would look about the country between here and Ellersdeane, now? And tell the farmers, and the cottagers, and so forth, and take a particular look round Ellersdeane Hollow. It would be a help."

"Excellent idea, Polke," said the Earl. "I'll ride home and set things going at once. And you'll let me know if anything turns up here during the evening or the night."

He strode off to the door and Neale followed. But on the threshold Neale was pulled up by the superintendent.

"Mr. Neale!" said Polke.

Neale turned to see his questioner looking at him with a rather quizzical expression.

"What precise message had you for me?" asked Polke.

"Just what I said," replied Neale. "I was merely to tell you Mr. Horbury disappeared from his house on Saturday evening, and has not been seen since."

"No further message...from your principals?" suggested Polke.

"Nothing," said Neale.

Polke nodded, and with a bow to the Earl sat down again to his desk. He took up a pen when the door had closed on his visitors, and for a while busied himself in writing. He was thus occupied when the telephone bell rang in the farthest corner of his room. He crossed over and laid hold of the receiver.

"Yes?" he said quietly. "Yes, this is Polke, superintendent, Scarnham. I rang you up twenty minutes since. I want you to send me, at once, the smartest man you have available. Case is disappearance, under mysterious circumstances, of a bank manager. Securities to a large amount are missing; valuables also. No expense will be spared here, money no object. You understand a first-class man? Tonight? Yes. Good train from town five-twenty, gets here nine-fifteen. He will catch that? Good. Tell him report here on arrival. All right. Good-bye."

Polke rang off and went back to his desk.

"What New Scotland Yard calls a first-class is very often what I should call a third-class," he muttered as he picked up his pen. "However, we'll live in hope something out of the usual will arrive. Now what are those two Chestermarkes after? Why didn't one of them come here? What are they doing? And what's the mystery? James Polke, my boy, here's a handful for you!"

If Polke had been able to look into Chestermarke's Bank just then, he would have failed to notice any particular evidences of mystery. It was nearly the usual hour for closing when Neale went back, and Gabriel immediately told him to follow out the ordinary routine. The clerks were to finish their work and go their ways, as if nothing had happened, and, as far as they could, they were to keep their tongues quiet. As for the partners, food was being sent over for them from the hotel. They would be obliged to remain at the bank for some time yet. But there was no need for Neale to stay. He could go when the day's balancing was done.

"You heard what instructions this Miss Fosdyke had given the police, I suppose?" asked Gabriel, as Neale was leaving the parlor. "Raising the whole town, no doubt?"

Neale briefly narrated all he knew. The partners listened with the expression characteristic of each, and made no comment. And in half an hour Neale handed over the keys to Joseph and went out into the hall, his labors over. That had been the most exciting day he had ever known in his life…was what was left of it going to yield anything still more exciting? He stood in the outer hall trying to make up his mind about something. He wanted to speak to Betty Fosdyke, to talk to her. She had evidently not recognized him when she came so suddenly into the dining-room of the bank-house. But why should she, he asked himself? They had only met once, when both were children, and she had no doubt forgotten his very existence. He rang the house bell at last and asked for Mrs. Carswell. The housekeeper came hurrying to him, a look of expectancy on her face.

"Has anything been heard, Mr. Neale?" she asked. "Or found out? Have the police been told yet?"

"The police know," answered Neale. "And nothing has been heard. Where is Miss Fosdyke, Mrs. Carswell? I should like to speak to her."

"Gone to the Scarnham Arms, Mr. Neale," replied the housekeeper. "She wouldn't stay here, though her room was all ready for her. Said she wouldn't stay two seconds in a house that belonged to men who suspected her uncle! So she's gone across there to take rooms. Do...do the partners suspect Mr. Horbury of something, Mr. Neale?"

Neale shook his head and turned away.

"I can't tell you anything, Mrs. Carswell," he answered. "If either Mr. Chestermarke or Mr. Joseph wish to give you any information, they'll give it themselves. But I can say this on my own responsibility, if you know of anything...anything, however small that would account for Mr. Horbury's absence, out with it!"

"But I don't...I know nothing but what I've told," said Mrs. Carswell. "Literally nothing!"

"Nobody knows anything," remarked Neale. "That's the worst of it. Well, we shall see."

He went away from the house and crossed the Market-Place to the Scarnham Arms, an old-world inn which had suffered few alterations during the last two centuries. And there inside its wide hall, superintending the removal of various articles of luggage which had just arrived from the station and in conversation with a much interested landlady, he found Betty.

"I may be here for weeks, and I shall certainly be here for days," the young lady was saying. "Put all these things in the bedroom, and I'll have what I want taken into the sitting-room later. Now, Mrs. Depledge, about my dinner. I'll have it in my sitting-room, and I'll have it early. I..."

At this moment Miss Fosdyke became aware of Neale's presence, and this eminently good-looking young man was not only smiling at her, but was holding out a hand which he evidently expected to be taken.

"You've forgotten me!" said Neale.

Miss Fosdyke's cheeks flushed a little and she held out her hand.

"Is it...is it Wallie Neale?" she asked. "But I saw you in the bank-house and you didn't speak to me!"

"You didn't speak to me," retorted Neale, smiling.

"Didn't know you," she answered. "Heavens! How you've grown! But, come upstairs. Mrs. Depledge, dinner for two, mind. Mr. Neale will dine with me."

Neale suffered his hostess to lead him upstairs to a private parlor. And when they were once within it, Miss Fosdyke shut the door and turned on him.

"Now, Wallie Neale!" she said, "out with it! What is the meaning of all this infernal mystery? And where's my uncle?"

Chapter 6

Neale dropped into a chair and lifted a despairing countenance to his downright questioner.

"I don't know!" he said. "I know nothing!"

"That is...beyond what I've already been told?" suggested the girl.

"Beyond what you've been told...exactly," replied Neale. "I'm literally bewildered. I've been going about all day as if...as if I were dreaming, or having a nightmare, or something. I don't understand it at all. I saw Mr. Horbury, of course, on Saturday, he was all right when I left him at the bank. He said nothing that suggested anything unusual. The whole thing is...a real facer! To me anyhow."

Betty devoted a whole minute to taking a good look at her companion. Neale, on his part, made a somewhat shyer examination of her. He remembered her as a long-legged little girl who had no great promise of good looks. He was not quite sure she had grown into good looks now. But she was an eminently bright and vivacious young woman, strong, healthy, vigorous, with fine eyes and teeth and hair, and a color that betokened an intimate acquaintance with outdoor life. And already, in the conversation at the bank, and in Polke's report of his interview with him, he had learnt she had developed certain characteristics which he faintly remembered in her as a child, when she had insisted on having her own way among other children.

"You've grown into quite a handsome young man, Wallie!" she observed suddenly, with a frank laugh. "I shouldn't have thought you would, somehow. Am I changed?"

"I should say...not in character," answered Neale shyly. "I remember you always wanted to be top dog!"

"It's my fate!" she said, with a sigh. "I've such a lot of people and things to look after. One has to be top dog, whether one wants to or not. But this affair...what's to be done?"

"I understand from Polke you've already done everything," replied Neale.

"I've given him orders to spare neither trouble nor expense," she asserted. "He's to send for the very best detective they can give him from headquarters in London, and search is to be made. Because...now, Wallie, tell me truthfully, you don't believe for one moment my uncle has run away with things?"

"Not for one second!" asserted Neale stoutly. "Never did!"

"Then...there's foul play!" exclaimed Betty. "And I'll spend my last penny to get at the bottom of it! Here I am, and here I stick, until I've found my uncle, or discovered what's happened to him. And listen, do you think those two men across there are to be trusted?"

Neale shook his head as if in appeal to her.

"I'm their clerk, you know," he replied. "I hate being there at all, but I am there. I believe they're men of absolute probity as regards business matters. Personally, I'm not very fond of either."

"Fond!" she exclaimed. "My dear boy! Joseph is a slimy sneak, and Gabriel is a bloodless sphinx. I hate both of them!"

Neale laughed and gave her a look of comprehension.

"You haven't changed, Betty," he said. "I'm to call you Betty, though you are grown up?"

"Since it's the only name I possess, I suppose you are," she answered. "But now what can we do...you and I? After all, we're the nearest people my uncle has in this town. Let's do something! I'm not the sort to sit talking. I want action! Can't you suggest something we can do?"

"There's one thing," replied Neale, after a moment's thought. "Lord Ellersdeane suggested possibly Mr. Horbury, hearing the they had returned home on Saturday, put the jewels in his pocket and started out to Ellersdeane with them. I know the exact path he'd have taken in that case, and I thought of following it this evening. One might come across something, or hear something, you know."

"Take me with you, as soon as we've had dinner," she said. "It'll be a beginning. I mean to turn this neighborhood upside down for news, you'll see. Some person or persons must have seen my uncle on Saturday night! A man can't disappear like that. It's impossible!"

"Um! But men do disappear," remarked Neale. "What I'm hoping is there'll eventually and quickly be some explanation of this disappearance, and Mr. Horbury hasn't met with...shall I put it plainly?"

"You'd better put anything plainly to me," she answered. "I don't understand other methods."

"It's possible he may have been murdered, you know," said Neale quietly.

Betty got up from her chair and went over to the window to look out on the Market-Place. She stood there some time in silence.

"It shall be a bad job for any man who murdered him if that is so," she said at last. "I was very fond of my uncle."

"So was I," said Neale. "But I say, no past tenses yet! Aren't we a bit previous? He may be all right."

"Ring the bell and let's hurry up that dinner," she commanded. "I didn't make it clear we want it as early as possible. I want to get out, and to see where he went...I want to do something active!"

But Betty was obliged to adapt herself to the somewhat leisurely procedure of highly respectable country-town hotels, whose cooks will not be hurried, and it was already dusk, and the moonlight was beginning to throw shadows of gable and spire over the old Market-Place, when she and Neale set out on their walk.

"All the better," said Neale. "This is just about the time he went out on Saturday night, and under very similar conditions. Now we'll take the precise path he'd have taken if he was on his way to Ellersdeane."

He led his companion to a corner of the Market-Place, and down a narrow alley which terminated on an expanse of open ground at the side of the river. There he made her pause and look round.

"Now if we're going to do the thing properly," he said, "just attend, and take notice of what I point out. The town, as you see, stands on this ridge above us. Here we are at the foot of the gardens and orchards which slope down from the backs of the houses on this side of the Market-Place. There is the gate of the bank-house orchard. According to Mrs. Carswell, Mr. Horbury came out of that gate on Saturday night.

What did he do then? He could have turned to the left,

along this river bank, or to the right, also along the river bank. But, if he meant to walk out to Ellersdeane...which he would reach in well under an hour, he would cross this foot-bridge and enter those woods. That's what we've got to do."

He led his companion across a narrow bridge, over a strip of sward at the other side of the river, and into a grove of fir which presently deepened and thickened as it spread up a gently shelving hillside. The lights of the town behind them disappeared and the gloom increased. Presently they were alternately crossing patches of moonlight and plunging into expanses of blackness. And Betty, after stumbling over one or two of the half-exposed roots which lay across the rough path, slipped a hand into Neale's arm.

"You'll have to play guide, Wallie, unless you wish me to break my neck," she laughed. "My town eyes aren't accustomed to these depths of gloom and solitude. And now," she went on, as Neale led her confidently forward through the wood, "let's talk some business. I want to know about those two...the Chestermarkes. For I've an uneasy feeling there's more in this affair than on the surface, and I want to know all about the people I'm dealing with. Just remember, beyond the mere fact of their existence and having seen them once or twice, years ago, I don't know anything about them. What sort of men are they...as individuals?"

"Queer!" replied Neale. "They're both queer. I don't know much about them. Nobody does. They're all right as business men, much respected and all that, you know. But as private individuals they're decidedly odd. They're both old bachelors, at least Gabriel's an old one, and Joseph is a youngish one. They live sort of hermit lives, as far as one can make out. Gabriel lives at the old house which I'll show you when we get out of this wood. You'll see the roofs, anyhow, in this moonlight. Joseph lives in another old house, but in the town, at the end of Cornmarket. What they do with themselves at home, Heaven knows! They don't go into such society as there is. They take no part in the town's affairs. There's a very good club here for men of their class...they don't belong to it. You can't get either of them to attend a meeting. They keep aloof from everything. But they both go up to London a great deal...they're always going. But they never go together. When Gabriel's away, Joseph's at home. When Joseph's off, Gabriel's on show. There's always one Mr. Chestermarke to be found at the bank. All the same, Mr. Horbury was the man who did all the business with customers in the ordinary way. So far as I know banking," concluded Neale, "I should say he was trusted and confided in more than most bank managers are."

"Did they seem very much astonished when they found he'd gone?" asked Betty. "Did it seem a great shock, a real surprise?"

"The cleverest man living couldn't tell what either Gabriel or Joseph thinks about anything," answered Neale. "You know what Gabriel's face is like, a stone image! And Joseph always looks as if he was sneering at you, a sort of soft, smiling sneer. No, I couldn't say they showed surprise, and I don't know what they've found out, they're the closest, most reserved men about their own affairs you could imagine!"

"But they say some of their securities are missing," remarked Betty. "They'll have to let the exact details be known, won't they?"

"Depends on them," replied Neale. "They'll only do what they like. And they don't love you for coming on the scene, I assure you!"

"But I'm here, nevertheless!" said Betty. "And here I stay! Wallie, haven't you got even a bit of a theory about all this!"

"Can't say I have!" confessed Neale woefully. "I'm not a very brilliant hand at thinking. The only thing I can think of is Mr. Horbury, knowing Lord Ellersdeane had returned home on Saturday, thought he'd hand back those jewels as soon as possible, and set off in the evening with that intention... possibly to be robbed and murdered on the way. Sounds horrible, but honestly I can't think of any other theory."

Betty involuntarily shivered and glanced about her at the dark cavernous spaces of the wood, which had now thickened into dense masses of oak and beech. She took a firmer grip of Neale's arm.

"And he'd come through here!" she exclaimed. "How dangerous with those things in his pocket!"

"Oh, but he'd think nothing of it!" answered Neale. "He was used to walking at night. He knew every yard of this neighborhood. Besides, he'd know very well nobody would know what he had on him. What I'd like to know is...supposing my theory's right, and he was taking these jewels to Ellersdeane, how did anybody get to know he had them? For the Chestermarkes didn't know they'd been given to him, and I didn't, nobody at the bank knew."

A sudden turn in the path brought them to the edge of the wood, and they emerged on a broad plateau of rough grass, from beneath which a wide expanse of landscape stretched away, bathed just then in floods of moonlight. Neale paused and waved his stick towards the shadowy distances and over the low levels which lay between.

"Ellersdeane Hollow!" he said.

Betty paused too, looking silently around. She saw an undulating, broken stretch of country, half-heath, half-covert, covering a square mile or so of land, house-less, solitary. In its midst rose a curiously shaped eminence or promontory, at the highest point of which some ruin or other lifted gaunt, shapeless walls against the moonlit sky. Far down beneath it, in a depression amongst the heath-clad undulations, a fire glowed red in the gloom. And on the further side of this solitude, amidst groves and plantations, the moonlight shone on the roofs and gables of half-hidden houses. Over everything hung a deep silence.

"A wild and lonely scene!" she said.

Neale raised his stick again and began to point.

"All this in front of us is called Ellersdeane Hollow," he remarked. "It's not just one depression, you see it's a tract of unenclosed land. It's dangerous to cross, except by the paths. It's honeycombed all over with disused lead-mines, some of the old shafts are a tremendous depth. All the same, you see, there's some tinker chap, or some gypsies, camped out down there and got a fire. That old ruin, up on the crag there, is called Ellersdeane Tower, one of Lord Ellersdeane's ancestors built it for an observatory. This path will lead us right beneath it."

"Is this the path he would have taken if he'd gone to Ellersdeane on Saturday night?" asked Betty.

"Precisely, straight ahead, past the Tower," answered Neale. "And there is Ellersdeane, right away in the distance, among its trees. There where the moonlight catches it. Now let your eye follow that far line of wood, over the tops of the trees about Ellersdeane village. Do you see where the moonlight shines on another high roof? That's Gabriel Chestermarke's place, the Warren."

"So he and Lord Ellersdeane are neighbors!" remarked Betty.

"Neighbors at a distance of a mile and who do no more than nod to each other," answered Neale. "Lord Ellersdeane and Mr. Horbury were what you might call friends, but I don't believe his lordship ever spoke ten words with either of the Chestermarke's until this morning. I tell you the Chestermarke's are regular hermits! When they're at home or about Scarnham, anyhow. Now let's go as far as the Tower and you can see all over the country from that point."

Betty followed her guide down a narrow path which led in and out through the undulations of the Hollow until it reached the foot of the promontory on which stood the old ruin that made such a prominent landmark. Seen at close quarters Ellersdeane Tower was a place of much greater size and proportion than it had appeared from the edge of the wood, and the path to its base was steep and rocky. And here the loneliness in which she and Neale had so far walked came to an end on the edge of the promontory, outlined against the moonlit sky, two men stood, talking in low tones.

Chapter 7

Neale's eye caught the gleam of silver braid on the clothing of one of the two men, and he hastened his steps a little as he and Betty emerged on the level ground at the top of the steep path.

"That's a policeman," he said. "It'll be the constable from Ellersdeane. The other man looks like a gamekeeper. Let's see if they've heard anything."

The two figures turned at the sound of footsteps, and came slowly in Neale's direction. Both recognized him and touched their hats.

"I suppose you're looking round in search of anything about Mr. Horbury?" suggested Neale. "Heard any news or found any trace?"

"Well, we're what you might call taking a preliminary observation, Mr. Neale," answered the policeman. "His lordship's sent men out all over the neighborhood. No, we've heard nothing, nor seen anything, either. But, then, there's not much chance of hearing anything hereabouts. The others have gone round asking at houses, and such-like to find out if he was seen to pass anywhere. Of course, his lordship was figuring on the chance Mr. Horbury might have had a fit, or something of that sort, and fallen somewhere along this path, between the town and Ellersdeane House, it's not much followed, this path. But we've seen nothing up to now."

Neale turned to the keeper.

"Were none of your people about here on Saturday night?" he asked. "You've a good many watchers on the estate, haven't you?"

"Yes, sir a dozen or more," answered the keeper. "But we don't come this way, this isn't our land. Our beats lie the other way... the other side of the village. We never come on to this part at all."

"This, you know, Mr. Neale," remarked the policeman, jerking his thumb over the Hollow, "this, in a manner of speaking, belongs to nobody. Some say it belongs to the Crown, I don't know. All I know is nobody has any rights over it. It's been what you might term common land ever since anybody can remember. This here Mr. Horbury that's missing, your governor, sir, I once met him out here, and had a bit of talk with him, and he told me it isn't even known who worked them old lead-mines down there, nor who has any rights over all this waste. That, of course," concluded the policeman, pointing to the glowing fire which Neale and Betty had seen from the edge of the wood, "that's why chaps like yonder man come and camp here just as they like, there's nobody to stop them."

"Who is the man?" asked Neale, glancing at the fire, whose flames made a red spot amongst the bushes.

"Most likely a traveling tinker chap, sir, that comes this way now and again," answered the policeman. "Name of Creasy...Tinner Creasy, the folks call him. He's come here for many a year, at odd times. Camps out with his pony and cart, and goes round the villages and farmsteads, seeing if there's anything to mend, and selling them pots and pans and such-like. Stops a week or two, sometimes longer."

"And poaches all he can lay hands on," added the gamekeeper. "Only he takes good care never to go off this Hollow to do it."

"Have you made any inquiry of him?" asked Neale.

"We were just thinking of doing that, sir," replied the policeman. "He roams up and down about here at nights, when he is here. But I don't know how long he's been camping this time. It's very seldom I ever come round this way myself, there's nothing to come for."

"Let's go across there and speak to him," said Neale.

He and Betty followed the two men down the side of the promontory and across the ups and downs of the Hollow, until they came to a deeper depression fringed about by a natural palisading of hawthorn. And as they drew near and could see into the dingle-like recess which the tinker had selected for his camping-ground they became aware of a savory and appetizing odor, and the gamekeeper laughed.

"Cooking his supper, is Tinner Creasy!" he remarked. "And good stuff he has in his pot, too!"

The tinker, now in full view, sat on a log near a tripod,

beneath which crackled a bright fire, burning under a black pot. The leaping flames revealed a shrewd, weather-beaten face which turned sharply towards the bushes as the visitors appeared. They also lighted up the tinker's cart in the background, the browsing pony close by, the implements of the tinner's trade strewn around on the grass. It was an alluring picture of vagabond life, and Neale suddenly compared it with the dull existence of folk who, like himself, were chained to a desk. He would have liked to sit down by Tinner Creasy and ask him about his doings, but the policeman had less poetical ideas.

"Hullo, Tinner!" said he, with easy familiarity. "Here again? I thought we should be seeing your fire some night this spring. Been here long?"

The tinker, who had remained seated on his log until he saw a lady was of the party, rose and touched the edge of his fur cap to Betty in a way which indicated his politeness was entirely for her.

"Since yesterday," he answered laconically.

"Only since yesterday!" exclaimed the policeman. "Ah, that's a pity, now. You wasn't here Saturday night, then?"

The tinker turned a quizzical eye on the four inquiring faces.

"How would I be here Saturday night when I only came yesterday?" he retorted. "You're the sort of chap that wants two answers to one question! What about Saturday night?"

The policeman took off his helmet and rubbed the top of his head as if to encourage his faculties.

"Nay!" he said. "There's a gentleman missing from Scarnham yonder, and it's thought he came out this way after dark, Saturday night, and something happened. But, of course, if you wasn't in these parts then..."

"I wasn't, nor within ten miles of them," said Creasy. "Who is the gentleman?"

"Mr. Horbury, the bank manager," answered the policeman.

"I know Mr. Horbury," remarked Creasy, with a glance at Neale and Betty. "I've talked to him a hundred-and-one times on this waste. So it's him, is it? Well, there's one thing you can be certain about."

"What?" asked Betty eagerly.

"Mr. Horbury wouldn't happen anything by accident, hereabouts," answered the tinker significantly. "He knew every inch of this Hollow. Some folks, now, might take a header into one of them old lead-mines. He wouldn't. He could had gone blind-fold over this spot."

"Well, he's disappeared," observed the policeman. "There's a search being made, all round. You heard naught last night, I suppose?"

Creasy gave Neale and Betty a look.

"Heard plenty of owls, and night-jars, and such-like," he answered, "and foxes, and weasels, and stoats, and beetles creeping in the grass. Naught human!"

The policeman resumed his helmet and sniffed audibly. He and the keeper moved away and talked together. Then the policeman turned to Neale.

"Well, we'll be getting back to the village, sir," he said. "If so be as you see our super, Mr. Neale, you might mention we're out and about."

He and his companion went off by a different path. At the top of a rise in the ground the policeman turned again.

"Tinner!" he called.

"Hullo?" answered Creasy.

"If you should hear or find anything," said the policeman, "come to me, you know."

"All right!" assented Creasy. He picked up some wood and replenished his fire. And glancing at Neale and Betty, who still lingered, he let fall a muttered whisper under his breath. "Bide a bit till those chaps have gone," he said. "I've a word or two."

He walked away to his cart after this mysterious communication, dived under its tilt, evidently felt for and found something, and came back, glancing over his shoulder to see the keeper and policeman had gone their ways.

"I never tell chaps of that sort anything, mister," he said, giving Neale a sly wink. "Them of my turn of life look on all gamekeepers and policemen as their natural enemies. They'd both of them turn me out of this if they could, only they know they can't. For some reason or other Ellersdeane Hollow is No Man's Land and therefore mine. And so I wasn't going to say anything to them...not me!"

"Then there is something you can say?" said Neale.

"You were here on Saturday!" exclaimed Betty. "You know something!"

"No, miss, I wasn't here Saturday," answered the tinker, "and I don't know anything about what the man asked, anyway I told him the truth about all that. But you say Mr. Horbury's missing, and he's considered to have come this way on Saturday night. So do either of you know that?"

He drew his right hand from behind him, and in the glare of the firelight showed them, lying across its palm, a briar tobacco-pipe, silver-mounted.

"I found that, last night, gathering dry sticks," he said. "It's letters engraved on the silver band 'J. H. from B. F.' 'J. H.' now? Does that mean John Horbury? You see, I know his Christian name."

Betty uttered a sharp exclamation and took the pipe in her hand. She turned to Neale with a look of sudden fear.

"It's the pipe I gave my uncle last Christmas!" she said. "Of course I know it! Where did you find it?" she went on, turning on Creasy. "Do tell us...do show us!"

"Foot of the crag there, miss...right beneath the old tower," answered Creasy. "And it's just as I found it. I'll give it to you, sir, to take to Superintendent Polke in Scarnham, he knows me. But just let me point something out. I ain't a detective, but in my forty-eight years I've had to keep my wits sharpened and my eyes open. Point out to Polke, and notice yourself whenever that pipe was dropped it was being smoked! The tobacco's caked at the surface, just as it would be if the pipe had been laid down at the very time the tobacco was burning well. Well if you're a smoker you'll know what I mean. That's one thing. The other is...just observe the silver band is quite bright and fresh, and there are no stains on the briar-wood. What's that indicate, young lady and young gentleman? Why, the pipe hadn't been lying so very long when I found it! Not above a day, I'll warrant."

"That's very clever of you, very observant!" exclaimed Betty. "But won't you show us the exact place where you picked it up?"

Creasy cast a glance at his cooking pot, stepped to it, and slightly tilted the lid. Then he signed to them to go back towards the tower by the path by which they had come.

"Don't want my supper to boil over, or to burn," he

remarked. "It's the only decent meal I get in the day, you see, miss. But it won't take a minute to show you where I found the pipe. Now what's the idea, sir," he went on, turning to Neale, "about Mr. Horbury's disappearance? Is it known that he came out here Saturday night?"

"Not definitely," replied Neale. "But it's believed he did. He was seen to set off in this direction, and there's a probability he crossed over here on his way to Ellersdeane. But he's never been seen since he left Scarnham."

"Well," observed Creasy, "as I said just now, he wouldn't happen anything by accident in an ordinary way. Was there any reason why anybody should set on him?"

"There may have been," replied Neal.

"He wouldn't be likely to have aught valuable on him, surely that time of night?" said the tinker.

"He may have had," admitted Neale. "I can't tell you more."

Creasy asked no farther question. He led the way to the foot of the promontory, at a point where a mass of rock rose sheer out of the hollow to the plateau crowned by the ruinous tower.

"Here's where I picked up the pipe," he said. "Lying among this rubbish, stones and dry wood, you see I just caught the gleam of the silver band. Now what should Mr. Horbury be doing down here? The path, you see, is a good thirty yards off. But, he may have fallen over or been thrown over and it's a sixty-feet drop from top to bottom."

Neale and Betty looked up the face of the rocks and said nothing. And Creasy presently went on, speaking in a low voice.

"If he met with foul play, if, for instance, he was thrown over here in a struggle or if, taking a look from the top there, he got too near the edge and something gave way," he said, "there's about as good means of getting rid of a dead man in this Ellersdeane Hollow as in any place in England! That's a fact!"

"You mean the lead-mines?" murmured Neale.

"Right, sir! Do you know how many of these old workings there is?" asked Creasy. "There's between fifty and sixty within a square mile of this tower. Some's fenced in, most isn't. Some of their mouths are grown over with bramble and bracken. And all of them are of tremendous depth. A man could be thrown down one of those mines, sir, and it would be a long job finding his body! But all that's very frightening to the lady, and we'll hope nothing of it happened. Still..."

"It has to be faced," said Betty. "Listen, I am Mr. Horbury's niece, and I'm offering a reward for news of him. Will you keep your eyes and ears open while you're in this neighborhood?"

The tinker promised he would do his best, and presently he went back to his fire, while Neale and Betty turned away towards the town. Neither spoke until they were half-way through the wood, then Betty uttered her fears in a question.

"Do you think the finding of the pipe shows he was there?" she asked.

"I'm sure of it," replied Neale. "I wish I wasn't. But...I saw him with this pipe in his lips at two o'clock on Saturday! I recognized it at once."

"Let's hurry on and see the police," said Betty. "We know something now, at any rate."

Polke, they were told at the police-station, was in his private house close by. A polite constable conducted them and presently they were shown into the superintendent's dining-room, where Polke, hospitably intent, was mixing a drink for a stranger. The stranger, evidently just in from a journey, rose and bowed, and Polke waved his hand at him with a smile, as he looked at the two young people.

"Here's your man, miss!" said Polke cheerily. "Allow me...Detective-Sergeant Starmidge, of the Criminal Investigation Department."

Chapter 8

Neale, who had never seen a real, live detective in the flesh, but cherished something of a passion for reading sensational fiction and the reports of criminal cases in the weekly newspapers, looked at the man from New Scotland Yard with a feeling of surprise. He knew Detective-Sergeant Starmidge well enough by name and reputation. He was the man who had unraveled the mysteries of the Primrose Hill murder. A particularly exciting and underground affair. It was he who had been intimately associated with the bringing to justice of the Camden Town Gang, a group of daring and successful criminals which had baffled the London police for two years.

Neale had read all about Starmidge's activities in both cases, and of the hairbreadth escape he had gone through in connection with the second. And he had formed an idea of him, which he now saw to be a totally erroneous one. For he did not look at all like a detective in Neale's opinion. Instead of being elderly, and sinister, and close of eye and mouth, he was a somewhat shy-looking, open-faced, fresh-colored young man, still under thirty, modest of demeanor, given to smiling, who might from his general appearance have been, say, a professional cricketer, or a young commercial traveler, or anything but an expert criminal catcher.

"Only just got here, and a bit tired, miss," continued Polke, waving his hand again at the detective. "So I'm just giving him a refresher to liven his brains up. He'll want them before we've done."

Betty took the chair which Polke offered her, and looked at the stranger with interest. She knew nothing about Starmidge, and she thought him quite different to any preconceived notion which she had ever had of men of his calling.

"I hope you'll be able to help us," she said politely, as Starmidge, murmuring something about his best respects to his host, took a whiskey-and-soda from Polke's hand. "Do you think you will and has Mr. Polke told you all about it?"

"Given him a mere outline, miss," remarked Polke. "I'll prime him before he goes to bed. Yes, he knows the main facts."

"And what do you propose to do first?" demanded Betty.

Starmidge smiled and set down his glass.

"Why, first," he answered, "first, I think I should like to see a photograph of Mr. Horbury."

Polke moved to a bureau in the corner of his dining-room.

"I can fit you up," he said. "I've a portrait here Mr. Horbury gave me not so long ago. There you are!"

He produced a cabinet photograph and handed it to Starmidge, who looked at it and laid it down on the table without comment.

"I suppose that conveys nothing to you?" asked Betty.

"Well," replied Starmidge, with another smile, "if a man's missing, one naturally wants to know what he's like. And if there's any advertising of him to be done by poster, I mean it ought to have a recent portrait of him."

"To be sure," agreed Polke.

"So far as I understand matters," continued Starmidge, "this gentleman left his house on Saturday evening, hasn't been seen since, and there's an idea he probably walked across country to a place called Ellersdeane. But up to now there's no proof he did. I think that's all, Mr. Polke?"

"All!" assented Polke.

"No!" said Neale. "Miss Fosdyke and I have brought you some news. Mr. Horbury must have crossed Ellersdeane Hollow on Saturday night. Look at this and I'll tell you all about it."

The superintendent and the detective listened silently to Neale's account of the meeting with Creasy, and Betty, watching Starmidge's face, saw he was quietly taking in all the points of importance.

"Is this tin-man to be depended upon?" he asked, when Neale had finished. "Is he known?"

"I know him," answered Polke. "He's come to this neighborhood for many years. Yes, an honest chap enough, bit given to poaching, no doubt, but straight enough in all other ways, no complaint of him that I ever heard of. I should believe all he says about this."

"Then, as that's undoubtedly Mr. Horbury's pipe, and as this gentleman saw him smoking it at two o'clock on Saturday, and as Creasy picked it up underneath Ellersdeane Tower on Sunday evening," said Starmidge, "there seems no doubt Mr. Horbury went that way, and dropped it where it was found. But, I can't think he was carrying Lord Ellersdeane's jewels home!"

"Why?" asked Neale.

"Is it likely?" suggested Starmidge. "One's got...always to consider probability. Is it probable a bank manager would put a hundred thousand pounds worth of jewels in his pocket, and walk across a lonely stretch of land at that time of night, just to hand them over to their owner? I think not, especially as he hadn't been asked to do so. I think if Mr. Horbury had been in a hurry to deliver up these jewels, he'd have driven out to Lord Ellersdeane's place."

"Good!" muttered Polke. "That's the more probable thing."

"Where are the jewels, then?" asked Neale.

Starmidge glanced at Polke with one expression, at Betty and Neale with another.

"They haven't been searched for yet, have they?" he asked quietly. "They may be somewhere about, you know."

"You mean to search for them?" exclaimed Betty.

"I don't know what I intend to do," replied Starmidge, smiling. "I haven't even thought. I shall have thought a lot by morning. But...the country's being searched, isn't it, for news of Mr. Horbury? Perhaps we'll hear something. It's a difficult thing for a well-known man to get clear away from a little place like this. No, what I'd like to know...what I want to satisfy myself about is, did Mr. Horbury go away at all? Is there really anything missing from the bank? Are those jewels really missing? You see," concluded Starmidge, looking round his circle of listeners, "there's an awful lot to take into account."

At that moment Polke's domestic servant tapped at the door and put her head inside the room.

"If you please, Mr. Polke, there's Mrs. Pratt, from the Station Hotel, would like a word with you," she said.

The superintendent hurried from the room, to return at

once with a stout, middle-aged woman, who, as she entered, raised her veil and glanced half-suspiciously at Polke's other visitors.

"All friends here, Mrs. Pratt," said the superintendent reassuringly. "You know young Mr. Neale well enough. This lady is Mr. Horbury's niece, anxious to find him. That gentleman's a friend of mine, you can say anything you like before him. Well, ma'am, you think you can tell me something about this affair? What might it be, now?"

Mrs. Pratt, taking the chair which Starmidge placed for her at the end of the table, nodded a general greeting to the company, and lifting her veil and untying her bonnet-strings, revealed a good-natured countenance.

"Well, Mr. Polke," she said, turning to the superintendent, "taking your word for it we're all friends, me being pretty sure, all the same, this gentleman's one of your own profession, which I don't object to. I'll tell you what it is I've come up for, special, as it were, and me not waiting until after closing-time to do it. But that town-crier's been down our way, and hearing him making his call between our house and the station, and learning what it was all about, thinks I to myself, 'I'd best go up and see the super and tell him what I know.' And," concluded Mrs. Pratt, beaming around her, "here I am!"

"Ay and what do you know, ma'am?" asked Polke. "Something, of course."

"Or I shouldn't be here," agreed Mrs. Pratt, smoothing out a fold of her gown. "Well Saturday afternoon, the time being not so many minutes after the 5.30 got in, and therefore you might say at the outside twenty minutes to six, a strange gentleman walked across from the station to our hotel, which is, as you're all well aware, exactly opposite. I happened to be in the bar-parlor window at the time, and I saw him crossing. Saw, likewise, from the way he looked about him, and up at the town above us, he'd never been in Scarnham before. And happen I'd best tell you what he was like, while the recollection's fresh in my mind. A little gentleman he was, very well dressed in what you might call the professional style; dark clothes and so forth, and a silk top-hat. I should say about fifty years of age, with a fresh complexion and a biggish grey moustache and a nicely rolled umbrella, quite the little swell he was. He made for our door, and I went to the bar-window to attend to him. He wanted to know if he could get some food, and I said of course he could, we'd some uncommon nice chops in the house. So he ordered three chops and a drink and then asked if we'd a telephone in the house, and could he use it. And, of course, I told him we had, and showed him where it was, after which he wanted a local directory, and I gave him Scammond's Guide. He turned that over a bit, and then, when he'd found what he wanted, he went to our telephone box, which, as you're well aware, Mr. Polke, is in our front hall. And into it he popped."

Mrs. Pratt paused a moment, and gave her listeners a knowing look, as if she was now about to narrate the most important part of her story.

"But what you mayn't be aware of, Mr. Polke," she continued, "is our telephone box, which has glass panels in its upper parts, has at this present time one of these panels broken, our pot-man did it, carrying a plank through the hall. So anyone passing to and fro, as it were, when anybody's using the telephone, can't help hearing a word or two of what's being said inside. Now, of course, I was passing in and out, giving orders for this gentleman's chops, when he was in the box. And I heard a bit of what he said, though I didn't, naturally, hear anything of what was said to him, nor who by. But it's in consequence of what I did hear, and of what Tolson, the town-crier, has been shouting down our way tonight, I come up here to see you."

"Much obliged to you, Mrs. Pratt," said Polke. "Very glad to hear anything that may have to do with Mr. Horbury's disappearance. Now, what did you hear?"

"What I heard," replied the landlady, "was this here disjointed, as you would term it. First of all I hear the gentleman ask for 'Town 23.' Now, of course, you know whose number that there is, Mr. Polke."

"Chestermarke's Bank," said Neale, turning to Betty.

"Chestermarke's Bank it is, sir," assented Mrs. Pratt. "Which you know very well, as also do I, having oft called it up. Very well, I didn't hear no more just then, me going into the dining-room to see our maid laid the table proper. But when I was going back to the bar, I heard more. 'Along the river-side?' says the gentleman, 'Straight on from where I am, all right.'

Then after a minute, 'At seven-thirty, then?' he says. 'All right...I'll meet you.' And after that he rings off and he went into the dining-room, and in due course he had his chops, and some tart and cheese, and a pint of our bitter ale, and took his time, and perhaps about a quarter past seven he came to the bar and paid, and he took a drop of Scotch whisky. After which he says, 'It's very possible, landlady, I may have to stay in the town all night, have you a nice room you can let me?' 'Certainly, sir,' says I. 'We've very good rooms, and bathrooms, and every convenience, shall I show you one?' 'No,' says he, 'this seems a good house, and I'll take your word for it, keep your best room for me, then.' And after that he lighted a cigar and went out, saying he'd be back later, and he crossed the road and went down on the river-bank, and walked slowly along towards the bottom of the town. And Mr. Polke and company," concluded Mrs. Pratt, solemnly turning from one listener to another, "that was the last I saw of him. For he never came back!"

"Never came back!" echoed Polke.

"Not even the ghost of him!" said Mrs. Pratt. "I waited up myself till twelve, and then I decided he'd changed his mind and was staying with somebody he knew, which person, Mr. Polke, I took to be Mr. Horbury. Why? 'Cause he'd rung up Chestermarke's Bank and who should he want at Chestermarke's Bank at six o'clock of a Saturday evening but Mr. Horbury? There wouldn't be nobody else there as Mr. Neale will agree."

"You never heard of this gentleman being in the town on Sunday or today?" asked Polke.

"Not a word!" replied Mrs. Pratt. "And never saw him go to the station, neither, to leave the town. Now, as you know, Mr. Polke, we've only two trains go away from here on Sundays, and there's only four on any week-day, us being nothing but a branch line, and as our bar-parlor window is exactly opposite the station, I see everybody that goes and comes. I always was one for looking out of window! And I'm sure that little gentleman didn't go away neither yesterday nor today. And that's all I know," concluded Mrs. Pratt, rising, "and if it's any use to you, you're welcome, and hopeful I am your poor uncle will be found, Miss, for a nicer gentleman I could never wish to meet!"

Mrs. Pratt departed a midst expressions of gratitude and police admonitions to keep her news to herself for a while. Betty and Neale turned eagerly to the famous detective. But Starmidge appeared to have entered upon a period of silence, and made no further observation than he would wait upon Miss Fosdyke in the morning, and presently the two young people followed Mrs. Pratt into the street and turned into the Market-Place. The last of the evening revelers were just coming out of the closing taverns, and to a group of them, Tolson, the town-crier, was dismally calling forth his announcement a one hundred pounds reward would be paid to any person who first gave news of having seen Mr. John Horbury on the previous Saturday evening or since. The clanging of his bell, and the strident notes of his cracked voice, sounded in the distance as Betty said goodnight to Neale and turned sadly into the Scarnham Arms.

Chapter 9

Chestermarke's clerks found no difficulty in obtaining access to the bank when they presented themselves at its doors at nine o'clock next morning. Both partners were already there, and appeared to have been there for some time. And Joseph at once called Neale into the private parlor, and drew his attention to a large poster which lay on a side-table, its ink still wet from the printing press.

"Let Patten put that up in one of the front windows, Neale," he said. "It's just come in, I gave the copy for it last night. Read it over, I think it's satisfactory, eh?"

Neale bent over the big, bold letters, and silently read the announcement:

"Messrs. Chestermarke, in view of certain unauthorized rumors, now circulating in the town and neighborhood, respecting the disappearance of their late manager, Mr. John Horbury, take the earliest opportunity of announcing all Customers Securities and Deposits in their hands are safe, and business will be conducted in the usual way."

"That make things clear?" asked Joseph, closely watching his clerk. "To our clients, I mean?"

"Quite clear, I should say," replied Neale.

"Then get it up at once, before opening hours, and save all the bother of questions," commanded Joseph. "And if people do come asking questions, as some of them will, tell them not to bother themselves, nor us. We don't want to waste our time interviewing fools all the morning."

Neale took the poster and went out, with no further remark. And presently the junior clerk, with the aid of a few wafers, fixed the announcement in the window which looked out on the Market-Place, and people began to gather round and to read it, and, after the usual fashion of country-born folk, then went away to talk about it. In half an hour it was known in every shop and tavern parlor in Scarnham Market-Place despite the town-crier's announcement, and the wild rumors of the night before, Chestermarke's Bank was all right, and they were already speaking of Horbury in the past tense. He was, wherever he might be, no longer the manager of that ancient concern, he was the late manager. At ten o'clock Superintendent Polke, bluff and cheery as usual, and Detective-Sergeant Starmidge, eyeing his new surroundings with appreciative curiosity, strolled round the corner from the police-station and approached the bank. Half a dozen loungers were gathered before the window, reading the poster. The two police officials joined them and also read in silence. Then, with a look at each other, they turned into the door which Patten had just opened. Neale hurried to the counter to meet them.

"Well, Mr. Neale," said Polke, as if he had called on the most ordinary business, "we'll just have a word with your principals, if they please. A mere interchange of views, you know, we shan't keep them."

"They don't want bothering," whispered Neale, bending over the counter. "Shan't I do instead?"

"No, sir!" answered Polke. "Nothing but principals will do! Here, Starmidge, give Mr. Neale one of your official cards."

Neale took the card and disappeared into the parlor, where he laid it before Gabriel.

"Mr. Polke is with him, sir," he said. "They say they won't detain you."

Gabriel tossed the card over to his nephew with a look of inquiry. Joseph sneered at it, and threw it into a waste-paper basket.

"Tell them we don't wish to see them," he answered. "We..."

"Stop a bit!" interrupted Gabriel. "I think perhaps we'd better see them. We may as well see them, and have done with it. Bring them in, Neale."

Polke and Starmidge, presently entering, found themselves coldly greeted. Gabriel made the slightest inclination of his head, in response to Polke's salutation and the detective's bow. Joseph pointedly gave no heed to either.

"Well?" demanded the senior partner.

"We've just called, Mr. Chestermarke, to hear if you've anything to say to us about this matter of Mr. Horbury's," said Polke. "Of course, you know it's been put in our hands."

"Not by us!" snapped Gabriel.

"Quite so, sir, by Lord Ellersdeane, and by Mr. Horbury's niece, Miss Fosdyke," assented Polke. "The young lady, of course, is naturally anxious about her uncle's safety, and Lord Ellersdeane is anxious about the Countess's jewels. And we hear securities of yours are missing."

"We haven't told you so," retorted Gabriel.

"We haven't even approached you," remarked Joseph.

"Just so!" agreed Polke. "But, under the circumstances..."

"We have nothing to say to you, superintendent," interrupted Gabriel. "We can't help anything Lord Ellersdeane has done, nor anything Miss Fosdyke likes to do. Lord Ellersdeane is not, and never has been, a customer of ours. Miss Fosdyke acts independently. If they call you in, as they seem to have done very thoroughly, it's their look out. We haven't! When we want your assistance, we'll let you know. At present we don't."

He waved one of the white hands towards the door as he spoke, as if to command withdrawal. But Polke lingered.

"You don't propose to give the police any information, then, Mr. Chestermarke?" he asked quietly.

"At present we don't propose to give any information to anybody whom it doesn't concern," replied Gabriel. "As regards the mere surface facts of Mr. John Horbury's disappearance, you know as much as we do."

"You don't propose to join in any search for him or any attempt to discover his whereabouts, sir?" inquired Starmidge, speaking for the first time.

Gabriel looked up from his paper, and slowly eyed his questioner.

"What we propose to do is a matter for ourselves," he answered coldly. "For no one else."

Starmidge bowed and turned away, and Polke, after hesitating a moment, said good-morning and followed him from the room. The two men nodded to Neale and went out into the Market-Place.

"Well?" said Polke.

"Queer couple!" remarked Starmidge.

Polke jerked his thumb at the poster in the bank window. "Of course!" he said, "so long as they can satisfy their customers that all's right so far as they're concerned, we can't get at what is missing that belongs to the Chestermarkes."

"There are ways of finding that out," replied Starmidge quietly.

"What ways, now?" asked Polke. "We can't make them tell us their private affairs. Supposing Horbury has robbed them, they aren't forced to tell us how much or how little he's robbed them of!"

"All in good time," remarked the detective. "We're only beginning. Let's go and talk to this Miss Fosdyke a bit. She doesn't mind what money she spends on this business, you say?"

"Not if it costs her last penny!" answered Polke.

"All right," said Starmidge. "Fosdyke's Entire represents a lot of pennies. We'll just have a word or two with her."

Betty, looking out of her window on the Market-Place, had seen the two men leave Chestermarke's Bank, and was waiting eagerly for their coming. She listened intently to Polke's account of the interview with the partners, and her cheeks glowed indignantly as he brought it to an end.

"Shameful!" she exclaimed. "To make accusations against my uncle, and then to refuse to say what they are! But...can't you make them say?"

"We'll try, in good time," answered Starmidge. "Slow and steady's the game here. For, whatever it is, it's a deep game."

"Nothing has been heard since I saw you last night?" asked Betty anxiously. "No one has brought you any news?"

"No news of any sort, miss," replied Polke.

"What's to be done, then, next?" she inquired, looking from one to the other. "Let us do something!"

"Oh, we'll do a lot, Miss Fosdyke, before the day's out," said Starmidge reassuringly. "I'm going to work just now. Now, the first thing is, publicity! We must have all this in the newspapers at once." He turned to the superintendent. "I suppose there's some journalist here in the town who sends news to the London press, isn't there?" he asked.

"Parkinson, editor of the Scarnham Advertiser, he does," replied Polke, with promptitude. "He's a sort of reporter-editor, you understand, and jolly glad of a bit of extra stuff."

"That's the first thing," said Starmidge. "The next, we must have a reward bill printed immediately, and circulated broadcast. It must have a portrait on it. I'll take the photograph you showed me last night. And we'll have to offer a specific reward in each. How much is it to be, Miss Fosdyke? For you'll have to pay it, you know."

"Anything you like!" said Betty eagerly. "A thousand pounds? Would that do, to begin with."

"We'll say half of it," answered Starmidge. "Very good. Now, Mr. Polke, if you'll tell me where this Mr. Parkinson's to be found, and where the best printing office in the place is, I'll go to work."

"Scammonds are the best printers and they're quick," said Polke. "But I'll come with you."

"Is there anything I can do?" asked Betty. "If I could only be doing something!"

Starmidge nodded his comprehension and mused a while.

"Just so!" he said. "You don't want to sit and wait. Well, there is something you might do, Miss Fosdyke, as you're Mr. Horbury's niece. Mr. Polke's been telling me about his household arrangements. Now, as you are a relation, suppose you call on his housekeeper, who was the last person to see him, and get all the information you can out of her? Draw her on to talk, you never know what interesting point you might get in that way. And are you Mr. Horbury's nearest relation?"

"Yes, the very nearest next-of-kin," answered Betty.

"Then ask to see his papers, his desk, his private belongings," said Starmidge. "Demand to see them! You've the legal right. And let us know, you'll always find me somewhere about Mr. Polke's how you get on. Now, superintendent, we'll get to work."

Outside the Scarnham Arms, Starmidge looked at his companion with a sly smile.

"Are you anything of a betting man?" he asked.

"Nothing much, odd half-crown now and then," replied Polke. "Why?"

"Lay you a fiver to a shilling Miss Fosdyke won't see anything of Horbury's nor get any information!" answered Starmidge, more slyly than ever. "She won't be allowed!"

Polke gave the detective a shrewd look.

"I dare say!" he said. "Whew, it's a queer game, this, Starmidge. First moves of it, anyway."

"Let's get on to the next," counseled Starmidge. "Where's this journalist?"

Mr. Parkinson, a high-brow, shock-headed young man, who combined the duties of editor and reporter with those of advertisement canvasser and business manager of the one four-page sheet which Scarnham boasted, received the two police officials in a small office in which there was just room for himself and his visitors to squeeze themselves.

"I was about coming round to you, Mr. Polke," he said. "Can you let me have the facts of this Horbury affair?"

"We've come to save you the trouble," answered Polke. "This gentleman, Detective-Sergeant Starmidge, of the C.I.D., Mr. Parkinson wants to have a bit of a transaction with you."

Parkinson eyed the famous detective with as much wonder as Neale had felt on the previous evening.

"Oh!" he exclaimed. "Pleased to meet you, sir I've heard of you. What can I do for you, Mr. Starmidge?"

"Can you wire, at our expense a full account of all that I shall tell you, to a London Press agency that'll distribute it amongst all the London papers at once?" asked Starmidge. "You know what I mean?"

"I can," answered Parkinson. "And principal provincials, too. It'll be in all the evening papers this very night, sir."

"Then come on," said Starmidge, dropping into a chair by the editorial desk. "I'll tell you all about it."

Polke listened admiringly while the detective carefully narrated the facts of what was henceforth to be known as the Scarnham Mystery. Nothing appeared to have escaped Starmidge's observation and attention. And he was surprised to find the detective's presentation of the case was not that which he would have made. Starmidge did no more than refer to the fact Lady Ellersdeane's jewels were missing. He said nothing whatever about the rumors some of Chestermarke's securities were said to have disappeared.

But on one point he laid great stress, the visit of the little gentleman with the large gray mustache to the Station Hotel at Scarnham on the evening where John Horbury disappeared, and to the fragments of conversation overheard by Mrs. Pratt. He described the stranger as Mrs. Pratt had described him, and appealed to him, if he read this news, to come forward at once. Finally, he supplemented his account with a full description of John Horbury, carefully furnished by the united efforts of Polke and Parkinson, and wound up by announcing the five hundred pounds reward.

"All over England, tonight, and tomorrow morning, sir," said Parkinson, gathering up his copy. "Now I'm off to wire this at once. Great engine the Press, Mr. Starmidge! I dare say you find it very useful in your walk of life."

Starmidge followed Polke into the Market-Place again.

"Now for that reward bill," he said. "I don't set so much store by it, but it's got to be done. It all helps. There's Miss Fosdyke, going to have a try at her bit."

He pointed down the broad pavement with an amused smile. Betty, attired in her smartest, was just entering the portals of Chestermarke's Bank.

Chapter 10

Mrs. Carswell opened the door of the bank-house in response to Miss Fosdyke's ring. She started a little at sight of the visitor, and her eyes glanced involuntarily and, as it seemed to Betty, with something of uneasiness, at the side-door which led into the Chestermarkes private parlor. And Betty immediately interpreted the meaning of that glance.

"No, Mrs. Carswell," she said, before the housekeeper could speak, "I haven't come to call on either Mr. Gabriel or Mr. Joseph Chestermarke. I came to see you. Might I come in?"

Mrs. Carswell stepped back into the hall, and Betty followed. For a moment the two looked at each other. And in the elder woman's eyes there was still the same expression, and it was with obvious uncertainty, if not with positive suspicion, she waited.

"You have not heard anything of Mr. Horbury?" asked Betty, who was not slow to notice the housekeeper's demeanor.

"Nothing!" replied Mrs. Carswell, with a shake of the head. "Nothing at all! No one has told me anything."

Betty turned to the door of the dining-room.

"Very well," she said. "I dare say you know, Mrs. Carswell, I am my uncle's nearest relation. Now I want to go through his papers and things. I want to see his desk, his last letters, anything and everything there is."

She laid a hand on the door and Mrs. Carswell suddenly found her tongue.

"Oh, miss!" she said, in a low, frightened voice, "you can't! That room's locked up. So is the study where all Mr. Horbury's papers are. So is his bedroom. Mr. Joseph Chestermarke locked them all up last night, he has the keys. Nobody's to go into them, nor into any other room without his permission."

Betty's cheeks began to glow, and an obstinate look to

settle about her lips.

"Oh!" she exclaimed. "But I think I shall have something to say to that, Mrs. Carswell. Ask Mr. Joseph Chestermarke to come here a minute."

The housekeeper shrunk back.

"I daren't, Miss Fosdyke!" she answered. "It would be as much as my place was worth!"

"I thought you were my uncle's housekeeper," suggested Betty. "Aren't you? Or are you employed by Mr. Joseph Chestermarke? Come, now?"

Mrs. Carswell hesitated. It was very evident she was afraid. But of what?

"So far as I know," continued Betty, "this is my uncle's house, and you're his servant. Am I right or wrong, Mrs. Carswell?"

"Right as regards my being engaged by Mr. Horbury," replied the housekeeper. "But the house belongs to them! Mr. Horbury, so I understand had the use of it...it was reckoned as part of his salary. It's their house, miss."

"But, anyway, my uncle's effects are his and I mean to see them," insisted Betty. "If you won't call Mr. Joseph or Mr. Gabriel out, I shall walk into the bank at the front door, and demand to see them. You'd better let one of them know I'm here, Mrs. Carswell I'm not going to stand any nonsense."

Mrs. Carswell hesitated a little, but in the end she knocked timidly at the private door. And presently Joseph Chestermarke opened it, looked out, saw Betty, and came into the hall. He offered his visitor no polite greeting, and for once he forgot his accustomed sneering smile. Instead, he gave the housekeeper a swift look which sent her away in haste, and he turned to Betty with an air of annoyance.

"Yes?" he asked abruptly. "What do you want?"

"I want to go into my uncle's house, into his rooms," said Betty. "I am his next-of-kin, I wish to examine his papers."

"You can't!" answered Joseph. "We haven't examined them ourselves yet."

"What right have you to examine them?" demanded Betty.

"Every right!" retorted Joseph.

"Not his private belongings!" she said firmly.

"This is our house, you're not going into it," declared

Joseph. "Nobody's going into it without our permission."

"We'll see about that, Mr. Joseph Chestermarke!" replied Betty. "If, supposing my uncle is dead, I've the right to examine anything he's left. I insist upon it! I insist on seeing his papers, looking through his desk. And at once!"

"No!" said Joseph. "Nothing of the sort. We don't know you've any right. We don't know you're his next-of-kin. We're not legally aware you're his niece. You say you are but we don't know it, as a matter of real fact. You'd better go away."

Betty's cheeks flamed hotly and her eyes flashed.

"So that's your attitude to me!" she exclaimed. "Very well! But you shall soon see whether I am what I say I am. What are you and your uncle implying, suggesting, hinting at?" she went on, suddenly letting her naturally hot temper get the better of her. "Do you realize what an utterly unworthy part you are playing? You accuse my uncle of being a thief and you dare not make any specified accusation against him! You charge him with stealing your securities and you daren't tell the police what securities! I don't believe you've a security missing! Nobody believes it! The police don't believe it. Lord Ellersdeane doesn't believe it. Why, your own clerk, Mr. Neale, who ought to know, if anybody does, doesn't believe it! You're telling lies, Mr. Joseph Chestermarke there! Lies! I'll denounce you to the whole town. I'll expose you! I believe my uncle has met with some foul play and as sure as I am his niece I'll probe the whole thing to the bottom. Are you going to admit me to those rooms?"

The door of the private room, which Joseph had left slightly ajar behind him, was pushed open a little, and Gabriel's colorless face looked out.

"Tell the young woman to go and see a solicitor," he said, and vanished again.

Joseph glanced at Betty, who was still staring indignantly at him.

"You hear?" he said quietly. "Now you'd better go away. You are not going in there."

Betty suddenly turned and walked out. She was across the Market-Place and at the door of the Scarnham Arms before her self-possession had come back to her. And she was aware then a gentleman, who had just alighted from a horse which a groom was leading away to the stable yard, was looking and smiling at her. "Oh!" she exclaimed. "Is it you, Lord Ellersdeane? I beg your pardon I was preoccupied."

"So I saw," said the Earl. "I'd watched you come across from the Bank. Is there any news this morning?"

"Come up to my sitting-room and let us talk," said Betty. She led the way upstairs and closed her door on herself and her visitor. "No news of my uncle," she continued, turning to the Earl. "Have you any?"

The Earl shook his head disappointingly.

"No!" he replied. "I wish I had! I myself and a lot of my men have been searching all round Ellersdeane practically all night. We've made inquiries at each of the neighboring villages without result. Have the police heard anything? I've only just come into town."

"You haven't seen Polke, then?" said Betty. "Oh, well, he heard something last night." She went on to tell the Earl of the meeting with the tinker, and of Mrs. Pratt's account of the mysterious stranger, and of what Starmidge was now doing. "It all seems such slow work," she concluded, "but I suppose the police can't move any faster."

"You heard nothing at the bank itself, from the Chestermarkes?" asked the Earl.

"I heard sufficient to make me as…as absent-minded as I was when you met me just now! I went there, as my uncle's nearest relation, with a simple request to see his papers and things…a very natural desire, surely. The Chestermarkes have locked up his rooms and they ordered me out showed me the door!"

"How very extraordinary!" exclaimed the Earl. "Really! In so many words?"

"I think Joseph had the grace to say I had better go away," said Betty. "And Gabriel, who called me a young woman told me to go and see a solicitor, which, of course," she added reflectively, "is precisely what I shall do as they will very soon find!"

The Earl stepped over to one of the windows, and stood for a moment or two silently looking out on the Market-Place.

"I don't understand this at all," he said at last. "What is the meaning of all this reserve on the Chestermarkes part? Why didn't they tell the police what securities are missing? Why don't they let you, his niece, examine Horbury's effects?

What right have they to fasten up his house?"

"Their house, so Mrs. Carswell says," remarked Betty.

"Oh, well it may be their house, strictly speaking," agreed the Earl, "but Horbury was its tenant, anyway, and the furniture and things in it are his, I'm sure of that, for he and I shared a similar taste in collecting old oak, and I know where he bought most of his possessions. I can't make the behavior of these people out at all and I'm getting more and more uneasy about the whole thing, Miss Fosdyke, as I'm sure you are. I wonder if the police will find the man who came to the Station Hotel on Saturday? Now, if they could lay hands on him, and get to know who he was, and what he wanted, and if he really met your uncle…"

The Earl suddenly paused and turned from the window with a glance at Betty.

"There's young Mr. Neale coming across from the bank," he observed. "I think he's coming here. By the by, isn't he a relation of Horbury's?"

"No," said Betty. "But my uncle was his guardian. Is he coming here, Lord Ellersdeane?"

"Straight here," replied the Earl. "Perhaps he's got some news."

Betty had the door open before Neale could knock at it. He came in with a smile, and glanced half-whimsically, half as if he had queer news to give, at the two people who looked so inquiringly at him.

"Well?" demanded Betty. "What is it, Wallie? Have these two precious principals sent you with news?"

"They're not my principals any longer," answered Neale. He laid down some books and an old jacket on the table. "That's my old working coat," he went on, with a laugh. "I've worn it for the last time at Chestermarke's. They've dismissed me."

Lord Ellersdeane turned sharply from the window, and Betty indulged in a cry of indignation.

"Dismissed…you?" she exclaimed. "Dismissed!"

"With a quarter's salary in lieu of notice," laughed Neale, slapping his pocket. "I've got it here…in gold."

"But why?" asked Betty.

Neale shook his head at her.

"Because you told Joseph that I didn't believe them

when they said some of their securities were missing," he answered. "You did it! As soon as you'd gone, they had me in, told me it was contrary to their principles to retain servants who took sides with other people against them, handed me a check and told me to cash it and depart. And here I am!"

"You don't seem to mind this very much, Mr. Neale," observed the Earl, looking keenly at this victim of summary treatment. "Do you?"

"If your lordship really wants to know," answered Neale, "I don't! I'm truly thankful. It's only what would have happened in another way. I meant to leave Chestermarke's. If it hadn't been for Mr. Horbury, I should have left ages ago. I hate banking! I hated the life. And I dislike Chestermarke's! Immensely! Now, I'll go and have a free life somewhere in Canada or some equally spacious climb where I can breathe."

"Not at all!" said Betty decidedly. "You shall come and be my manager in London. The brewery wants one, badly. You shall have a handsome salary, Wallie much more than you had at that beastly bank!"

"Very kind of you, I'm sure," laughed Neale. "But I think I'm inclined to put breweries in the same line with banks. Don't you be too rash, Betty I'm not exactly cut out for commercialism. Not," he added reflectively, "not that I haven't been a very good servant to Chestermarke's. I have! But Chestermarkes are…what they are!"

The Earl, who had been watching the two young people with something of amused interest, suddenly came forward from the window.

"Mr. Neale!" he said.

"My lord!" responded Neale.

'What's your honest opinion about your late principals?" asked the Earl.

Neale shook his head slowly and significantly.

"I don't know," he answered.

"Do you know they've just now refused Miss Fosdyke permission to examine her uncle's belongings?" continued the Earl. "That they wouldn't even let her enter the house?"

"No, I didn't know," replied Neale. "But I'm not surprised. Nothing those two could do would ever surprise me."

"Feeling that, what do you advise in this case?" asked

the Earl. "Come! You're no longer in their employ, you can speak freely now. What do you think?"

"Well," said Neale, after a pause, and speaking with unusual gravity, "I think the police ought to make a thorough examination of the bank-house. I'm surprised it hasn't been thought of before."

The Earl picked up his hat.

"I've been thinking of it all the morning!" he said. "Come, let us all go round to Polke."

Chapter 11

As they turned out of the Market-Place into the street leading to the police-station, Lord Ellersdeane and his companions became aware of a curious figure which was slowly preceding them. A very old man whose massive head and long white hair, falling in thick shocks about his neck, was innocent of covering, whose tall, erect form was closely wrapped about in a great, many-caped horseman's cloak which looked as if it had descended to him from some early Georgian ancestor. In one hand he carried a long staff; the other clutched an ancient folio; altogether he was something very much out of the common, and Neale, catching sight of him, nudged Betty's elbow and pointed ahead.

"One of the sights of Scarnham!" he whispered. "Old Batterley, the antiquary. Never seen with a hat, and never without that cloak, his staff, and a book under his arm. You needn't be astonished if he suddenly stops and begins reading his book in the open street, it's a habit of his."

But the antiquary apparently had other business. He turned into the police-station, and when the three visitors followed him a moment later, he was already in Polke's private office, and Polke and Starmidge were gazing speculatively at him. Polke turned to the newcomers, as the old man, having fitted on a pair of large spectacles, recognized the Earl and executed a deep bow.

"Mr. Batterley's just called with a suggestion, my lord," observed Polke, good-humoredly. "He's heard of Mr. Horbury's disappearance, and of the loss of your lordship's jewels, and he says an explanation of the whole thing may be got if we search the bank-house."

"Thoroughly!" said Batterley, with a warning shake of his big head. "Thoroughly...thoroughly, Mr. Polke! No use just walking through the rooms, and seeing what any housemaid would see, the thing must be done properly. Your lordship," he continued, turning to the Earl, "knows many houses in our Market-Place possess secret passages, double-staircases, and the like, Horbury's house is certainly one of those that do. It has, of course, been modernized. My memory is not quite as good as it was, but I have a recollection when I was a boy, well over seventy years ago. I am, as your lordship is aware, nearer ninety than eighty, there were hiding-places discovered in the bank-house at the time Matthew Chestermarke, grandfather of the present Gabriel, had it altered. In fact, I am quite sure I was taken by my father to see them. Now, of course, many of these places were bricked up, and so on, but I think...it is my impression a double staircase was left untouched, and some recesses in the paneling of the garden-room. That garden-room, Mr. Polke, if you know what I mean?"

"Mr. Batterley," remarked the Earl, "means the paneled room which looks out on the garden. Mr. Horbury has used it as a study."

"The garden-room," continued the old antiquary, "should be particularly examined. It is into that room the double staircase opens by a door concealed in the recess at the side of the fire-place. There were, I am sure, recesses behind the paneling in that room. Now, Horbury may have known of them, he had tastes of an antiquarian disposition, in an amateur way, you know. At any rate, Mr. Polke, you should examine the house and especially that room, for Horbury may have hidden Lord Ellersdeane's property there. A deeply interesting room that!" added the old man musingly. "I haven't been in it for some sixty years or so, but I remember it quite well. It was in that room Jasper Chestermarke murdered Sir Gervase Rudd."

Starmidge, who, like the rest of them, had been listening eagerly to Batterley's talk, turned sharply to him.

"Did you say murdered, sir?" he said.

"A well-known story!" answered the old man half-impatiently, as he rose from his chair. "An ancestor of these Chestermarkes, he killed a man in that very room. Well, that's why I suggest, Mr. Polke. And for another reason. As Lord Ellersdeane there knows, being, as his lordship is, a member of our society, the bank-house is so old that underneath it there may be such matters as old wells, old drains. Now, supposing Horbury had discovered some way under the present house, some secret passage or something, and he went down into it on Sunday? He may have fallen into one of these places and be lying there dead or helpless. It's possible, Mr. Polke, it's quite possible. I make the suggestion to you for what it's worth, you know."

The old man bowed himself out and went away, and Polke turned to Lord Ellersdeane and Betty.

"I'm glad your lordship's come in," he said. "Quite apart from what Mr. Batterley suggests, we'll have to examine that bank-house. It's all nonsense allowing the Chestermarkes to have their own way about everything! It's time we examined Horbury's effects."

Starmidge turned to Betty.

"Did you succeed in getting in there, Miss Fosdyke?" he asked.

"No!" replied Betty. "Mr. Joseph Chestermarke absolutely refused me admittance, and his uncle told me to go to a solicitor."

"Good advice, certainly," remarked Polke drily. "You'd better take it, miss. But what's Mr. Neale doing here?"

"Mr. Neale," said the Earl, "has just been summarily dismissed for...to put it plainly taking sides with Miss Fosdyke and myself."

"Ho, ho!" exclaimed Polke. "Ah! Well, my lord, there's only one thing to be done, and as your lordship's in town, let us do it at once."

"What?" asked the Earl.

"You must come with me before the borough magistrates, they're sitting now," said Polke, "and make application for a search-warrant. Your lordship will have to swear you have lost your jewels, and you have good cause to believe they may be on the premises occupied lately by Mr. Horbury, to whose care you entrusted them. It's a mere matter of form, we shall get the warrant at once. Then Starmidge and I will go and execute it. Miss Fosdyke just do what I suggest, if you please. Mr. Neale will take you to Mr. Pellworthy, the solicitor, he was your uncle's solicitor, and a friend of his. Tell him all about your visit to the bank this morning. Say that you insist, as next-of-kin, on having access to your uncle's belongings. Get Mr. Pellworthy to go with you to the bank. Meet Detective-Sergeant Starmidge and me outside there, in, say, half an hour. Then we'll see what happens. Now, my lord, if you'll come with me, we'll apply for that search-warrant."

As the Scarnham clocks were striking twelve, Gabriel and Joseph looked up from their desks to see Shirley's eyes, large with excitement, gazing at them from the threshold of their private parlor.

"Well?" demanded the senior partner.

The clerk moved nearer to his principal's desk.

"Mr. Polke's outside, sir, with the gentleman who came in with him before," announced Shirley. "He says he must see you at once. And there's Mr. Pellworthy, sir, with Miss Fosdyke. Mr. Pellworthy says, sir, he must see you at once, too."

Gabriel glanced at his nephew. And Joseph spoke without looking up from his writing-pad, and as if he knew that his partner was regarding him.

"Bring them all in," he said.

He criticized his writing as the four callers were ushered in; he did not even look round at them. Gabriel, more sphinx like than ever, regarded each in order with an air of distinct disapproval. And he took care to speak first.

"Now, Mr. Pellworthy?" he said sharply. "What do you want?"

Pellworthy, an elderly man, looked at Gabriel with as much disapproval as Gabriel had bestowed on him.

"Mr. Chestermarke," he said quietly, "Miss Fosdyke, as next-of-kin to Mr. John Horbury, my client desires to see and examine her uncle's effects. As you know very well, she is quite within her rights. I must ask you to give her access to Mr. Horbury's belongings."

"And what do you want, Mr. Polke?" demanded Gabriel.

Polke produced a formal-looking document and held it before the banker's eyes.

"Merely to show you that, Mr. Chestermarke," he answered. "That's a search-warrant, sir! It empowers me and Mr. Starmidge here to search, but I needn't read it to you, Mr. Chestermarke, I think. I suppose we can go into the house now?"

Faint spots of color showed themselves on Gabriel's cheeks. And again he turned to his nephew. Joseph, however, did not speak. Instead, he turned to the wall at his side and pressed a bell. A moment later a maid-servant opened the private door which communicated with the house, and looked inquiringly and a little nervously inside. Joseph frowned at her.

"I rang twice!" he said. "That meant Mrs. Carswell. Send her here."

The girl hesitated.

"If you please, sir," she said at last, "Mrs. Carswell isn't in, sir, she's out."

Joseph turned sharply, up to this he had remained staring at the papers on his desk, now he twisted completely round in his chair.

"Where is she?" he demanded. "Fetch her!"

"If you please, sir, Mrs. Carswell hasn't been in for quite an hour, sir," said the girl. "She put on her things and went out, sir, just...just after that young lady called this morning. She...she's never come back, sir."

Polke, who was standing close to Starmidge, quietly nudged the detective's elbow. Both men watched the junior partner. And both saw the first signs of something that was very like doubt and anxiety show in his face.

"That'll do!" he said to the servant. He rose slowly from his desk, put a hand in his pocket, and drew out some keys. Without a word, he slightly motioned the visitors to follow him. Out in the hall stood two men, who in spite of their plain clothes, were obviously policemen. Joseph started and turned to Polke.

"Damn you!" he snarled under his breath. "Are you going to pester us with your whole crew? Send those fellows off at once!"

"Nothing of the sort, Mr. Chestermarke!" replied Polke, in a similar whisper, "I shall bring as many of my men here as I please. It's your own fault, you should have been reasonable this morning. Now, sir, you'll open any door in this house that's locked."

Joseph suddenly paused and handed over the keys he was dangling.

"Open them yourself!" he said.

He turned on his heel, and without another word or look went back into the private parlor. And Polke, opening the door of the dining-room, ushered his party inside, and then stepped back to the two men who were waiting in the hall.

"Smithson," he said to one of them, "you'll stay at the house-door here, inside, mind, so as not to attract attention from any customers coming up this hall to the bank. Jones, come out here with me a minute," he continued, taking the second man outside. "Look here, I've a quiet job for you. You know the housekeeper here...Mrs. Carswell? She's disappeared. May be all right and it mayn't. Now, you go out and take a look round for her. And go to the cab-stand at the corner of the Moot Hall, and just find out if she's taken a taxi from them, and if so, where she wanted to be driven to. And then come back and tell me and when you come back, stay inside the house with Smithson."

The policeman nodded his comprehension of these instructions and went out, and Polke turned back to the dining-room and closed the door. He looked at Starmidge.

"Now I'm in your hands," he said quietly. "You take charge of this. What do you wish to do?"

"One thing particularly at first," answered Starmidge. "And we can all work at it. Never mind these secret passages and dark corners and holes in the panels, at present we may have a look at these later on. What I do want to find out is if there's any letter among Mr. Horbury's papers making an appointment with him last Saturday evening. To put matters briefly, I want some light on that man who came to the Station Hotel on Saturday, and who presumably came to meet Mr. Horbury."

"I see," said Polke. "Good! Then...first?"

"Here's his desk and its drawers," suggested Starmidge. "Now, let us all four take a drawer each and see if we can find any such letter. I'm going on the presumption this stranger came down to see Mr. Horbury, and on his arrival he telephoned up to let him know he was here. If that presumption is correct, then, in all probability, there'd been previous correspondence between them as to the man's visit."

"If that man came to see Mr. Horbury," remarked the solicitor, "why didn't he come straight here to the bank-house?"

"That's just where the mystery lies, sir," replied Starmidge. "All the mystery of the affair lies in that man's coming at all! Let me find out who that man was, and what he came for, and if he and Mr. Horbury met, and where they went when they did meet and I'll soon tell you what would probably make your hair stand on end!" he muttered to himself, as he pulled a drawer out of the desk and placed on a center table before Betty. "Now, Miss Fosdyke, you get to work on that."

For over an hour the four curiously assorted searchers examined the contents of the missing man's desk, of another desk in the study, of certain letter-racks which hung above the mantelpieces in both rooms, of drawers in these rooms, of drawers and small cabinets in his bedroom. Starmidge turned out the pockets of all the clothing he could find, opened suitcases, trunks, dressing-cases. They found nothing of the nature desired. And just as half-past one came, and Polke was wondering what Starmidge would do next, Jones came back and called him into the inner hall.

"I've got some news of her," he whispered. "She's off from Scarnham, anyway, sir! I couldn't get any word of her in the town, nor at the cab-places, in fact, it's only within this last five minutes that I've got it."

"Well?" demanded Polke eagerly. "And what is it?"

"Young Mitchell, who has a taxi-cab of his own, you know," said Jones. "He told me...heard I was inquiring. He says at half-past ten, just as he was coming out of his shed in River Street, Mrs. Carswell came up and asked him to drive her into Ecclesborough. He did, they got there at half-past eleven. He set her down at the Exchange Station. Then he came back alone. So she's got two hours good start, sir if she really is off!"

Chapter 12

Polke took a step or two on the pavement outside the bank, meditating on this latest development of a matter that was hourly growing in mystery. Why had this woman suddenly disappeared? Had she merely gone to Ecclesborough for the day Or had she made it her first stage in a further journey? Why had she taken a taxi-cab for an eighteen-miles ride, at considerable expense, when, at twelve o'clock, she could have taken a train which would have carried her to Ecclesborough for fifteen pence? It seemed as if she had fled. And if she had fled, she had got, as the constable said, two hours good start. And in Ecclesborough, too! A place with a population of half a million, where there were three big railway stations, from any one of which a fugitive could set off east, west, north, south, at pleasure, and with no risk of attracting attention. Two hours! Polke knew from long experience what can be done in two hours by a criminal escaping from justice. He turned back to speak to his man and as he turned, Joseph came out of the bank. Joseph gave him an insolent stare, and was about to pass him without recognition. But Polke stopped him.

"Mr. Chestermarke, you heard the housekeeper here has disappeared?" he asked sharply. "Can you tell anything about it?"

"What have I to do with Horbury's housekeeper?" retorted Joseph. "Do your own work!"

He passed on, crossing the Market-Place to the Scarnham Arms, and Polke, after gazing at him in silence for a moment, beckoned to his policeman.

"Come inside, Jones," he said. He led the way into the house and through the hall to the kitchens at the back, where two women servants stood whispering together. Polke held up a finger to the one who had answered Joseph's summons to the parlor earlier in the morning. "Here!" he said, "a word with you. Now, exactly when did Mrs. Carswell go out? You needn't be afraid of speaking, my girl it'll go no further, and you know who I am."

"Not so very long after that young lady was here, Mr. Polke," answered the girl, readily enough. "Within oh, a quarter of an hour at the most."

"Did she say where she was going to either of you?" asked Polke.

"No, sir, not a word!"

"To neither of us," said the other, an older woman, drawing nearer. "She just went, Mr. Polke."

"Had she any messages...telegram, or anything of that sort come for her?" asked Polke. "Had anybody been to see her?"

"There was no message that I know of," said the housemaid. "But Mr. Joseph came to speak to her."

"When?" demanded Polke.

"Just after the young lady had gone. He called her out of the kitchen, and they stood talking in the passage there a bit," answered the elder woman. "Of course, Mr. Polke, we didn't hear nothing, but we saw them."

"What happened after that?" asked Polke.

"Nothing, but Mr. Joseph went away, and she came back in here for a minute or two and then went upstairs. And next thing she came down dressed up and went out. She said nothing to us," replied the woman.

"You saw her go out?" said Polke.

Both women pointed to the passage which communicated with the hall.

"When this door's open as it was," said one, "you can see right through. Yes, we saw her go through the hall door. Of course we thought she'd just slipped out into the town for something."

Polke hesitated and meditated. What use was it, at this juncture, to ask for more particular details of this evident flight? Mrs. Carswell was probably well away from Ecclesborough by that time. He turned back to the hall and then looked at the women again.

"I suppose neither of you ever saw or heard anything of Mr. Horbury on Saturday night after he'd gone out?" he inquired.

The two women glanced at each other in silence.

"Did you?" repeated Polke. "Come, now!"

"Well, Mr. Polke," said the elder woman, "we didn't. But, of course, we know what's going on, couldn't very well not know, now could we, Mr. Polke? And we can tell you something that may have to do with things."

"Out with it, then!" commanded Polke. "Keep nothing back."

"Well," said the woman, "there was somebody stirring about this house in the middle of Saturday night between, say, one and two o'clock in the morning...Sunday morning, of course. Both me and Jane here heard them quite plain. And we thought naught of it, then...least-ways, what we did think it was Mr. Horbury. He often came in very late. But when we found out next morning he'd never come home, why then, we did think it was queer that we'd heard noises."

"Did you mention it to Mrs. Carswell?" asked Polke.

"Of course, but she said she'd heard nothing, and it must have been rats," replied the elder woman.

"But I've been here three years and I've never seen a rat in the place."

"Nor me!" agreed the housemaid. "And it wasn't rats. I heard a door shut twice. Plain as I'm speaking to you, Mr. Polke."

Polke reflected a minute and then turned away.

"All right, my lasses!" he said. "Well, keep all this to yourselves. Here I'll tell you what you can do. Send Miss Fosdyke a nice cup of tea into the study...send us all one we can't leave what we're doing just yet. And a mouthful of bread and butter with it. Come along, Jones," he continued, leading the constable away. "Here, you step round to old Mr. Batterley's, you know where he lives near the Castle. Mr. Polke's compliments, and would he be so good as to come to the bank-house and help us a bit? He'll know what I mean. Bring him back with you."

The constable went away, and Polke, after rubbing one of his mutton-chop whiskers for a while with an air of great abstraction, returned to the study. There Mr. Pellworthy and Betty were talking earnestly in one of the window recesses. Starmidge, at the furthest end of the room, was examining the old oak paneling.

"I've sent for Mr. Batterley to give us a hand," said

Polke. "I suppose we'd best examine this room in the way he suggested?"

Starmidge betrayed no enthusiasm.

"If he can do any good," he answered. "But I don't attach much importance to that. However, if there are any secret places around..."

"There's a nice cup of tea coming in for you and Mr. Pellworthy in a minute, Miss Fosdyke," said Polke. "We'll all have to put our dinner off a bit, I reckon." He motioned to the detective to follow him out of the room. "Here's a nice go!" he whispered. "The housekeeper's off! Bolted without a doubt! And she's got a clear start, too."

Starmidge turned sharply on the superintendent.

"Got any clue to where she's gone?" he demanded.

"She's gone amongst five hundred thousand other men and women," replied Polke ruefully. "I've found out that much. Drove off in a taxi-cab to Ecclesborough, as soon as Miss Fosdyke had been here this morning. And mark you! After a few minutes conversation with Joseph Chestermarke. Ecclesborough, indeed! Might as well look for a drop of water in the ocean as for one woman in Ecclesborough! She was set down at the Exchange Station. Why, she may be half-way to London or Liverpool, or Hull, by now!"

Starmidge was listening intently. And passing over the superintendent's opinions and regrets, he fastened on his facts.

"After a few minutes conversation with Joseph Chestermarke, you say?" he observed. "How do you know that?"

"The servants told me, just now," replied Polke.

Starmidge glanced at the door of the private parlor.

"He's gone out," said Polke.

Just then the door opened and Gabriel emerged, closing and locking it after him. He paid no attention to the two men, and was passing on towards the outer hall when Polke hailed him.

"Mr. Chestermarke," he said, "sorry to trouble you, do you know the housekeeper, Mrs. Carswell, has disappeared? You heard what that girl said this morning? Well, she hasn't come back, and..."

"No concern of mine, Mr. Police-Superintendent!' interrupted Gabriel. "Nothing of this is any concern of mine. I shall be obliged to you if you'll confine your very unnecessary operations to the interior of the house, and not stand about this outer hall, or keep this door open between outer and inner halls. I don't want my customers interfered with as they come and go."

With that the senior partner passed on, and Starmidge smiled at his companion.

"I'm glad he interrupted you, all the same, Mr. Polke," he said. "I was afraid you were going to say you knew this woman had gone, in a hurry, to Ecclesborough."

"No, I wasn't," replied Polke. "I told him what I did because I wanted to know what he'd say."

"Well you heard!" said Starmidge. "And what's to be done, now? That woman's conduct is very suspicious. I think, if I were you, Mr. Polke, I should get in touch with the Ecclesborough police. Why not? No harm done. Why not call them up, give them a description of her, and ask them to keep their eyes open. She mayn't have left Ecclesborough, mayn't intend leaving. For look here!" he drew Polke further away from the two doors between which they were standing, and lowered his voice to a whisper. "Supposing," he went on, "supposing there is any secret understanding between this Mrs. Carswell and Joseph Chestermarke, and it looks like it, if she went off immediately after a conversation with him, she may have gone to Ecclesborough simply so they could meet there, safely, later on. Eh?"

"Good notion!" agreed Polke. "Well, we can watch him."

"I'm beginning to think we must watch him, thought so for the last two hours," said Starmidge. "But in the meantime, why not put the Ecclesborough police on to keeping their eyes open for her? Can you give them a good description?"

"Know her as well as I know my own wife by sight," answered Polke. "And her style of dressing, too. All right I'll go and do it, now. Well, there'll be Mr. Batterley coming along in a few minutes, Jones has gone for him. If he can show you any of their secret places he talked about..."

"He's here," said Starmidge, as the old antiquary and the constable entered the hall. "All right I'll attend to him."

But when Polke had gone, and Batterley had been conducted into the study, or garden-room as he insisted on calling it, Starmidge left the old man with Mr. Pellworthy and

Betty and made an excuse to go out of the room after the housemaid, who had just brought in the tea for which Polke had asked. He caught her at the foot of the staircase, and treated her to one of his most ingratiating smiles.

"I say!" he said, "Mr. Polke's just been telling me about what you and the cook told him about Mrs. Carswell you know. Now, I say, you needn't say anything except to cook, but I just want to take a look round Mrs. Carswell's room. Which is it?"

The cook, who kept the kitchen door open so as not to lose anything of these delightful proceedings, came forward. Both accompanied Starmidge upstairs to show him the room he wanted. And Starmidge thanked them profusely and in his best manner after which he turned them politely out and locked the door. Meanwhile Polke went to the police-station and rang up the Ecclesborough police on the telephone. He gave them a full, accurate, and precise description of Mrs. Carswell, and a detailed account of her doings that morning, and begged them to make inquiry at the three great stations in their town.

The man with whom he held conversation calmly remarked as each station at Ecclesborough dealt with a few thousands of separate individuals every day, it was not very likely booking-clerks or platform officials would remember any particular persons, and Polke sorrowfully agreed with him. Nevertheless, he begged him to do his best, the far-off partner in this interchange of remarks answered they would do a lot better if Mr. Polke would tell them something rather more definite. Polke gave it up at that, and went off into the Market-Place again, to return to the bank. But before he reached the bank he ran across Lord Ellersdeane, hanging about the town to hear some result of the search, had been lunching at the Scarnham Club, and now came out of its door.

"Any news so far?" asked the Earl.

Polke glanced round to see that nobody was within hearing. He and Lord Ellersdeane stepped within the doorway of the club-house. Polke narrated the story of the various happenings since the granting of the search-warrant, and the Earl's face grew graver and graver.

"Mr. Polke," he said at last, "I do not like what I am hearing about all this. It's a most suspicious thing the housekeeper should disappear immediately after Miss

Fosdyke's first call this morning, and she should have had some conversation with Mr. Joseph Chestermarke before she went. Really, one dislikes to have to say it of one's neighbors, and of persons of the standing of the Chestermarkes, but their behavior is...is..."

"Suspicious, my lord, suspicious!" said Polke. "There's no denying it. And yet, they're what you might call so defiant, so brazen-faced and insolent, that..."

"Here's your London man," interrupted the Earl. "What is he after now?"

Starmidge came out of the door of the bank-house alone. He caught sight of Polke and Lord Ellersdeane, smiled, and hurried towards them. He carried something loosely wrapped in brown paper in his hand. As he stepped into the doorway of the club-house, he took the wrapping off, and showed a small morocco-covered box on which was a coronet in gold.

"Does your lordship recognize that?" he asked.

"My wife's jewel-casket, of course!" exclaimed the Earl. "Of course it is! Bless me! Where did you find it?"

"In the chimney, in Mrs. Carswell's bedroom," answered Starmidge, with a grimace at Polke. "It's empty!"

Chapter 13

The Earl took the empty casket from the detective's hand and looked at it, inside and outside, with doubt and wonder.

"Now what do you take this to mean?" he asked.

"That we've got three people to find, instead of two, my lord," answered Starmidge promptly. "We must be after the housekeeper."

"You found this in her room?" asked Polke. "So you went up there?"

"As soon as you'd left me," replied the detective, with a shrewd smile. "Of course! I wanted to have a look round. I didn't forget the chimney. She'd put that behind the back of the grate, a favorite hiding-place. I say she...but, of course, someone else may have put it there. Still we must find her. You telephoned to the police at Ecclesborough, superintendent?"

"Ay, and got small comfort!" answered Polke. "It's a stiff job looking for one woman amongst half a million people."

"She wouldn't stop in Ecclesborough," said Starmidge. "She'll be on her way further afield, now. You can get anywhere from Ecclesborough, of course."

"Of course!" assented Polke. "She would be in any one of half a dozen big towns within a couple of hours, in some of them within an hour, in London within three. This'll be another case of printing a description. I wish we'd thought of keeping an eye on her before!"

"We haven't got to the stage where we can think of everything," observed Starmidge. "We've got to take things as they come. Well there's one thing can be done now," he went on, looking at the Earl, "if your lordship will be kind enough to do it."

"I'll do anything I can," replied Lord Ellersdeane. "What is it?"

"If your lordship would just make a call on the two Mr. Chestermarkes," suggested Starmidge. "To tell them, of course," he added, pointing to the empty casket. "Your lordship will get some attention I suppose. They won't give any attention to Polke or myself. If your lordship would just tell them your casket emptied of its valuable contents, had been found hidden in Mrs. Carswell's room, perhaps they'll listen, and what is much more important give you their views on the matter." concluded Starmidge, drily, "I should very much like to hear them!"

The Earl made a wry face.

"Oh, all right!" he answered. "If I must, I must. It's not a job that appeals to me, but...very well. I'll go now."

"And we," said Starmidge, turning to Polke, "had better join the others and see if the old antiquary gentleman has found any of these secret places he talked of."

Lord Ellersdeane found no difficulty in obtaining access to the partners. He was shown into their room with all due ceremony as soon as Shirley announced him. He found them evidently relaxing a little after their lunch, from which they had just returned. They were standing in characteristic attitudes, Gabriel, smoking a cigar, bolt upright on the hearth-rug beneath the portrait of his ancestor. Joseph, toying with a scented cigarette, leaning against the window which looked out on the garden. For once in a way both seemed more amenable and cordial.

The Earl held out the empty casket.

"This," he said, "is the casket in which I handed my wife's jewels to Mr. Horbury. It is, as you see, empty. It has just been found by the Scotland Yard man, Starmidge."

Gabriel glanced at the casket with some interest, Joseph, with none, neither spoke.

"In the housekeeper's room hidden in her fire-place," continued the Earl, looking from one partner to the other. "That shows, gentlemen, the jewels were, after all, in this house on these premises."

"There has never been any question of that," said Gabriel quickly. "We, of course, never doubted what your lordship was good enough to tell us naturally!"

"Not for a moment!" said Joseph. "We felt at once you had given the jewels to Horbury."

The Earl set the casket down on Gabriel's desk and looked a little uncertain and uncomfortable. Gabriel indicated the chair which he had politely moved forward on his visitor's entrance.

"Won't your lordship sit down?" he said.

The Earl accepted the invitation and looked from one man to the other. A sudden impression crossed his mind never, he thought, were there two men from whom it was so difficult to get a word as these Chestermarkes, who had such a queer habit of staring in silence at one!

"The...the housekeeper appears to have run away," he said haltingly. "That's...somewhat queer, isn't it?"

"We understand Mrs. Carswell has left the house and the town," replied Gabriel. "As to it's being queer...well, all this is queer!"

"And all of a piece!" remarked Joseph.

The Earl was glad the junior partner made that remark, and he turned to him.

"I understand you saw her and spoke to her just before she left, this morning?" he said hesitatingly. "Did she give you the impression of being...shall we say, uneasy?"

"I certainly saw her and spoke to her," asserted Joseph. "I went to scold her. I had given her orders no one was to be allowed access to certain rooms in the house, and we were not to be bothered by callers. She fetched me out to see Miss Fosdyke, I went to scold her for that. We had our reasons for not permitting access to those rooms. They have, of course, been frustrated."

"But at any rate some good's come of it," observed the Earl, pointing to his casket. "This has been found. And in the housekeeper's bedroom. Hidden! And she's gone. What do you think of it, gentlemen?"

Gabriel spread his hands and shook his head. But Joseph answered readily.

"I should think," he replied, "she's gone to meet Horbury."

The Earl started, glancing keenly from one partner to the other.

"Then you still think Horbury is guilty of...of dishonesty!" he exclaimed. "Really, I...dear me, such an absolutely upright, honorable man..."

"Surface!" said Joseph quietly. "Surface! On the surface, my lord."

The Earl's face flushed a little with palpable displeasure, and he turned from the junior to the senior partner.

"Very good of your lordship," said Gabriel, with the faintest suggestion of a smile. "But a man's honesty is bounded by his necessity. We, of course, are better acquainted with our late manager's qualities now."

"You have discovered something?" asked the Earl anxiously.

"Up to now," replied Gabriel, "we have kept things to ourselves. But we don't mind giving your lordship a little...just a little information. There is no doubt Horbury had, for some time past, engaged in speculation in stocks and shares...none whatever!"

"To a considerable extent," added Joseph.

"And unsuccessfully?" inquired the Earl.

"We are not yet quite sure of the details," answered Gabriel. "The mere fact is enough. Of course, no man in his position has any right to speculate. Had we known he speculated..."

"He would have been discharged from our service," said Joseph. "No banker can retain the services of a manager who gambles."

The Earl began to feel almost as uncomfortable as if these two men were charging him with improper transactions. He was a man of simple mind and ideas, and he supposed the Chestermarkes knew what they were talking about.

"Then you think this sudden disappearance..." he said.

"In the history of banking...unwritten, possibly," remarked Joseph, "there are many similar instances. No end of them, most likely. Bank managers enjoy vast opportunities of stealing, my lord! And the man who is best trusted has more opportunities than the man who's watched. We never suspected and so we never watched."

"You have heard of the stranger who came to the town on Saturday night, and is believed to have telephoned from the Station Hotel to Horbury?" asked the Earl. "What of him?"

"We have heard," answered Gabriel. "We don't know anymore. We don't know any such person from the description. But we have no doubt he did meet Horbury and his visit had something...probably everything to do with Horbury's disappearance."

"But how could he disappear?" asked the Earl. "I mean to say, how could such a well-known man disappear so completely, without anybody knowing of it? It seems impossible!"

"If your lordship will think for a moment," said Joseph, "you will see it is not merely not impossible, but very easy. Horbury was a great pedestrian, he used to boast of his thirty and forty mile walks. Now we are well within twenty miles of Ecclesborough. Ecclesborough is a very big town. What was there to prevent Horbury, during Saturday night, from walking across country to Ecclesborough? Nothing! If, after interviewing that strange man, he decided to clear out at once, he'd nothing to do but set off over a very lonely stretch of country, every inch of which he knew to Ecclesborough. He would be in Ecclesborough by an early hour in the morning. Now in Ecclesborough there are three stations...big stations. He could get away from any one of them, what booking-clerk or railway official would pay any particular attention to him? The thing is ridiculously easy!"

"What of the other man?" asked the Earl. "If there were two men together at an early hour?"

"They need not have caught a train at a very early hour," replied Joseph. "They need not have been together when they caught any train. I don't say they went together. I don't say they went to Ecclesborough. I don't say they caught a train. I only say what, it must be obvious, they easily could do without attracting attention."

"The fact of Horbury's disappearance is not challengeable," remarked Gabriel quietly. "We know why he disappeared."

"I should think," said Joseph, still more quietly, "Lord Ellersdeane also knows by now."

"No, I don't!" exclaimed the Earl, a little sharply. "I wish I did!"

Joseph pointed to the casket.

"Why have the police been officially searching the house, then?" he asked.

"To see if they could get any clue to his disappearance," replied the Earl.

"And they found that!" retorted Joseph.

"In the housekeeper's room," said the Earl. "She may

have appropriated the jewels."

"I think your lordship must see that is very unlikely without collusion between Horbury and herself," remarked Gabriel.

"Mrs. Carswell," said Joseph, "has always been more or less of a mysterious person. We know nothing about her. I don't even know where Horbury got her from. But the probability is they were in collusion, and when he went, she stayed behind, to ascertain how things turned out on his disappearance; and she fled when it began to appear searching inquiries were to be made into which she might be drawn."

The Earl made no reply. He recognized the Chestermarke observations and suggestions were rather more than plausible, and much as he fought against the idea of the missing manager's dishonesty, he could not deny the circumstances as set forth by the bankers were suspicious.

"Your lordship will, of course, follow up this woman?" said Gabriel, after a brief silence.

"I suppose the police will," replied the Earl. "But aren't you going to do anything yourselves, Mr. Chestermarke? You told me, you know, certain securities of yours were missing."

Gabriel glanced at his nephew and Joseph nodded.

"Oh, well!" answered Gabriel. "We don't mind telling your lordship and if your lordship pleases, you may tell the police, we are doing something. We have, in fact, been doing something from an early hour. We have a very clever man at work just now, he has been at work since he heard from us twenty-four hours ago. But our ideas are not those of Polke. Polke begins his inquiries here. Our inquiries...based on our knowledge begin elsewhere."

"You think Horbury will be heard of elsewhere?" suggested the Earl.

"Much more likely to be heard of elsewhere than here, my lord!" asserted Gabriel.

"But, of course, what we do need not interfere with anything your lordship does, or what Miss Fosdyke does, or the police do."

"All any of us want, I suppose, is to find Horbury," said the Earl, as he rose. "If he's found, then, I conclude, some explanation will result. You don't believe in searching about here, then?"

"Let Polke and his men have their way, my lord," replied Gabriel, with a wave of his hand. "My impression of police methods is those who follow them can only follow that particular path. We are not looking for Horbury here. He's elsewhere."

"So, by this time, are your lordship's jewels," added Joseph significantly. "They, one may be sure, are not going to be found in or about Scarnham."

The Earl said good-day and went out, troubled and wondering. In the hall he met the search party. Mr. Batterley had failed to find anything in the way of secret stairs or passages or openings beyond those already known to the occupants, and though he was still confident they existed, the police had wound up their present investigations to turn to more palpable things. Polke and the detective listened to the Earl's account of his interview, and the superintendent sniffed at the mention of the inquiries instituted by the partners.

"Ah!" he said incredulously. "Just so! Private inquiry agent, no doubt. All right let them do what they like. But we're going to do what we like, my lord, and what we do will be on very different lines. First thing now we want that woman!"

Chapter 14

The search-party separated outside the bank, not too well satisfied with the result of its labors. The old antiquary walked away obviously nettled he was not allowed to pursue his investigations further. Betty and the solicitor went across to the hotel in deep conference. The Earl accompanied Starmidge and Polke to the police station. And there the detective laid down a firm outline of the next immediate procedure. It was of no use to half-do things, he said they must rouse wholesale attention. Once more the press must be made use of, the sudden disappearance of Mrs. Carswell must be noised abroad in the next morning's papers. A police notice describing her must be got out and sent all over the kingdom. And last, but certainly not least, Lord Ellersdeane must offer a substantial reward for the recovery of, or news of, his missing property. Let the Chestermarke's adopt their own method, if they had any of finding the alleged absconding manager. He, preferred to solve these mysteries by ways of his own.

It was growing near to dusk when all their necessary arrangements had been made, and Starmidge was free to seek his long-delayed dinner. He had put himself up, of his own choice, at a quiet and old-fashioned inn near the police station, where he had engaged a couple of rooms and found a landlady to his liking. He repaired to this retreat now, and ate and drank in quiet, and smoked a peaceful pipe afterwards, and was glad of a period of rest. But as he took his ease, he thought and pondered, and by the time evening had fairly settled over the little town, he went out into the streets and sought the ancient corner of Scarnham which was called Cornmarket. Starmidge wanted to take a look at the house in which Joseph spent his bachelor existence. Since his own arrival in the town, he had been learning all he could about the two Chestermarke's, and he was puzzled about them. For a man who was still young, Starmidge had seen a good deal of the queer side of life, and had known a good many strange people, but so far he had never come across two such apparently curious characters as the uncle and nephew who ran the old-fashioned bank. Their evident indifference to public opinion puzzled him. He could not understand their ice-cold defiance of what he called law. He never remembered being treated as they had treated him. For Starmidge, when on duty, considered himself as much the representative of Justice as any ermined and coifed judge could be, and he had been accustomed so far to attentive and respectful consideration. But neither Gabriel nor Joseph appeared to have any proper appreciation of the dignity of a detective-sergeant of the Criminal Investigation Department, and their eyes had regarded him as if he were something very inferior indeed.

Starmidge, though by no means a vain man, felt nettled by such treatment, and he accordingly formed something very like a prejudice against the two partners. That prejudice was quickly followed by suspicion, especially in the case of Joseph. According to Starmidge's ideas, the bankers, if they really believed Horbury to have absconded, if certain securities of theirs really were missing, if they really thought Horbury had carried them off, and the Countess of Ellersdeane's jewels with him, ought to have placed every information in their power at the disposal of the police. It was suspicious, and strange, and not at all proper, they didn't.

And it was suspicious, too, the housekeeper, Mrs. Carswell, should take herself off after a brief exchange of words with Joseph. It looked very much as if the junior partner had either warned her to go, or had told her to go. hy had she gone *then*? When she might have gone before. And why in such haste? Clearly, considering every-thing, there were grounds for believing there was some secret between Mrs. Carswell and Joseph. Anyway, rightly or wrongly, Starmidge was suspicious of the junior partner in Chestermarke's Bank, and he wanted to know everything he could find out about him. He had already learnt Joseph, like his uncle, was a confirmed bachelor, and lived in an old house at the corner of Cornmarket. Somewhat so far as the town-folk could judge after the fashion of a hermit. Starmidge would have given a good deal for a really good excuse to call on Joseph at that house, so he might see the inside of it. Indeed, if he had only met with a better reception at the bank, he would have invented such an excuse. But if Gabriel was icily stand-offish, Joseph was openly sneering and contemptuous, and the detective knew no excuse would give him admittance. Still, there was the outside, he would take a look at that. Starmidge was a young man of ideas as well as of ability, and without exactly shaping his thought in so many words, he felt vaguely perhaps, but none the less strongly just as you can size up some men by the clothes they wear, so you can get an idea of others by the outer look of the houses which shelter them.

Cornmarket in Scarnham lay at the further end of the street called Finkleway. It was a queer, open space which sloped downhill from the center of the ridge on which the middle of the town was built to the valley through which the little river meandered. Where the streets, and the road leading out to the open country and Ellersdeane cut into it, it was completely enclosed by old houses of the sort which Starmidge had already admired in the Market-Place.

Many of them half-timbered, all of them very ancient. One or two of them were inns; some were evidently workmen's cottages; others were better-class dwelling-houses. From the description already furnished to him by Polke, Starmidge at once recognized Joseph' abode. It was a corner house, abutting on the road which ran out at the lower angle of this irregular space and led down to the river and Scarnham Bridge. It was by far the biggest house thereabouts, a tall, slender, stone-built house of many stories, towering high above any of the surrounding gables.

And save for a very faint, dull glow which shone through the transom window of the front door, there was not a vestige of light in a single window of the seven stories. Cornmarket was a gloomy commonplace, thought Starmidge, but the little oil lamps in the cottages were riotously cheery in comparison with the darkness of the tall, gaunt Chestermarke mansion. It looked like the abode of dead men. Starmidge longed to knock at that door, if only to get a peep inside the hall. But he curbed his desires and went quietly round the corner of the house. There was a high black wall there which led down to the grassy bank of the river. From its corner another wall ran along the river-side, separated from the stream by a path. There was a door set in this wall, and Starmidge, after carefully looking round in the gloom, quietly tried it and found it securely locked. An intense desire to see the inside of Joseph's garden seized the detective. Near the door, partly overhanging the garden wall, partly overshadowing the path and the river-bank, was a tree. Starmidge, after listening carefully and deciding no one was coming along the path, made shift to climb the tree, just then bursting into full leaf. In another minute he was amongst its middle branches, and peering inquisitively into the garden which lay between him and the gaunt outline of the gloom-stricken house.

The moon was just then rising above the roofs and gables of the town, and by its rapidly increasing light Starmidge saw the garden was of considerable size, raining back quite sixty yards from the rear of the house, and having a corresponding breadth. Like all the gardens which stretched from the backs of the Market Place houses to the river-bank, it was rich in trees. High elms and beeches rose from its lawns, and made deep shadows across them. But Starmidge was not so much interested in those trees, fine as they were, as in a building; obviously modern, which was set in their midst, completely isolated.

That it was a comparatively new building he could see; the moonbeams falling full on it showed that the stone of which it was built was fresh and unstained by time or smoke. But what was it? Of what nature, for what purpose? It was neither stable, nor coach-house, nor summer-house, nor a grouping of domestic offices. No drive or path led to it. It was built in the middle of a grass-plot, round it ran a stone-lined trench. Its architecture was plain but handsome; it possessed two distinctive features which the detective was quick to notice. One, was at any rate on the two sides which he could see its windows were set at a height of quite twelve feet from the ground. The other, from its flat parapet roof rose a conical structure something like the rounded stacks of glass foundries and potteries. This was obviously a chimney, and from its mouth at that moment was emerging a slight column of smoke which threw back curiously colored reflections, blue, and yellow, and red, to the moonlight which fell on its thickening spirals. Starmidge felt just as much desire to get inside this queer structure as into the house behind it, and if he could have seen any prospect of taking a peep through its windows he would have risked detection and dropped from his perch into the garden. But he judged if the windows were twelve feet from the ground on the two sides of the building which he could see, they would be the same height on the sides which he couldn't see; moreover, he observed they were obscured by either dull red glass or red curtains. Clearly no outsider was intended to get a peep into this temple of mystery. What was it? What went on within it? He was about to climb down from the tree when he got some sort of an answer to these questions. From within the building, muffled by the evidently thick walls, came the faintest sound of metal beating on metal a mere rippling, tinkling sound, light and musical, such as might have been made by fairy blacksmiths beating on a fairy anvil.

But far away as it sounded, it was clear and unmistakable. Starmidge regained the path between the wall and the river and went slowly forward. The place, he decided, was evidently some sort of a workshop, in which was a forge. Probably Joseph amused himself with a little amateur work in metals. He thought no more of the matter just then. He wanted to explore the river bank along which he now walked. For according to the story of the landlady of the Station Hotel, it was on that river bank the mysterious stranger was to meet whoever it was he spoke to over the telephone, and so far Starmidge had not had an opportunity of examining its geography. There was not much to examine. The river, a mere ditch, eight or ten yards in breadth, wandered through a level mead at the base of the valley, separated from the gardens by a wide path. Between Scarnham Bridge, at the foot of Cornmarket and the corner of Joseph's big garden, and the end of Cordmaker's Alley, a narrow street which ran down from the further end of the Market Place to the riverside, there were no features of any note or interest.

On the other side of the river lay the deep woods through which Neale and Betty had passed on their way to Ellersdeane Hollow. Starmidge had heard all about the expedition, and he glanced curiously at the black depths of the trees, wondering if John Horbury and the mysterious stranger, supposing they had met, had turned into these woods to hold their conference. He presently came to the foot-bridge by which access to the woods and the other bank of the river was gained, and by it he lingered for a moment or two, looking at it in its bearings to the bank-house garden and orchard on his left hand, and to the Station Hotel, the lights of which he could plainly see down the valley. Certainly, if John Horbury and the stranger desired to meet in secret, here was the place.

The stranger had nothing to do but stroll along the river-bank from the hotel. Horbury had only to step out of his orchard and meet him. Once together, they had only to cross that foot-bridge into the woods to be immediately in surroundings of great privacy. Starmidge turned up Cordmaker's Alley, regained the Market Place, and strolled on to Polke's private house. The superintendent was taking his ease after his day's labors and reading the Ecclesborough evening newspapers, he tossed one of them over to his visitor.

"All there!" he said, pointing to some big headlines. "Got it all in, just as you told it to Parkinson. Full justice to the descriptions of both Horbury and the Station Hotel stranger. Smart work, eh?"

"Power of the Press as Parkinson said," answered Starmidge, with a laugh. "It's very useful, the Press. I don't know how they managed without it in the old days of criminal catching, Mr. Polke. Press and telegraph, eh? They're valuable adjuncts."

"You think all that would be in the London papers this evening?" asked Polke.

"Sure to be," replied Starmidge. "I'm hoping we'll hear something from London tomorrow. I say, I've been taking a bit of a look round one or two places tonight, quietly, you know. What's that curious building in Joseph's garden?"

Polke put down his paper and looked unusually interested.

"I don't know!" he answered. "How did you see it? I've never seen inside his garden."

"Climbed a tree on the river bank and looked over the wall," replied Starmidge.

"Well," said Polke, "I did hear, some few years ago, he was building something in that garden, but the work was done by Ecclesborough contractors, and nobody ever knew much about it here. I believe Joseph's a bit of an amateur experimenter, but I don't know what he experiments in. Nobody ever goes inside his house...he's a hermit."

"He's got some sort of a forge there, anyhow," said Starmidge. "Or a furnace, or something of that sort."

Then they talked of other things until half-past ten, when the detective retired to his inn and went to bed. He was sleeping soundly when a steady knocking at his door roused him, to hear the voice of his landlady outside. And at the same time he heard the big clock of the parish church striking midnight.

"Mr. Starmidge!" said the voice, "there's a policeman wanting you. Will you go round at once to Mr. Polke's? There's a man come from London about that piece in the newspapers."

Chapter 15

Starmidge hastily pulled some garments about him, and flinging a travelling coat over his shoulders, hurried downstairs, to find a sleepy-looking policeman in the hall.

"How did this man get here at this time of night?" he asked, as they set off towards the police-station.

"Came in a taxi-cab from Ecclesborough," answered the policeman. "I haven't heard any particulars, Mr. Starmidge, except he'd read the news in the London paper this evening and set off here in consequence. He's in Mr. Polke's house, sir."

Starmidge walked into the superintendent's parlor, to find him in company with a young man, whom the detective at once sized up as a typical London clerk. A second glance assured him that his clerkship was of the legal variety.

"Here's Detective-Sergeant Starmidge," said Polke. "Starmidge, this gentleman's Mr. Simmons, from London. Mr. Simmons says he's clerk to a Mr. Hollis, a London solicitor. And, having read the description in the papers this last evening, he's certain the man who came to the Station Hotel here on Saturday is his governor."

Starmidge sat down and looked again at the visitor, a tall, sandy-haired, freckled young man, who was obviously a good deal puzzled.

"Is Mr. Hollis missing, then?" asked Starmidge.

Simmons looked as if he found it somewhat difficult to explain matters.

"Well," he answered. "It's this way. I've never seen him since Saturday. And he hasn't been at his rooms...his private rooms since Saturday. In the ordinary course he ought to have been at business first thing yesterday. We'd some very important business on yesterday morning, which wasn't done because of his absence. He never turned up yesterday at all nor today either, we never heard from or of him. And so, when I read the description in the papers this evening, I caught the first express I could get down here...at least to Ecclesborough I had to motor from there."

"That description describes Mr. Hollis, then?" asked Starmidge.

"Exactly! I'm sure it's Mr. Hollis...it's him to a T!" answered the clerk. "I recognized it at once."

"Let's get everything in order," said Starmidge, with a glance at Polke. "To begin with, who is Mr. Hollis?"

"Mr. Frederick Hollis, solicitor, 59b South Square, Gray's Inn," replied Simmons promptly. "Andwell & Hollis is the name of the firm, but there isn't any Andwell, hasn't been for many a year, he's dead, long since, is Andwell. Mr. Hollis is the only proprietor."

"Don't know him at all," remarked Starmidge. "What's his particular line of practice?"

"Conveyancing," said Simmons.

"Then, naturally, I shouldn't," observed Starmidge. "My acquaintance is chiefly with police court solicitors. And you say he'd private rooms somewhere? Where, now?"

"Paper Buildings, Temple," replied the clerk. "He'd a suite of rooms there...he's had them for years."

"Bachelor, then?" inquired the detective.

"Yes, he's a bachelor," agreed Simmons.

"You know he hasn't been at his rooms since Saturday, you've ascertained that?" continued Starmidge.

"He's never been at his rooms since he left them after breakfast on Saturday morning," replied Simmons. "I went there at eleven o'clock Monday, that was yesterday, again at four, twice on Tuesday. I was coming away from the Temple when I got the paper and read about this affair."

"When did you see him last?" asked Starmidge.

"Half-past-twelve Saturday. He went out dressed just as it says in your description. And," concluded the clerk, with a shake of his head which suggested his own inability to understand matters, "he never said a word to me about coming down here."

"Did he say anything to anybody at his rooms about going away? For the weekend, for instance?" asked the detective. "There'd be somebody there, of course."

"Only a woman who tidied up for him and got his breakfast ready of a morning," said Simmons. "He took all his other meals out. No, he said nothing to her. But he wasn't a weekender. He very rarely left his rooms except for the office."

"Any of his relations been after him?" inquired Starmidge.

"I don't know anything about his relations nor friends, either," answered the clerk. "Don't even know the address of one of them, or I'd have gone to seek him on Monday, everything's at a standstill. He was a lonely sort of man. I never heard of his relations or friends."

'How long have you been with him, then?" asked the detective. "Some time?"

"Six years," replied Simmons.

"And you've no doubt, from the description in the papers, the gentleman who came here on Saturday last is Mr. Hollis?" asked Starmidge.

The clerk shook his head with an air of conviction.

"None!" he answered. "None whatever!"

Starmidge helped himself to a cigar out of an open box which lay on Polke's table. He lighted it carefully, and smoked for a minute or two in silence. Then he looked at Polke.

"Well, there's a very obvious question to put to Mr. Simmons after all that," he remarked. "Have you any idea," he continued, turning to the clerk, "of any reason that would bring Mr. Hollis to Scarnham?"

Simmons shook his head more vigorously than before.

"Not the ghost of an idea!" he exclaimed.

"There was no business being done with anybody at Scarnham?" asked Starmidge.

"Not in our office!" asserted Simmons. "I'm sure of that. I know all the business we have in hand. To tell you the truth, gentlemen, though you may think me very ignorant, I never even heard of Scarnham myself until I read the paper this evening."

"Quite excusable," said Starmidge. "I never heard of it myself until Monday. Well, this is all very queer, Mr. Simmons. What does Mr. Polke think? And what's Mr. Polke got to suggest!"

Polke, who had been listening silently, turned to the clerk.

"Did you chance to look at Mr. Hollis's letters...recent letters, I mean..." he asked, "to see if you would find anything inviting him down here?"

"I did," replied Simmons promptly. "I looked through all the letters on his desk and in his drawers yesterday afternoon. I didn't find anything that explained his absence. And when I was at his rooms this evening I looked at some letters on his mantelpiece, nothing there. I tell you, I haven't the least notion as to what could bring him to Scarnham."

"And I suppose none of your fellow-clerks have, either?" asked Polke.

Simmons smiled and glanced at Starmidge.

"We've only myself and another, a junior clerk and a boy," he said. "It's not a big practice, only a bit of good conveyancing now and then, and some family business. Mr. Hollis isn't dependent on it, he's private means of his own."

"Aye, just so!" observed Polke. "And I should say, Starmidge, it was private business brought him down here, if he's the man, as he certainly seems to be. But whose?"

Starmidge turned again to the clerk.

"You've a good memory, I can see," he said. "Now, did you ever hear Mr. Hollis mention the name of Horbury?"

"Never!" replied Simmons.

"Did you ever hear him speak of Chestermarke's Bank?" asked Starmidge.

"No, never! Never heard either name in my life until I saw them in the papers," asserted Simmons.

"Who looks after the banking account at Hollis's?" asked the detective. "I mean, the business account you know. Not his private one."

"I do," said Simmons. "Always have done since I went there."

"You never saw any checks paid to those names or any checks from them?" inquired Starmidge. "Think, now!"

"No, I'm absolutely sure of it," said the clerk. "Horbury, perhaps, I might not remember, but I should have remembered Chestermarke, it's an uncommon name, to me, anyway."

"Well," said Starmidge, after a pause, during which all three looked at each other as men look who have come to a dead stop in the progress of things, "there's one thing very certain, Mr. Simmons. If that was your governor who came down to the Station Hotel here on Saturday evening last, he certainly telephoned from there to Chestermarke's Bank as soon as he arrived. And he got a reply from there, and he evidently went out to meet whoever sent it...that sender seeming to be Mr. Horbury, the manager. And so," he concluded, turning to Polke, "what we've got to find out is, what did Hollis come here at all for?"

"We shan't find that out tonight," said Polke, with a yawn.

"Quite so...so we'll adjourn till morning, when Mr. Simmons shall see Mrs. Pratt just to establish things," remarked Starmidge. "In the meantime he'd better come round with me to my place, and I'll get him a bed."

Neither the police superintendent nor the detective had the slightest doubt after hearing Simmons story the man who presented himself at the Station Hotel at Scarnham on the evening of John Horbury's disappearance was Mr. Frederick Hollis, solicitor, of Gray's Inn. If they had still retained any doubt it would have disappeared next morning when they took the clerk down to see Mrs. Pratt. The landlady described her customer even more fully than before. Simmons had no doubt whatever she described his employer. He wouldn't have been more certain, he said, Mrs. Pratt was talking about Mr. Hollis, if she'd shown him a photograph of that gentleman.

"So we can take that for settled," remarked Polke, as the three left the hotel and went back to the town. 'The man who came here last Saturday night was Mr. Frederick Hollis, solicitor, of South Square, Gray's Inn, London. That's established, I take it, Starmidge?"

"Seems so," agreed the detective.

"Then the next question is. Where's he got to?" said Polke.

"I think the next question is. Has anybody ever heard of him in connection with Mr. Horbury, or the Chestermarkes?" observed Starmidge. "There's no doubt he came down here to see one or other of them, Horbury, most likely."

"And who's to tell us anything?" asked Polke.

"Miss Fosdyke's a relation of Horbury's," replied Starmidge. "She may know Hollis by name. Mr. Neale's always been in touch with Horbury, he may have heard of Hollis. And so may the bankers."

"The difficulty is to make them say anything," said

Polke. "They'll only tell what they please."

'Let's try the other two, anyway," counseled Starmidge. "They may be able to tell something. For as sure as I am what I am, the whole secret of this business lies in Hollis's coming down here to see Horbury, and in what followed on their meeting. If we could only get to know what Hollis came here for...ah!"

But they got no further information from either Betty or Neale. Neither had ever heard of Mr. Frederick Hollis, of Gray's Inn. Betty was certain, beyond doubt, he was no relation of the missing bank-manager. She had the whole family-tree of the Horbury's at her finger-ends, she declared. No Hollis was connected with even its outlying twigs. Neale had never heard the name of Hollis mentioned by Horbury. And he added he was absolutely sure during the last five years no person of that name had ever had dealings with Chestermarke's Bank... open dealings, at any rate.

Secret dealings with the partners, severally or collectively, or with Horbury, for that matter, Mr. Hollis might have had, but Neale was certain he had no ordinary business with any of them. Polke took heart of grace and led Simmons across to the bank. To his astonishment, the partners now received him readily and politely. They even listened with apparent interest to the clerk's story, and asked him some questions arising out of it. But each declared he knew nothing about Mr. Frederick Hollis, and was utterly unaware of any reason that could bring him to Scarnham. It was certainly on no business of theirs, as a firm, or as private individuals, he came.

"He came, of course, to see Horbury," said Joseph at last. "That's dead certain. No doubt they met. And after that... well, they seem to have vanished together."

Gabriel followed Polke into the hall and drew him aside.

"Did this clerk tell you whether his master was a man of standing?" he asked.

"Man of private means, Mr. Chestermarke, with a small, highly respectable practice, a conveyancing solicitor," answered Polke.

"Oh!" replied Gabriel. "Just so. Well, we know nothing about him."

Polke and his companion returned to the Scarnham

Arms, where Starmidge was in consultation with Betty and Neale.

"They know nothing at all over there," he reported. "Never heard of Hollis. What's to be done now!"

"Mr. Simmons must do the next thing," answered the detective. "Get back to town, Mr. Simmons, and put yourself in communication with every single one of Mr. Hollis's clients, you know them all, of course. Find out if any of them gave Mr. Hollis any business that would send him to Scarnham. Don't leave a stone unturned in that way! And the moment you have any information, however slight, wire to me, here on the instant."

Chapter 16

Starmidge and Polke presently left to walk down to the railway station with the bewildered clerk. When they had gone, Betty turned to Neale, who was hanging about her sitting-room with no obvious intention of leaving it.

"While these people are doing what they can in their way, is there nothing we can do in ours?" she asked. "I hate sitting here doing nothing at all! You're a free man now, Wallie can't you suggest something?"

Neale was thoroughly enjoying his first taste of liberty. He felt as if he had just been released from a long term of imprisonment. To be absolutely free to do what he liked with himself, during the whole of a spring day, was a sensation so novel he was holding closely to it, half-fearful it might all be a dream from which it would be a terrible thing to awake, to see one of Chestermarke's ledgers under his nose. And this being a wonderfully fine morning, he had formed certain sly designs of luring Betty away into the country, and having the whole day with her. A furtive glance at her, however, showed him Betty's thoughts and ideas just then were entirely business-like, but a happy inspiration suggested to him business and pleasure might be combined.

"We ought to go and see if that tinker chap's found out or heard anything," he said. "You remember he promised to keep his eyes and ears open. And we might do a little looking round the country for ourselves. I haven't much faith in those local policemen and gamekeepers. Why not make a day of it, going round? I know a place, nice old inn, the other side of Ellersdeane where we can get some lunch. Much better making inquiries for ourselves," he concluded insinuatingly, "than sitting about waiting for news."

"Didn't I say so?" exclaimed Betty. "Come on, then! I'm ready. Where first?"

"Let's see the tinker first," said Neale. "He's a sharp man, he may have something else to tell by now."

He led his companion out of the town by way of Scarnham Bridge, pointing out Joseph's gloomy house to her as they passed it.

"I'd give a lot," he remarked, as they turned on to the open moor which led towards Ellersdeane Hollow, "to know if either of the Chestermarke's really did know anything about that chap Hollis coming to the town on Saturday. I shouldn't be a bit surprised if they did. Those detective fellows like Starmidge are very clever in their way, but they always seem to me to stop thinking a bit too soon. Now both Starmidge and Polke seem to take it for certain this Hollis went to meet Horbury when he left the Station Hotel. There's no proof he went to meet Horbury...none!"

"Whom might he have gone to meet, then?" demanded Betty.

"You listen to me a bit," said Neale. "I've been thinking it over. Hollis comes to the Station Hotel and uses their telephone. Mrs. Pratt overhears him call up Chestermarke's Bank that's certain. Then she goes away, about her business. An interval elapses. Then she hears some appointment made, with somebody, along the river bank, for that evening. But that interval during which Mrs. Pratt didn't overhear? How do we know the person with whom Hollis began his conversation was the same person with whom he finished it? Come, now!"

"Wallie, that's awfully clever of you!" exclaimed Betty. "How did you come to think of such an ingenious notion?"

"Worked it out," answered Neale. "This way! Hollis comes down to Scarnham to see Chestermarke's Bank, which means one of the partners. He rings up the bank. He speaks to somebody there. How do we know that somebody was Horbury? We don't! It may have been Mrs. Carswell. Now supposing the real person Hollis wanted to see was either Gabriel or Joseph Chestermarke? Very well, this person who answered from the bank would put Hollis on to either of them at once. Gabriel has a telephone at the Warren. Joseph has a telephone at his home yonder behind us. It may have been with either Gabriel or Joseph that Hollis finished his conversation. And if it was finished with one of them, it was, in my opinion, whatever that's worth, with Master Joseph!"

"What makes you think that?" asked Betty, startled by the suggestion.

Neale laid a hand on the girl's arm and turned her round to face the town. He lifted his stick and pointed at Joseph's high roof, towering above the houses around it. Then he swept the stick towards the river and its course, plainly to be followed, in the direction of the station.

"You see Joseph's house there," he said. "You see the river, the path along its bank going right down to the meadow opposite the Station Hotel? Very well now, supposing it was Joseph with whom Hollis wound up that telephone talk, suppose it was Joseph whom Hollis was to see. What would happen? Joseph knew Hollis was at the Station Hotel. The straightest and easiest way from the Station Hotel to Joseph's house is straight along the river bank. Now then, call on your memory! What did Mrs. Pratt tell us? 'When I was going back to the bar,' says Mrs. Pratt, 'I heard more. "Along the riverside," says the gentleman. "Straight on from where I am, all right." Then, after a minute, "At seven-thirty, then?" he says. "All right I'll meet you." And after that,' concludes Mrs. Pratt, 'he rings off.' Now, why shouldn't it be Joseph he was going to meet? Remember, again, the river-side path leads straight to Joseph's house. Come! Mrs. Pratt's story doesn't point conclusively to Horbury at all. It's as I say, the telephone conversation may have begun with Horbury, but it may have ended with somebody else. And what I say is...who was the precise person whom Hollis went to meet?"

"Are you going to tell all that to Starmidge?" asked Betty admiringly. "Because I'm sure it's never entered his head so far."

"Depends," replied Neale. "Let's see if the tinker has anything to tell. He's at home, anyway. There's his fire."

A spiral of blue smoke, curling high above the green and gold of the gorse bushes, revealed Creasy's whereabouts. He had shifted his camp since their first meeting with him. His tilted cart, his tethered pony, and his fire, were now in a hollow considerably nearer the town. Neale and Betty looked down into his retreat to find him busily mending a collection of pots and pans, evidently gathered up during his round of the previous day. He greeted his visitors with a smile, and fetched a three-legged stool from his cart for Betty's better accommodation.

"Heard anything?" asked Neale, seating himself on a log of wood.

The tinker pointed to several newspapers which lay near at hand, kept from blowing away by a stone placed on the uppermost.

"Only what's in these," he answered. "I've read all that so I'm pretty well posted up, mister. I've just read this morning's, bought it in the town when I went to fetch some bread. Queer affair altogether, I call it!"

"Have you looked round about at all?" asked Betty.

"I've been a good bit over the Hollow, miss," answered Creasy. "But it's a stiff job seeking anything here. There's nobody knows what a wilderness this Hollow is until they begin exploring it. Holes, corners, nooks, crannies, bracken and bushes, it is a wilderness, and that's a fact! I'd engage to hide myself safely in this square mile for many a week, against a hundred seekers. It wouldn't a bit surprise me, you know, if it comes out in the end Mr. Horbury, after all, did fall down one of these old shafts. I couldn't believe it possible at first, knowing he knew every in and out of the place, but I'm beginning to think he may have done. There's only one thing against that theory."

"What?" asked Betty.

"Where's the other gentleman?" answered the tinker. "If they came together on to this waste, one couldn't fall down a shaft without the other knowing it, eh? And it's scarcely likely they'd both fall down."

Neale glanced at Betty and shook his head.

"There you are, you see!" he muttered. "They all hang to the notion Hollis did meet Horbury! Mr. Horbury may have been alone, after all, you know," he went on, turning to Creasy. "There's no proof the other gentleman was with him."

"Aye, well I'm going on what these paper accounts say," answered Creasy. "They all take it for granted those two were together. Well, about these old shafting's, I did notice something very early this morning I thought might be looked into."

"What is it?" asked Neale. "Don't let's lose any chance of finding anything out, however small it may be."

The tinker finished mending a kettle and set it aside

amongst other renovated articles. He lifted the pan of solder off the fire, set it aside, too, and got up.

"Come this way, then," he said. "I was going in to Scarnham this noon to tell Mr Polke about it, but as long as you're here..."

He led the way through the thick gorse and heather until he came to a narrow track which wound across the moor in the direction of the town. There he paused, pointing towards Ellersdeane on the one hand, towards Scarnham on the other.

"You see this track, mister?" he said. "You'll notice it goes to Ellersdeane village that way, and to Scarnham this. Of course, you can't see it all the way in either direction, but you can take my word for it...it does. It comes out at Ellersdeane by the duck-pond, at Scarnham by the bridge at the foot of Cornmarket. People who know it would follow it if they wanted a short cut across the moor from the town to the village or the opposite, as you might say. Now then, look here a bit this way."

He preceded them along the narrow track until, on an open space in the moorland, they came to one of the old lead-mine shafts, the mouth of which had been fenced in by a roughly built wall of stone gathered from its immediate surroundings. In this wall, extending from its parapet to the ground, was a wide gap. The stones which had been displaced to make it had disappeared into the cavernous opening.

"Now then!" said the tinker, turning on his companions with the inquiring look of a man who advances a theory which may or may not be accepted as reasonable, "you see that? What I'd like to know is...is that a recently made gap? It's difficult to tell. If this bit of a stone fence had been built with mortar, one could have told. But it's never had mortar or lime in it! It's just rough masonry, as you see stones picked up off the moor, like all these fences round the old shafts. But there's the gap right enough! Do you know what I'm thinking?"

"No!" murmured Betty, with a glance of fear and doubt at the black vista which she saw through the gap. "But don't be afraid to speak."

"I'm thinking this," continued the tinker. "Supposing a man was following this track from Ellersdeane to Scarnham, or the other way about, as it might be, supposing he was curious to look down one of these old shafts, supposing he looked down this one, which stands, as you see, not two yards off the very track he was following, supposing he leaned his weight on this rotten bit of fencing, supposing it gave way? What?"

Neale, who had been listening intently, made a movement as if to lay his hand on the grey stones. Betty seized him impulsively.

"Don't, Wallie!" she exclaimed. "That frightens me!"

Creasy lifted his foot and pressed it against the stones at one edge of the gap. Before even that slight pressure three or four blocks gave way and dropped inward the sound of their fall came dully from the depths beneath.

"You see," said the tinker, "it's possible. It might be. And as you can tell from the time it takes a stone to drop, it's a long way down there. They're very deep, these old mines."

Neale turned from the broken wall and looked narrowly at the ground about it.

"I don't see any signs of anybody being about here recently," he remarked. "There are no footmarks."

"There couldn't be, mister," said Creasy. "You could march a regiment of soldiers over this moorland grass for many an hour, and there'd be no footprints on it when they'd gone, it's that wiry and strong. No! If half a dozen men had been standing about here when one fell in or if two or three men had come here to throw another man in," he added significantly, "there'd be no footmarks. Try it, you can't grind an iron-shod heel like mine into this turf."

"It's all very horrible!" said Betty, still staring at the black gap with its suggestions of subterranean horror. "If one only knew..."

The tinker turned and looked at the two young people as if he were estimating their strength.

"What are you wondering about?" asked Neale.

Creasy smiled as he glanced again at Betty.

"Well," he replied, "you're a pretty strong young fellow, mister, I take it, and the young lady looks as if she'd got a bit of good muscle about her. If you two could manage one end of a rope, I'd go down into that shaft at the other end a bit of the way, at any rate. And then I'd let down a lantern and see if there's anything to be seen."

Betty turned anxiously to Neale, and Neale looked the tinker over with appraising eyes.

"I could pull you up myself," he answered. "You're no

great weight. And haven't those shafts got props and stays down the side?"

"Aye, but they'll be thoroughly rotten by this," said Creasy. "Well, we'll try it. Come to my cart I've plenty of stuff there."

"You're sure there's no danger?" asked Betty. "Don't imperil yourself!"

"No danger, so long as you two will stick to this end of the rope," said Creasy. "I shan't go too far down."

The tilted cart proved to contain all sorts of useful things. They presently returned to the shaft with two coils of stout rope, a crowbar, a lantern attached to a length of strong cord, and a great sledge-hammer, with which the tinker drove the crowbar firmly into the ground some ten or twelve feet from the edge of the gap.

He made one end of the first rope fast to this; the other end he securely knotted about his waist; one end of the second rope he looped under his armpits, and handed the other to Neale; then, lighting his lantern, he prepared to descend, having first explained the management of the ropes to his assistants.

"All you've got to do," he said reassuringly to Betty, "is to hold on to this second rope and let me down, gradual-like. When I say 'Pull,' draw up. I'll help, hand over hand, up this first rope. Simple enough and I shan't go too far."

Nevertheless, he exhausted the full length of both ropes, and it seemed a long time before they heard anything of him. Betty, frightened of what she might hear, fearful lest Neale should go too near the edge of the shaft, began to get nervous at the delay, and it was with a great sense of relief that she at last heard the signal. The tinker came hand over hand up the stationary rope, helped by the second one. His face, appearing over the edge of the gap, was grave and at first inscrutable. He shook himself when he stepped above ground, as if he wanted to shake off an impression. Then he turned and spoke in a whisper.

"It's as I thought it might be!" he said. "There's a dead man down there!"

Chapter 17

Betty checked the cry of horror which instinctively started to her lips, and turned to Neale with a look which he was quick to interpret. He moved nearer to the tinker, who was unwinding the rope from his waist.

"You couldn't tell...what man?" he asked, in low tones.

Creasy shook his head with a look of dislike for what he had seen by the light of his lantern.

"No!" he answered. "It wasn't possible, mister. But a man there is! And dead, naturally. And a long way it is, too, down to the bottom of that place!"

"What's to be done?" asked Neale.

The tinker slowly coiled up his ropes, and laid them in order by the crowbar.

"There's only one thing to be done," he answered, after a reflective pause. "We shall have to get him up. That'll be a job! You and the young lady go back to Scarnham, and tell Polke what we've found, and let him come out here with a man or two. I'll go into Ellersdeane yonder and get some help and a windlass...can't do without that. There's a man that sinks wells in Ellersdeane, I'll get him and his men to come back with me. Then we can set to work."

Creasy moved away as he finished speaking, untethered his pony, threw an old saddle across its back, and without further remark rode off in the direction of the village, while Neale and Betty turned back to Scarnham. For a while neither broke the silence which had followed the tinker's practical suggestions; when Betty at last spoke it was in a hushed voice.

"Wallie!" she said, "do you think that can possibly be... Uncle John?"

"No!" answered Neale sharply, "I don't! I don't believe it possible he would be so foolish as to lean over a rotten bit of walling like that, he'd know the danger of it."

"Then it must be the other man, Hollis!" said Betty.

"Maybe," agreed Neale. "If it is..."

He paused, and Betty looked at his set face as if she were wondering what he was thinking of.

"What?" she asked timidly. "You're uneasy about something."

"It's a marvel to me, if it is Hollis, however he comes to be there," answered Neale at last. "According to all we know, he certainly went to meet somebody on Saturday night. I can't think how anybody who knew the district would have let a stranger do such a risky thing as to lean over one of those shafts. Besides, if anybody was with him, and there was an accident, why hasn't the accident been reported? Betty! It's more like murder!"

"You think he may have been thrown down there?" she asked fearfully.

"Thrown down or forced down, it's all the same," said Neale. 'There may have been a struggle...a fight. But there, what's the use of speculating? We don't even know whose body it is yet. Let's get on and tell those police chaps."

Turning off the open moor on to the highway at the corner of Scarnham Bridge, they suddenly came face to face with Gabriel, who, for once in a way, was walking instead of driving into the town. The two young people, emerging from the shelter of a high hedgerow which bordered the moorland at that point, started at sight of the banker's colorless face, cold and set as usual. But Gabriel betrayed no surprise, and was in no way taken aback. He lifted his hat in silence, and was marching on when Neale impulsively hailed him.

"Mr. Chestermarke!" he exclaimed.

Gabriel halted and turned, looking at his late clerk with absolute impassiveness. He made no remark, and stood like a statue, waiting for Neale to speak.

"You may like to know," said Neale, coming up to him, "we have just found the body of a man on the moor... Ellersdeane Hollow."

Gabriel showed no surprise. No light came into his eyes, no color to his cheek. It seemed a long time before his firmly set lips relaxed.

"A man?" he said quietly. "What man?"

"We don't know," answered Neale. "All we know is, there's a man's body lying at the bottom of one of the old shafts up there...near Ellersdeane Tower. The tinker who camps out there has just seen it...he's been partly down the shaft."

"And did not recognize it?" asked Gabriel.

"No, it was too far beneath him," replied Neale. "He's gone into the village to get help."

Gabriel lingered a moment, and then, lifting his hat again, began to move forward towards the town.

"I should advise you to acquaint the police, Mr. Neale," he said. "Good-morning!"

He marched away, stiffly upright, across the bridge and up the Cornmarket, and Neale and Betty followed.

"Why did you tell him?" asked Betty.

Neale threw a glance of something very like scorn after the retreating figure.

"Wanted to see how he'd take it!" he answered. "Bah! Gabriel's no better than a wax figure! You might as well tell a marble image any news of this sort as tell him! You'd have thought he'd have had sufficient human feeling in him to say he hoped it wasn't your uncle, anyhow!"

"No, I shouldn't," said Betty. "I sized Gabriel up and Joseph, too when I walked into their parlor the other afternoon. They haven't any feelings, you might as well expect to get feeling out of a fish."

They met Starmidge in the Market Place talking to Parkinson. Neale told the news to both. The journalist dashed into his office for his hat, and made off to Ellersdeane Hollow. Starmidge turned to the police-station with his information.

"No one else knows, I suppose?" he remarked, as they went along.

"Gabriel knows," answered Neale. 'We met him as we were coming off the moor and I told him."

"Show any surprise?" asked the detective.

"Neither surprise nor anything else," said Neale. "Absolutely unaffected!"

Polke, hearing the news, immediately bustled into activity, sending for a cab in which to drive along the road to a point near Ellersdeane Tower, from which they could reach the lead mine. But he shook his head when he saw Betty meant to return. "Don't, miss!" he urged. "Stay here in town, you'd far better. It's not a nice job for ladies, aught of that sort. Wait at the hotel, do, now!"

"Doing nothing!" exclaimed Betty. "That would be far

worse. Let me go. I'm not afraid of anything. And to hang about, waiting and wondering..."

Neale, who had been about to enter the cab with the police, drew back.

"You go on," he said to Polke. "Get things through, Miss Fosdyke and I will walk slowly back there. We won't come close up till you can tell us something definite. Don't you see she's anxious about her uncle? We can't keep her waiting."

He rejoined Betty as Polke and his men drove off. Together they turned again in the direction of the bridge. Once across it and on the moor, Neale made the girl sit down on a ledge of rock at some distance from the lead mine, but within sight of it. While he talked to her, stood watching the figures grouped about the shaft. Creasy had evidently succeeded in getting help at once. Neale saw men fixing a windlass over the mouth of the old mine; saw a man at last disappear into its depths. And after a long pause he saw from the movements of the other men the body had been drawn to the surface and they were bending over it. A moment later, Starmidge separated himself from the rest, and came in Neale's direction. He nodded his head energetically at Betty as he drew within speaking distance.

"All right, Miss Fosdyke!" he said. "It's not your uncle. But...it's the other man, Mr. Neale...no doubt of it!"

"Hollis!" exclaimed Neale.

"It's the man described by Mrs. Pratt and Simmons that's certain," answered the detective. "So there's one mystery settled, though it makes all the rest stranger than ever. Now, Miss Fosdyke, that'll be some relief to you, so don't come any nearer. But just spare Mr. Neale a few minutes, I want to speak to him."

Betty obediently turned back to the ledge of rock, and Neale walked with Starmidge towards the group around the shaft.

"Can you tell anything?" he asked. "Are there any signs of violence? I mean, does it look as if he'd been..."

"Thrown in there?" said the detective calmly. "Ah, it's a bit early to decide. The only thing I'm thinking of now is the fact this is Hollis! That's certain, Mr. Neale. Now what could he be doing on this lonely bit of ground? Where does this track lead?"

"It's a short cut from Scarnham Bridge corner to the middle of Ellersdeane village," answered Neale, pointing one way and then the other.

"And Gabriel lives in Ellersdeane, doesn't he?" asked Starmidge. "Or close by?"

Neale indicated certain chimneys rising amongst the trees on the far side of the Hollow. "He lives there. The Warren," he replied.

"Um!" mused Starmidge. "I wonder if this poor fellow was making his way there to see him?"

"How should he...a stranger know of this short cut?" demurred Neale. "I don't think that's very likely."

"That's true, unless he'd had it pointed out to him," rejoined Starmidge. "It's odd, anyway, his body should be found half-way, as it were, between Gabriel's place and Joseph' house isn't it now? But, Lord bless you! We're only on the fringe of this business as yet. Well just take a look at him."

Neale walked within the group of bystanders, feeling an intense dislike and loathing of the whole thing. In obedience to Starmidge's wish, he looked steadily at the dead man and turned away.

"You don't know him? Never saw him during the five years you were at the bank?" whispered the detective. "Think... make certain, now."

"Never saw him in my life!" declared Neale, stepping back. "I neither know him nor anything about him."

"I wanted you to make sure," said Starmidge. "I thought you might possibly recollect him as somebody who'd called at the bank during your time."

"No!" said Neale. "Certainly not! I've never set eyes on him until now. Of course, he's Hollis, I suppose?"

"Oh, without doubt!" answered Polke, who caught Neale's question as he came up. "He's Hollis, right enough. Mr. Neale, here's a difficulty. It's a queer thing, but there isn't one of us here who knows if this spot is in Scarnham or in Ellersdeane. Do you? Is it within our borough boundary, or is it in Ellersdeane parish? The Ellersdeane policeman there doesn't know, and I'm sure I don't! It's a point of importance, because the inquest will have to be held in the parish in which the body was found."

The Ellersdeane constable who had followed Polke

suddenly raised a finger and pointed across the heather.

"Here's a gentleman coming as might know, Mr. Polke," he said. "Mr. Chestermarke!"

Neale and Starmidge turned sharply to see the banker advancing quickly from the adjacent road. A cab, drawn up a little distance off, showed he had driven out to hear the latest news. Polke stepped forward to meet the new-comer. Gabriel greeted him in his usual impassive fashion.

"This body been recovered?" he asked quietly.

"A few minutes ago, Mr. Chestermarke," answered Polke. "Will you look at it?"

Gabriel moved aside the group of men without further word, and the others followed him. He looked steadily at the dead man's face and withdrew.

"Not known to me," he said, in answer to an inquiring glance from Polke. "Hollis, I suppose, of course."

He went off again as suddenly as he had come and Starmidge drew Neale aside.

"Mr. Neale!" he whispered, with a nearer approach to excitement than Neale had yet seen in him. "Did you see Gabriel's eyes? He's a liar! As sure as my name's Starmidge, he's a liar! Mr. Neale! He knows that dead man!"

Chapter 18

Neale, startled and amazed by this sudden outburst on the part of a man whom up to that time he had taken to be unusually cool-headed and phlegmatic, did not immediately answer. He was watching the Ellersdeane constable, who was running after Gabriel's rapidly retreating figure. He saw Gabriel stop, listen to an evident question, and then lift his hand and point to various features of the Hollow. The policeman touched his helmet, and came back to Polke.

"Mr. Chestermarke, sir, says the moorland is in three parishes," he reported panting. "From Scarnham Bridge corner to Ellersdeane Tower yonder is in Scarnham parish, this side the Hollow is in Ellersdeane; everything beyond the Tower is in Middlethorpe."

"Then we're in Scarnham," said Polke. "He'll have to be taken down to the town mortuary. We'd better see to it at once. What are you going to do, Starmidge?" he asked, as the detective turned away with Neale.

"I'll take this short cut back," said Starmidge. "I want to get to the post office. Yes, sir!" he went on, as he and Neale slowly walked towards Betty. "I say, he knew him! knew him, Mr. Neale, knew him as soon as ever he clapped his eyes on him!"

"You're very certain about it," said Neale.

"Dead certain!" exclaimed the detective. "I was watching him purposely. I've taught myself to watch men. The slightest quiver of a lip, the least bit of light in an eye, the merest twitch of a little finger, don't I know them all, and know what they mean! And, when Gabriel stepped up to look at that body, I was watching that face of his as I've never watched mortal man before!"

"And you saw what?" asked Neale.

"I saw...recognition!" said Starmidge. "Recognition, sir! I'll stake my reputation as a detective officer Mr. Gabriel Chestermarke has seen that dead man before. He mayn't know him personally. He may never have spoken to him. But he knew him! He'd seen him!"

"Will your conviction of that help at all?" inquired Neale.

"It'll help me," replied the detective quickly. "I'm gradually getting some ideas. But I shan't tell Polke, nor anybody else of it. You can tell Miss Fosdyke if you like, she'll understand. Women have more intuition than men. Now I'm off I want to get a wire away to London. Look here drop in at the police station when you get back. We shall examine Hollis's clothing, you know there may be some clue to Horbury."

He hurried off towards the town, and Neale rejoined Betty. And as they slowly followed the detective, he told her what Starmidge had just said with such evident belief and Betty understood, as Starmidge had prophesied, and she grew more thoughtful than ever.

"When are we going to find a way out of all this miserable business!" she suddenly exclaimed. "Are we any nearer a solution because of what's just happened? Does that help us to finding out what's become of my uncle?"

"I suppose one thing's sure to lead to another," said Neale. "That seems to be the detective's notion, anyhow. If Starmidge is so certain Gabriel knew Hollis, he'll work that for all it's worth. It's my opinion, whatever that's worth, Hollis came down here to see the Chestermarke's. Did he see them? There's the problem. If one could only find out!"

"I wish you and I could do something apart from the police," suggested Betty. "Isn't there anything we could do?"

Neale pointed ahead to the high roof of Joseph's house across the river.

"There's one thing I'd like to do, if I could," he answered. "I'd just like to know all the secrets of that place! There are some I'm as certain as that we're crossing this moor. You see that queer-shaped structure, sort of conical chimney sticking up among the trees in Joseph's garden? That's a workshop, or a laboratory, or something, in which Joseph spends his leisure moments. I'd like to know what he does there. But nobody knows! Nobody is ever allowed in that house, nor in the garden.

I don't know a single soul in all Scarnham that's ever been inside either. I'm perfectly certain Mr. Horbury was never asked there. Once Joseph's across his thresholds, back or front, there's an end of him till he comes out again!"

"But he doesn't live entirely alone, does he?" asked Betty.

"As near as can be," replied Neale. "His entire staff consists of an old man and an old woman, man and wife who've been with him...oh, ever since he was born, I believe! You may have seen the old man about the town, old Palfreman. Everybody knows him...queer, old-fashioned chap. He goes out to buy in whatever's wanted. The old woman never shows. That's the trio that live in there, a queer lot, aren't they?"

"It's all queer!" sighed Betty. "But now this unfortunate man's body has been found Wallie! do you think it possible he was thrown down that mine? That would mean murder!"

"If he was thrown down there, already dead," answered Neale grimly, "it would not only mean murder but more than one person was concerned in it. We shall know more when they've examined the body and searched the clothing. I'm going round to the police station when I've seen you back to the hotel. I'm hoping they'll find something that'll settle the one point that's so worrying."

"Which point?" asked Betty.

"The real critical point in my opinion," answered Neale. "Who it was Hollis came to see on Saturday? There may be letters, papers, on him that will settle that. And if we once know that it will make a difference! Because then...then..."

"What then?" demanded Betty.

"Then the police can ask that person if Hollis did meet him!" exclaimed Neale. "And they can ask, too, what that person did with Hollis. Solve that, and we'll see daylight!"

But Betty shook her head with clear indications of doubt as to the validity of this theory.

"No!" she said. "It won't come off, Wallie. If there's been foul play, the guilty people will have had too much cleverness to leave any evidences on their victim. I don't believe they'll find anything on Hollis that'll clear things up. Daylight isn't coming from that quarter!"

"Where are we to look for it, then?" asked Neale dismally.

"It's somewhere far back," declared Betty. "I've felt that all along. The secret of all this affair isn't in anything that's been done here and lately it's in something deep down. And how to get at it, and to find out about my uncle, I don't know."

Neale felt it worse than idle to offer more theories, speculation was becoming useless. He left Betty at the Scarnham Arms, and went round to the police-station to meet Starmidge and together they went over to the mortuary. And before noon they knew all the medical examination and careful searching could tell them about the dead man.

Hollis, said the police surgeon and another medical man who had been called in to assist him, bore no marks of violence other than those which were inevitable in the case of a man who had fallen seventy feet. His neck was broken; he must have died instantaneously. There was nothing to show there had been any struggle previous to his fall. Had such a struggle taken place, the doctors would have expected to find certain signs and traces of it on the body, there were none. Everything seemed to point to the theory he had leaned over the insecure fencing of the old shaft to look into its depths.

Probably to drop stones into them. The loose, unmortar parapet had given way with his weight, and he had plunged headlong to the bottom. He might have been pushed in from behind of course, but that was conjecture. Under ordinary circumstances, agreed both doctors, everything would have seemed to point to accident. And one of them suggested it was very probable what really had happened was this. Hollis, on his way to call on some person in the neighborhood, or on his return from such a call, had crossed the moor, been attracted by inquisitiveness to the old mine, had leaned over its parapet, and fallen in. Accident...it all looked like sheer accident.

In one of the rooms at the police-station, Neale anxiously watched Polke and Starmidge examine the dead man's clothing and personal effects. The detective rapidly laid aside certain articles of the sort which he evidently expected to find, a purse, a cigar-case; the usual small things found in a well-to-do man's pockets. A watch and chain, a ring or two. He gave no particular attention to any of these beyond ascertaining there was a good deal of loose money in the purse, some twelve or fifteen pounds in gold and pointing out the watch had stopped at ten minutes to eight.

"That shows the time of the accident," he remarked.

"Are you sure?" suggested Polke doubtfully. "It may

merely mean the watch ran itself out then."

Starmidge picked up the watch, a stem winder and examined it.

"No," he said, "it's broken by the fall. See there the spring's snapped. Ten minutes to eight, Saturday night, Mr. Polke that's when this affair happened. Now then, this is what I want!"

From an inner pocket of the dead man's smart morning-coat, he drew a morocco-leather letter-case, and carefully extracted the papers from it. With Neale looking on at one side, and Polke at the other, Starmidge examined every separate paper. Nothing he found bore any reference to Scarnham. There were one or two bills from booksellers made out to Frederick Hollis, Esquire. There was a folded playbill which showed Mr. Hollis had recently been to a theatre, and because of some penciled notes on its margins had taken an unusual interest in what he saw there. There were two or three letters from correspondents who evidently shared with Mr. Hollis a taste for collecting old books and engravings. There were some cuttings from newspapers. They, too, related to collecting. And Neale suddenly got an idea.

"I say!" he exclaimed. "Mr. Horbury was a bit of a collector of that sort of thing, as you probably saw from his house. This man may have run down to see him about some affair of that sort."

But at that moment Starmidge unfolded a slip of paper which he had drawn from an inner pocket of the letter-case. He gave one glance at it, and laid it flat on the table before his companions.

"No!" he said. "That's probably what brought Hollis down to Scarnham! A check for ten thousand pounds! And incomplete!"

The three men bent wonderingly over the bit of pink paper. Neale's quick eyes took in its contents at a glance.

London: May 12th, 1912.
Vanderkiste, Mullineau & Company,
563 Lombard Street, E.C.
Pay .... or Order
the sum of Ten Thousand Pounds
£10,000.00.

By..

"That's extraordinary!" exclaimed Neale. "Date and amount filled in and the names of payee and drawer omitted! What does it mean?"

"Ah!" said Starmidge, "when we know that, Mr. Neale, we shall know a lot! But I'm pretty sure of one thing. Mr. Hollis came down here intending to pay somebody ten thousand pounds. And he wasn't exactly certain who that somebody was!"

"Good!" muttered Polke. "Good! That looks like it."

"So," said Starmidge, "he didn't fill in either the name of the payee or his own name until he was sure! See, Mr. Neale!"

"Why did he fill in the amount?" remarked Neale, skeptically.

Starmidge winked at Polke.

"Very likely to dangle before somebody's eyes," he answered slyly. "Can't you reconstruct the scene, Mr. Neale? 'Here you are!' says Hollis, showing this check. 'Ten thousand of the very best, lying to be picked up at my bankers. Say the word, and I'll fill in your name and mine!' Lay you a pound to a penny that's been it, gentlemen!"

"Good!" repeated Polke. "Good, sergeant! I believe you're right. Now, what'll you do about it?"

The detective carefully folded up the check and replaced it in the slit from which he had taken it. He also replaced all the other papers, put the letter-case in a stout envelope and handed it to the superintendent.

"Seal it up and put it away in your safe till the inquest tomorrow," he said. "What shall I do? Oh, well you needn't mention it, either of you, except to Miss Fosdyke, of course, but as soon as the inquest is adjourned, as it'll have to be I shall slip back to town and see those bankers. I don't know, but I don't think it's likely Mr. Hollis would have ten thousand pounds always lying at his bank. I should say this ten thousand has been lodged there for a special purpose. And what I shall want to find out from them, in that case, is what special purpose? And what had it to do with Scarnham, or anybody at Scarnham? See? And I'll tell you what, Mr. Polke I don't know whether we'll produce that check at the inquest on Hollis at first, anyhow. The coroner's bound to adjourn, he'll want tomorrow will be formal identification of the body, all other evidence can be left till later. I've wired for Simmons, he'll be able to identify. No, we'll keep this check business back till I've been to London. I shall find out something from Vanderkistes, they're highly respectable private bankers, and they'll tell me..."

At that moment a policeman entered the room and presented Polke with a card.

"Gentleman's just come in, sir," he said. "Wants to see you particular."

Polke glanced at the card, and read the name aloud, with a start of surprise. "Mr. Leonard Hollis!"

Chapter 19

Polke hastily followed the policeman from the room to return immediately with a quiet-looking elderly gentleman in whom Neale and Starmidge saw a distinct likeness to the dead man.

"His brother!" whispered Polke, as he handed a chair to the visitor. "So you've seen about this in the newspapers, sir?" he went on, turning to Mr. Leonard Hollis. "And you thought you'd better come over, I suppose?"

"I have not only read about it in the newspapers," answered the visitor, "but last night, very late received a telegram from my brother's clerk, Mr. Simmons who evidently found my address at my brother's rooms. So I left Birmingham where I now live, at once, to see you. Now, have you heard anything of my brother?"

Polke shook his head solemnly and warningly.

"I'm sorry to say we have, sir," he replied. "You'd better prepare for the worst news, Mr. Hollis. We found the body this morning not two hours ago. And we don't know, as yet, how he came by his death. The doctors say it may have been pure accident. Let's hope it was! But there are strange circumstances, sir...very strange!"

Hollis quietly rose from his chair.

"I suppose I can see him?" he asked.

Polke led him out of the room, and Starmidge turned to Neale.

"We're gradually getting at something, Mr. Neale," he said. "All this leads somewhere, you know. Now, since we found that incomplete check, there's a question I wanted to ask you. You've left Chestermarke's Bank now, and under the circumstances we're working in you needn't have any delicacy about answering questions about them. Do you know of any recent transaction of theirs which involved ten thousand pounds?"

"No!" replied Neale. "I certainly don't."

"Nor any sum approaching it?" suggested Starmidge. "Or exceeding it?"

"Nothing whatever!" reiterated Neale. "I know of all recent banking transactions at Chestermarke's, and I can't think...I've been thinking since we saw that check...of anything the check had to do with."

"Well, it's a queer thing," remarked the detective meditatively. "I'll lay anything Hollis brought that check down here for some specific purpose and who on earth is there in this place he could bring it to but Chestermarke's? However, we'll see if I don't trace something about it when I get up to town, and then..."

Polke and the dead man's brother came back, talking earnestly. The superintendent carefully closed the door, and begging his visitor to be seated again, turned to Starmidge.

"I've told Mr. Hollis all the main facts of the case," he said. "Of course, he identified his brother at once."

"When did you see him last, sir!" asked Starmidge.

"Some eight or nine months ago," replied Hollis. "He came to see me, in Birmingham. Previous to that, I hadn't seen him for several years. I ought to tell you," he went on, turning to Polke, "for a great many years I have lived abroad tea-planting in Ceylon. I came back to England about a year ago, and eventually settled down at Edgbaston. I suppose my brother's clerk found my address on an old letter or something last night, and wired to me in consequence."

"When Simmons was here," observed Starmidge, "he said your brother seemed to have no relations."

"I daresay Simmons would get that impression," remarked Hollis. "My brother was a very reserved man, who was not likely to talk much of his family. As a matter of fact, I am about the only relation he had except some half-cousins, or something of that sort."

"Can you tell us anything about your brother's position?" asked Starmidge. "The clerk said he didn't practice very much, and had means of his own."

"Quite true," assented Hollis. "I believe he had a comfortable income, apart from his practice, perhaps five or six hundred a year. He mentioned to me that he only did business for old clients."

"Do you think he'd be likely to have a sum of ten

thousand pounds lying at his bankers?" inquired Starmidge.

Hollis looked sharply at the detective and then shook his head.

"Not unless it was for some special purpose," he answered. "He might have such a sum if he'd been selling out securities for re-investment. But my impression is...in fact, it's more than an impression I'm sure he bought himself an annuity of about the amount I mentioned just now, some years ago. You see, he'd no children, and he knew I was a well-to-do man, so he used his capital in that a way."

"Would you be surprised to see a check of his drawn for ten thousand pounds?" asked Starmidge suddenly.

"Frankly, I should!" replied Hollis, with a smile. "That is, if it was on his private account."

"Do you happen to know who kept his private account?" inquired Starmidge.

"Yes," answered Hollis. "He banked with an old private firm called Vanderkiste, Mullineau & Company, of Lombard Street."

Starmidge, after a whispered word with Polke, took up the envelope in which he had placed the dead man's letter-case, and produced the check.

"Look at that, sir," he said, laying it before the visitor. "Is that your brother's handwriting?"

"His handwriting...oh, yes!" exclaimed Hollis. "Most certainly! But there's no signature!"

"No and there's no name of any payee," said Starmidge. "That's where the mystery comes in. But this and this letter-case and its contents was found on him, and there's no doubt he came down to Scarnham intending to pay that check to somebody. You can't throw any light on that, sir?"

The visitor, who continued to regard the check with evident amazement, at last turned away from it and glanced at his three companions.

"Well," he said, "I don't know I can. But one principal reason why I hurried here, after getting Simmons telegram last night, is this. In the newspapers there is a good deal of mention of a Mr. John Horbury, manager of a bank in this town. He, too, you tell me, has disappeared. Now, I happen to possess a remarkably good memory, and it was at once stirred by seeing that name.

"My brother Frederick and I were at school together at Selburgh...Selburgh Grammar School, you know quite thirty-five or six years ago. One of our schoolmates was a John Horbury. And he came from this place, Scarnham."

The three listeners looked at each other. And Neale started, as if at some sudden reminiscence, and he spoke quickly.

"I've heard Mr. Horbury speak of his school-days at Selburgh!" he said. "And now I come to think of it he had some books with the school coat-of-arms on the sides prizes."

"Just so!" remarked Hollis. "I remember Jack Horbury very well indeed, though I never saw him after I left school, nor heard of him either, until I saw all this news about him in the papers. Of course, your missing bank manager is the John Horbury my brother and I were at school with! And I take it the reason my brother came down to Scarnham last Saturday was to see John Horbury."

Starmidge had been listening to all this with close attention. He was now more than ever convinced he was at last on some track, but so far he could not see many steps ahead. Nevertheless, his next step was clearly enough discernible.

"You say you saw your brother some eight or nine months ago, sir?" he remarked. "Did he mention Mr. Horbury to you at that time?"

"No, he didn't," replied Hollis.

"Did he ever...recently, I mean ever mention his name to you in a letter?" asked Starmidge.

"No never! I don't know," said Hollis, "he or I ever spoke to each other of John Horbury from the time we left school. John Horbury was not, as it were, a very particular chum of ours. We knew him as we knew a hundred other boys. As I have already told you, the two names, Horbury, Scarnham, in the newspapers yesterday, immediately recalled John Horbury, our schoolmate, to me. Up to then, I don't suppose I'd ever thought of him for years! And I don't suppose he'd ever thought of me, or of my brother. Yet, I feel sure my brother came here to see him. For business reasons, I suppose?"

"The odd thing about that, Mr. Hollis," remarked Polke, "is we can't find the slightest reason, either from anybody here, or from your brother's clerk in London, why your brother should come to see Horbury, whether for business, or for any other purpose. And as to his remembering Mr. Frederick Hollis, well, here's Mr. Neale. Mr. Horbury was his guardian and Mr. Neale, of course, has known him all his life. Now, Mr. Neale never heard him mention Mr. Frederick Hollis by name at any time. And there's now staying in the town Mr. Horbury's niece, Miss Fosdyke; she, too, never heard her uncle speak of any Mr. Hollis. Then, as to business, the partners at Chestermarke's Bank declare they know nothing whatever of your brother. Mr. Gabriel, the senior partner, has seen the poor gentleman, and didn't recognize him. So we at any rate, are as wise as ever. We don't know what your brother came here for!"

Hollis bowed his head in full acceptance of the superintendent's remarks. But he looked up at Starmidge and smiled.

"Exactly!" he said. "I quite understand you, Mr. Polke. But I am convinced my brother came here to see John Horbury. Why he came, I know no more than you do, but I hope to know!"

"You'll stay in the town a bit, sir?" suggested Polke. "You'll want to make arrangements for your poor brother's funeral, of course. Anything we can do, sir, to help, shall be done."

"I'm much obliged to you, Mr. Polke," replied Hollis. "Yes, I shall certainly stay in Scarnham. In fact," he went on, rising and looking quietly from one man to the other, "I shall stay in Scarnham until I, or you, or somebody have satisfactorily explained how my brother came to his death! I shall spare neither effort nor money to get at the truth, that's my determination!"

"There's somebody else in like case with you, Mr. Hollis," observed Polke. "Miss Fosdyke's just as concerned about her uncle as you are about your brother. She declares she'll spend a fortune on finding him or finding out what's happened to him. It was Miss Fosdyke insisted on having Detective-Sergeant Starmidge down at once."

Hollis quietly scrutinized the detective.

"Well?" he asked. "And what do you make of it?"

But Starmidge was not in the mood for saying anything more just then, and he put his questioner off, asking him, at the same time, to keep the matter of the check to himself. Presently Hollis went away with Neale, to whom he wished to talk, and Starmidge, after a period of what seemed to be profound thought, turned to Polke.

"Superintendent!" he said earnestly. "With your leave, I'd like to try an experiment."

"What experiment?" demanded Polke.

Starmidge pointed to the ten thousand pound check, which was still lying on the table.

"I'd like to take that check across to Chestermarke's Bank, and show it to the partners," he answered.

"Good heavens! Why?" exclaimed Polke. "I thought you didn't want anybody to know about it."

"Never mind I've an idea," said the detective. "I'd just like them to see it, anyway, and," he added, with a wink, "I'd like to see them when they do see it!"

"You know best," said Polke. "If you think it well, do it."

Starmidge put the check in an envelope and walked over to the bank. He was shown into the partners room almost immediately, and the two men glanced at him with evident curiosity.

"Sorry to trouble you, gentlemen," said Starmidge, in his politest manner. "There's a little matter you might help us in. We've been searching this unfortunate gentleman's clothing, you know, for papers and so on. And in his letter-case we found...this!"

He had the check ready behind his back, and he suddenly brought it forward, and laid it immediately before the partners, on Gabriel's desk, at the same time stepping back so he could observe both men.

"Queer, isn't it, gentlemen?" he remarked quietly. "Incomplete!"

Gabriel, in spite of his habitual control, started. Joseph, bending nearer to the desk, made a curious sound of surprise. A second later they both looked at Starmidge...each as calm as ever. "Well?" said Gabriel.

"You don't know anything about that, gentlemen?" asked Starmidge, affecting great innocence.

"Nothing!" answered Gabriel.

"Of course not!" murmured Joseph, a little derisively.

"I thought you might recognize the handwriting,"

suggested Starmidge, using one of his previously invented excuses.

"No!" replied Gabriel. "Don't know it!"

"From Adam's writing," added Joseph.

"You know the name of the bankers, I suppose, gentlemen?" asked the detective.

"Vanderkiste? Oh, yes!" assented Gabriel. "Well-known city firm. But I don't think we've ever done business with them," he added, turning to his nephew.

"Never!" replied Joseph. "In my time, at any rate."

Starmidge picked up the check and carefully replaced it in its envelope. "Much obliged to you, gentlemen," he said, retreating towards the door. "Oh, you'll be interested in hearing, no doubt, the dead man's brother, Mr. Leonard Hollis, of Birmingham, has come. He's identified the body."

"And what does he think, or suggest?" asked Joseph, glancing out of the corners of his eyes at Starmidge. "Has he any suggestions or ideas?"

"He thinks his brother came here to meet Mr. Horbury," answered Starmidge.

"That's so evident it's no news," remarked Joseph. "Perhaps he can suggest where Horbury's to be found."

Starmidge bowed and went out and straight back to Polke. He handed him the check and the letter-case.

"Lock them up!" he said. "Now then, listen! You can do all that's necessary about that inquest. I'm off to town. Sit down, and I'll tell you why. And what I tell you, keep to yourself."

That evening, Starmidge, who had driven quietly across the country from Scarnham to Ecclesborough, joined a London express at the Midland Station in the big town. The carriages were unusually full, and he had some difficulty in finding the corner seat he particularly desired. But he got one, at last, at the very end of the train, and he had only just settled himself in it when he saw Gabriel hurry past. Starmidge put his head out of the window and watched Gabriel entered a first-class compartment in the next coach.

"First stop Nottingham!" mused the detective. And he pulled a sheaf of telegram forms out of his pocket, and leisurely began to write a message which before he signed his name to it had run into many words.

Chapter 20

Starmidge sent off his telegram when the train stopped at Nottingham, and thereafter went to sleep, secure in the knowledge it would be promptly acted upon by its recipients. And when, soon after eleven o'clock, the express ran into St. Pancras, he paid no particular attention to Gabriel. He had no desire, indeed, the banker should see him, and he hung back when the crowded carriages cleared, and the platform became a scene of bustle and animation. But he had no difficulty in distinguishing Gabriel's stiffly erect figure as it made its way towards the hall of the station, and his sharp eyes were quick to notice a quietly dressed, unobtrusive sort of man who sauntered along, caught sight of the banker, and swung round to follow him. Starmidge watched both pass along towards the waiting lines of vehicles then he turned on his heel and went to the refreshment room and straight to a man who evidently expected him.

"You got the wire in good time, then?" said Starmidge.

"Plenty!" answered the other man laconically. "I've put a good man on to him. See anything of them?"

"Yes, but I didn't know our man," remarked Starmidge. "Who is he? Will he do what I want?"

"He's all right fellow who's just been promoted, and, of course, he's naturally keen," replied Starmidge's companion. "Name of Gandam. That was a pretty good and full description of the man you want followed, Starmidge," he went on, with a smile. "You don't leave much out!"

"I didn't want him to be overlooked, and I didn't want to show up myself," said Starmidge. "I noticed our man spotted him quick. Now, look here I'll be at headquarters first thing tomorrow morning, I want this chap Gandam's report. Nine-thirty sharp! Now we'll have a drink, and I'll get home."

"Good case?" asked the other man, as they pledged each other. "Getting on with it?"

"Tell you more tomorrow," answered Starmidge. "When

and if I know more. Nine-thirty, mind!"

But when Starmidge met his companion of the night before at nine-thirty next morning, it was to find him in conversation with the other man, and to see dissatisfaction on the countenances of both. And Starmidge, a naturally keen observer, knew what had happened. He frowned as he looked at Gandam.

"You don't mean to say he slipped you!" he exclaimed.

"I don't know about slipped," muttered Gandam. "I lost him, anyway, Mr. Starmidge, and I don't see how I can be blamed, either. Perhaps you might have done differently, but..."

"Tell about it!" interrupted Starmidge. "What happened?"

"I spotted him, of course, from your description, as soon as he got out of the train," replied Gandam. "No mistaking him, naturally, he's an extra good one to watch. He'd no luggage, not even a handbag. I followed him to the taxi-cabs. I was close by when he stepped into one, and I heard what he said. 'Stage door Adalbert Theater.' Off he went, I followed in another taxi. I stopped mine and got out, just in time to see him walk up the entry to the stage-door. He went in. It was then half-past eleven; they were beginning to close. I waited and waited until at last they closed the stage-door. I'll take my oath he'd never come out! Never!"

Starmidge made a face of intense disgust.

"No, of course he hadn't!" he exclaimed. "He'd gone out at the front. I suppose that never struck you? I know that stage-door of the Adalbert, it's up a passage. If you'd stood at the end of that passage, man, you could have kept an eye on the front and stage-door at the same time. But, of course, it never struck you a man could go in at the back of a place and come out at the front, did it? Well that's off for the present. And so am I."

Vexed and disappointed Gabriel had not been tracked to wherever he was staying in London, Starmidge went out, hailed a taxi-cab, and was driven down to the city. He did not particularly concern himself about Gabriel's visit to the stage-door of the Adalbert Theatre. It was something, after all, to know he had gone there. If need arose, he might be traced from that theater, in which, very possibly, he had some financial interest. What Starmidge had desired to ascertain was the banker's London address. He had already learned in Scarnham Gabriel was constantly in London for days at a time, he must have some permanent address at which he could be found. And Starmidge foresaw he might wish to find him, perhaps in a hurry. But just then his chief concern was with another banking firm...Vanderkiste's. He walked slowly along Lombard Street until he came to the house, a quiet, sober, eminently respectable-looking old business place, quite unlike the palatial affairs in which the great banking corporations of modern origin carry on their transactions.

There was no display of marble and plaster and plate glass and mahogany and heavy plethoric fittings, a modest brass plate affixed to the door was the only sign and announcement banking business was carried on within. Equally old-fashioned and modest was the interior and Starmidge was quick to notice the clerks were all elderly or middle-aged men, solemn and grave as undertakers. The presentation of the detective's official card procured him speedy entrance to a parlor in which sat two old gentlemen, who were evidently greatly surprised to see him.

They were so much surprised indeed, as to be almost childishly interested, and Starmidge had never had such attentive listeners in his life as these two elderly city men, to whom crime and detention were as unfamiliar as higher finance was to their visitor. They followed Starmidge's story point by point, nodding every now and then as he drew their attention to particular passages, and the detective saw they comprehended all he said. He made an end at last and Mr. Vanderkiste, a white-bearded, benevolent-looking gentleman, looked at Mr. Mullineau, a little, rosy-faced man, and shook his head.

"It would be an unusual thing, certainly," he observed, "for Mr. Frederick Hollis to have ten thousand pounds lying here to his credit. Mr. Hollis was an old customer, we knew him very well, but he didn't keep a lot of money here. We know his circumstances. He bought himself a very nice annuity some years ago, it was paid into his account here twice a year. But ten thousand pounds!"

Mr. Mullineau leaned forward.

"We don't know if Frederick Hollis paid any large

amount in lately, you know," he observed. "Hadn't you better summon Linthwaite?"

"Our manager," remarked Mr. Vanderkiste, as he touched a bell. "Ah, yes, of course he'll know. Mr. Linthwaite," he continued, as another elderly man entered the room, "can you tell us what Mr. Frederick Hollis's balance in our hands is?"

"I have just been looking it up, sir," replied the manager, "in consequence of this sad news in the papers. Ten thousand, eight hundred, seventy-nine, five, four, Mr. Vanderkiste."

"Ten thousand eight hundred and seventy-nine pounds, five shillings and four-pence," repeated Mr. Vanderkiste. "Ah! An unusually large amount, I think, Mr. Linthwaite?"

"Just so, sir," agreed the manager. "The reason is rather more than a week ago Mr. Hollis called here himself with a check for ten thousand pounds which he paid into his account, explaining to me it had been handed to him for a special purpose, and he should draw a check for his own against it, for the same amount, very shortly."

"Ah!" remarked Mr. Vanderkiste. "Has the check which he paid in been cleared?"

"We cleared it at once," replied the manager. "Oh, yes! But the check which Mr. Hollis spoke of drawing against it has not come in and now, of course..."

"Just so," said Mr. Vanderkiste. "Now that he's dead, of course, his check is no good. Um! That will do, thank you, Mr. Linthwaite."

He turned and looked at Starmidge when the manager had withdrawn.

"That explains matters," he said. "The ten thousand pounds had been paid to Mr. Frederick Hollis for a special purpose."

"But by whom?" asked Starmidge. "That's precisely what I want to know! The knowledge will help me. I don't know how much it mayn't help me! For there's no doubt about it, gentlemen, Hollis went down to Scarnham to pay ten thousand pounds to somebody on somebody else's account! He was, I am sure, as it were, ambassador for somebody. Who was...who is...that somebody? Almost certainly, the person who gave Hollis the check your manager has just mentioned and whose ten thousand pounds is, as a matter of fact, still lying in your hands! Who is that person? What bank was the check drawn on? Let me have an answer to both these questions, and..."

The two old gentlemen exchanged looks, and Mr. Mullineau quietly rose and left the room. In his absence Mr. Vanderkiste shook his head at the detective.

"A very, very queer case, officer!" he remarked.

"An extraordinary case, sir," agreed Starmidge. "Before we get to the end of it there will be some strange revelations, Mr. Vanderkiste."

"So I should imagine, so I should imagine!" assented the old gentleman. "Very remarkable proceedings altogether! We shall be deeply interested in hearing how matters progress. Of course, this affair of the ten thousand pounds is very curious. We..."

Mr. Mullineau came back with a slip of paper, which he handed to the detective.

"That gives you the information you want," he said.

Starmidge read aloud what the manager had written down on his principal's instructions.

"Drawer...Helen Lester," he read. "Bank...London & Universal: Pall Mall Branch." He looked up at the two partners. "I suppose you gentlemen don't know who this Mrs. or Miss Helen Lester is?" he inquired.

"No, not at all," answered Mr. Mullineau. "Nor does Linthwaite. I thought Mr. Hollis might have told him something about that special purpose. But he told him nothing."

"You'll have to go to the London & Universal people," observed Mr. Vanderkiste. "They, of course, will know all about this customer."

Mullineau looked inquiringly at his partner.

"Don't you think as there are almost certain to be some complications about this matter, Linthwaite had better go with Detective Starmidge?" he suggested. "The situation, as regards the ten thousand pounds, is a somewhat curious one. This Miss or Mrs. Lester will want to recover it. Now, according to what Mr. Starmidge tells us, no body, so far as he's aware, is in possession of any facts, papers, letters, anything, relating to it. I think there should be some consultation between ourselves and this other bank which is concerned."

"Excellent suggestion!" agreed Mr. Vanderkiste. "Let him go by all means."

Half an hour later, Starmidge found himself closeted with another lot of bankers. But these were younger men, who were quicker to grasp situations and comprehend points, and they quickly understood what the detective was after. Moreover, they were already well posted up in those details of the Scarnham mystery which had already appeared in the newspapers.

"What you want," said one of them, a young and energetic man, addressing Starmidge at the end of their preliminary conversation, "is to find out for what purpose Mrs. Lester gave Mr. Frederick Hollis ten thousand pounds?"

"Precisely," replied Starmidge. "It will go far towards clearing up a good many things."

"I have no doubt Mrs. Lester will tell you readily enough," said the banker. "In fact, as things are, I should say she'll only be too glad to give you any information you want. That ten thousand pounds being in Messrs. Vanderkiste's hands, in Hollis's name, and Hollis being dead, there will be bother, not serious, of course, but still formal bother about recovering it. Very well, Mrs. Lester, who, I may tell you, is a wealthy customer of ours, lives in the country as a rule, and I happen to know she's there now. I'll write down her address. Tell her, by all means, you have been to see us on the matter."

Starmidge left Mr. Linthwaite talking with the London & Universal people. Now that he had got the desired information, had no more to say. Outside the bank he opened the slip of paper which had just been handed to him, and saw that another journey lay before him. Mrs. Lester lived at Lowdale Court, near Chesham.

Chapter 21

Starmidge, lingering a moment on the steps of the bank to consider whether he would go straight to Chesham or repair to headquarters for a consultation with his superior, was suddenly joined by the manager who had just given him his information.

"You are going down to Lowdale Court?" asked the manager.

"During the morning, yes," answered Starmidge.

"If it will be any help to you," said the manager, "I'll ring up Mrs. Lester on the telephone, and let her know you're coming. She's rather a nervous woman and it will pave the way for you if I give you a sort of introduction. Besides..." here he paused, and looked at the detective with an inquiring air, "don't you think Mrs. Lester had better be warned at once not to speak of this matter until she's seen you?"

"You think she may be approached?" asked Starmidge.

The manager wagged his head and smiled knowingly.

"I think there's something so very queer about this affair and Mrs. Lester ought to be seen at once," he said.

"She shall be!" answered Starmidge. "Tell her I'll be down there within two hours, I'll motor there. Thank you for your suggestion. Now I'll just run to headquarters and then be straight off."

He hailed a passing taxi-cab and drove to New Scotland Yard, where he was presently closeted with a high personage in deep and serious consultation, the result of which was that by twelve o'clock, Starmidge and a fellow-officer, one Easleby, in whom he had great confidence, were spinning away towards the beech-clad hills of Buckinghamshire, and discussing the features and probabilities of the queer business which took them there. Before two, they were in the pleasant valley which lies between Chenies and Chesham and pulling up at the door of a fine old Jacobean house, which, set in the midst of delightful lawns and gardens, looked down on the winding of the river Chess. And practical as both men were, and well experienced in their profession, it struck both as strange they should come to such a quiet and innocent-looking place to seek some explanation of a mystery which had surely some connection with crime. The two detectives were immediately shown into a morning room in which sat a little, middle-aged lady in a widow's cap and weeds, who looked at her visitors half-timidly, half-welcomingly. She sat by a small table on which lay a heap of newspapers, and Starmidge's sharp eyes saw at once she had been reading the published details of the Scarnham affair.

"You have no doubt been informed by your bankers we were coming, ma'am?" began Starmidge, when he and Easleby had seated themselves near Mrs. Lester. "The manager there was good enough to say he'd telephone you."

Mrs. Lester, who had been curiously inspecting her callers and appeared somewhat relieved to find they were quite ordinary-looking beings, entirely unlike her own preconceived notions of detectives, bowed her head.

"Yes," she answered, "my bankers telephoned an officer from Scotland Yard would call on me this morning, and I was to speak freely to him, and in confidence, but I really don't quite know what it is I'm to talk to you about, though I suppose I can guess."

"This, ma'am," answered Starmidge, bending towards the pile of newspapers and tapping a staring head-line with his finger. "I see you've been reading it up. I have been in charge of this affair since Monday last, and I came up to town last night about it specially. You will have read in this morning's paper the body of Mr. Frederick Hollis was found at Scarnham yesterday?"

"Yes," said Mrs. Lester, with a sigh. "I have read of that. Of course, I knew Mr. Hollis, he was an old friend of my husband. I saw him last week. But what took Mr. Hollis down to Scarnham? I have been in the habit of seeing Mr. Hollis constantly regularly and I never even heard him mention Scarnham, nor any person living at Scarnham. There are many persons mentioned in these newspaper accounts," continued Mrs. Lester, "in connection with this affair whose names I never heard before, yet they are mentioned as if Mr. Hollis had something to do with them. Why did he go there?"

"That, ma'am, is precisely what we want to find out from you!" replied Starmidge, with a side glance at his fellow-detective. "It's just what we've come for!"

He was watching Mrs. Lester very closely as he spoke, and he saw up to that moment she had certainly no explanation in her own mind as to the reason of this police visit.

"But what can I tell you?" she exclaimed. "As I have said, I don't know why Frederick Hollis went to Scarnham! He never mentioned Scarnham to me when he was here last week."

"Let me tell you something that is not in the papers yet ma'am," said Starmidge. "I think it will explain matters to you. When we examined Mr. Hollis's effects at Scarnham, yesterday morning, after the finding of his body, we found in his letter-case a check for ten thousand pounds..."

Starmidge stopped suddenly. Mrs. Lester had started, and her pale face had grown paler. Her eyes dilated as she looked at the two men.

"A check!" she exclaimed. "For ten thousand pounds. On him? And whose check?"

"It was a curious check, ma'am," replied Starmidge. "It was drawn on Mr. Hollis's bankers, Vanderkiste, Mullineau & Company, of Lombard Street. It was dated and was filled in for ten thousand pounds, in words and in figures. But it was not signed and it was not made out to anybody. No name of payee, you understand, ma'am, no name of payer. But it is very evident Mr. Hollis made out the check intending to pay it to somebody. What we want to know is, who is or was, that somebody? I came up to town to try to find that out! I went to Mr. Hollis's bankers this morning. They told me last week Mr. Hollis paid into his account there a check for ten thousand pounds, drawn by Helen Lester, and told their manager he should be drawing a check for his own against it in a day or two. I then went to your bank, ma'am, saw your bankers, and got your address. Now, Mrs. Lester, there's no doubt whatever the check which we found on Mr. Hollis is the check he spoke of to Vanderkiste's manager. And we want you, if you please, to tell us two things: For what purpose did you give Mr. Hollis ten thousand pounds? To whom was he to pay it? Tell us, ma'am and we shall have gone a long way to clearing this affair! And it's more serious than you'd think."

Mrs. Lester, who had listened to Starmidge with absorbed and almost frightened attention, looked anxiously at both men before she replied to the detective's direct inquiry.

"You will respect my confidence, of course?" she asked at last. "Whatever I say to you will be in strict confidence?"

"Whatever you tell us, Mrs. Lester," answered Starmidge, "we shall have to report to our superiors at the Criminal Investigation Department. You may rely on their discretion fully. But if there is any secret in this, ma'am, it will all have to come out, now that it's an affair of police investigation. Far better tell us here and now!"

"There'll be no publication of anything without Mrs. Lester's knowledge and consent," remarked Easleby, who guessed at the reason of the lady's diffidence. "This is a private matter, so far. All she can tell us will be for police information only."

"I shall have to mention the affairs of some other person," said Mrs. Lester. "But, I suppose it's absolutely necessary? Now that you know what you do, for instance, I suppose I could be made to give evidence, eh!"

"I'm afraid you're quite right, ma'am," admitted Starmidge. "The mystery of Mr. Hollis's death will certainly have to be cleared up. Now this check affair is out, you could be called as a witness at the inquest. Better tell us, ma'am and leave things to us."

Mrs. Lester, after a moment's reflection, looked steadily at her visitors. "Very well!" she answered, "I suppose I had better. Indeed, I have been feeling, ever since my bankers rang me up this morning, I should have to tell you, though I still can't see how anything I can tell you has to do...that is, precisely with Mr. Hollis's visit to Scarnham. Yet, it may... perhaps must have. The fact is, I recently called in Mr. Hollis, as an old friend, to give me some advice. I must tell you that my husband died last year...now about eight months ago. We have an only son who is an officer in the Army."

"You had better give us his name and regiment, ma'am," suggested Starmidge.

Mrs. Lester hesitated a little.

"Very well," she said at last. "He is Lieutenant Guy Lester, of the 55th Lancers. Stationed where? At present at

Maychester. Now I have got to tell you what is both painful and unpleasant for me to tell. My husband, though a very kind father, was a very strict one. When our son went into the Army, his father made him a certain yearly allowance which he considered a very handsome one. But my husband," continued Mrs. Lester, with a faint smile, "had been engaged in commercial pursuits all his life, until a year or two before his death, and he did not know the expenses, and the...well, the style of living in a crack cavalry regiment are what they are. More than once Guy asked his father to increase his allowance considerably. His father always refused, he was a strict and, in some ways, a very hard man about money. And so my son had recourse to a money-lender."

Starmidge, who was sitting close by his fellow-detective, pressed his elbow against Easleby's sleeve, at last they were getting at something.

"Just so, ma'am," he said encouragingly. "Nothing remarkable in all this so far, quite an everyday matter, I assure you! Nothing for you to distress yourself about, either, all that can be kept quiet."

"Well," continued Mrs. Lester, "my son borrowed money from a money-lender in London, expecting, of course, to pay it back on his father's death. I must tell you that my husband married very late in life, he was quite thirty years my senior. No doubt this money-lender acquainted himself with Mr. Lester's age and state of health."

"He would, ma'am, he would!" agreed Starmidge.

"He'd take particular good care of that, ma'am," added Easleby. "They always do in such cases."

"Yes," said Mrs. Lester, "but, you see, when my husband died, he did not leave Guy anything at all! He left everything to me. So Guy had nothing to pay the money-lender with. Then, of course, the money-lender began to press him, and in the end Guy was obliged to come and tell me all about it. That was only a few weeks ago. And it was very bad news, because the man claimed much...very much...more money than he had ever advanced. His demands were outrageous!"

Starmidge gave Mrs. Lester a keen glance, and realized an idea of her innocence in financial matters.

"Ah!" he observed, "they are very grasping, ma'am, some of these money-lenders! How much was this particular one asking of your son, now?"

"He demanded between fourteen and fifteen thousand pounds," replied Mrs. Lester. "An abominable demand, for my son assured me at the very outside he had not had more than seven or eight thousand."

"And what happened, ma'am?" inquired Starmidge sympathetically. "The man pestered you, of course!"

"Guy made him one or two offers," answered Mrs. Lester. "Of course I would have made them good to get rid of the affair. It was no use, he had papers and things signed by Guy who had borrowed all the money since he came of age and he refused to abate a penny. The last time Guy called on him, he told him flatly he would have his fifteen thousand to the last shilling. It was, of course, extortion!"

Starmidge and Easleby exchanged looks. Both felt they were on the very edge of a discovery.

"To be sure, ma'am," asserted Starmidge. "Absolute extortion! And what is the name of the money-lending gentleman?"

"His name," replied Mrs. Lester, "is Godwin Markham."

"Did you ever see him, ma'am?" asked Starmidge.

Mrs. Lester looked her astonishment.

"I?" she exclaimed. "No, never!"

"Did your son ever describe him to you? His personal appearance, I mean," inquired Starmidge.

Mrs. Lester shook her head.

"No!" she replied. "Indeed, I have heard my son say he never saw Markham but once. He did his...business, I suppose you would call it with the manager who always said when this recent pressing began he was powerless he could only do what Mr. Markham bade him do."

"Precisely!" said Starmidge. "There generally is a manager whose chief business is to say that sort of thing, ma'am. Dear me and where, ma'am, is this Mr. Godwin Markham's office? You know that, no doubt?"

"Oh, yes it is in Conduit Street, off New Bond Street," replied Mrs. Lester.

"Of course you never went there?" asked Starmidge. "No, of course not. All was done through your son, until you called in Mr. Hollis. Now, when did you call in Mr. Hollis, Mrs. Lester? The date's important."

"About a fortnight ago," replied Mrs. Lester. "I sent for him, I told him all about it, I asked his advice. At his suggestion I gave him a check for ten thousand pounds. He said he would make an endeavor to settle the whole thing for that amount, and have everything cleared up. He took the check away with him."

"Between then and that day when he was here and you gave him the check," asked Starmidge, "and last Saturday, when we know Mr. Hollis went to Scarnham, did you hear of or from Mr. Hollis at all?"

"Only in this way," replied Mrs. Lester. "When he left me, he said before approaching Markham, as intermediary, he should like to see Guy, and hear what his account of the transactions was, and he would ask my son to come up to town from Maychester and meet him. I heard from Guy at the end of last week...last Saturday morning, as a matter of fact he had been to town, he had lunched with Mr. Hollis at Mr. Hollis's club, and after discussing the whole affair, Mr. Hollis said he would make a determined effort to settle the matter at once. And after that," concluded Mrs. Lester, "I heard no more or anything until I read of this Scarnham affair in the newspapers."

"And now that you have read it, ma'am, and have heard what I have to tell," said Starmidge, "do you connect it in any way with Mr. Guy Lester's affair?"

Mrs. Lester looked puzzled. She considered the detective's proposition in silence for a time.

"No!" she answered at last. "Really, I don't!"

Starmidge got up, and Easleby followed his lead.

"Well, ma'am," said Starmidge, "there is a connection, without doubt, and I think within a very short time we shall have discovered what it is. What you have told us has been of great assistance...the very greatest assistance. And you can make your mind easy for the present, I don't see any reason for any unpleasant publicity just now in fact, I think you'll find there won't be any. The unpleasant publicity, ma'am," concluded Starmidge, with an almost imperceptible wink at Easleby, "will be for some other people."

The two detectives bowed themselves out, re-entered their car, and were driven on to Chesham. Neither had touched food since breakfast-time and each was hungry. They discovered an old-fashioned hotel in the main street of the little town, and were presently confronting a round of cold beef, a cold ham, and two foaming tankards, in the snug parlor which they had to themselves.

"One result of our profession, young Starmidge," observed the middle-aged Easleby, bending towards his companion over a well-filled plate, "is that it makes a man indulge in a tremendous lot of what you might call intellectual speculation!"

"What are you speculating about?" asked Starmidge.

"This...on information received," replied Easleby, as he lifted his tankard. "There are the names of three Scarnham gentlemen before me, Gabriel Chestermarke, Joseph Chestermarke, John Horbury. Now, then which of the three sports the other name of Godwin Markham?"

Chapter 22

Starmidge ate and drank in silence for a while, evidently pondering his companion's question.

"Yes," he said at last, "there's all that in it. It may be any one of the three. You never know! Yet, according to all I've been told, Horbury's a thoroughly straight man of business."

"According to all I've been told," remarked Easleby, "and all I've been told about anything has been told by yourself, the two Chestermarke's have the reputation of being thoroughly straight men of business outwardly. But one thing is certain, my lad, after what we've just learned, Hollis went down to Scarnham to offer that check to one of these three men. And whichever it was, that man's Godwin Markham! It's a double-life business, Jack...the man's Godwin Markham here in London, and he's somebody else in somewhere else. Dead certainty, my lad!"

"It's not Horbury," said Starmidge, after some reflection. "I'll stake my reputation, such as it is, on that!"

"You don't know," replied Easleby. "Remember, Mrs. Lester said this son of hers always did business with a manager. That's a usual thing with these big money-lending offices, the real man doesn't show. For anything you know, Horbury may have been running a money-lender's office in town, unknown to anybody, under the name of Godwin Markham. And he may have wanted new funds for it, and he may have collared those securities which the Chestermarke's say are missing, and he may have appropriated Lord Ellersdeane's jewels? You never can tell in any of these cases. You see, my lad, you've been going, all along, on the basis, the supposition, Horbury's an innocent man, and the victim of foul play. But he may be a guilty man! Lord bless you! I don't attach any importance to reputation and character, not I! It isn't ten years since Jim Chambers and myself had a case in point, a bank manager who was churchwarden, Sunday-School teacher, this, that, and the other in the way of piety and respectability, all a cloak to cover as clever a bit of thievery and fraud as ever I heard of! He gotten years, that chap, and he ought to have been hanged. As I say, you never can make certain. Hollis may have found out Godwin Markham of Conduit Street was in reality John Horbury of Scarnham, and then…"

"I'll tell you what!" interrupted Starmidge, who had been thinking as well as listening. "There's a very sure and certain way of finding out who Godwin Markham is! Do you remember? Mrs. Lester said her son had only seen him once. Well, once is enough he'd remember him. We must go to Maychester right away and see this young Lester, and get him to describe the man he saw."

"Good notion, of course," assented Easleby. "Where is Maychester, now?"

"Essex," replied Starmidge.

"That would certainly be a solver," said Easleby. "But there's something else we could do, following up your special line of thought. Now, honor bright, which of these men do you take Godwin Markham to be?"

"Gabriel Chestermarke!" answered Starmidge promptly. "It's established he's constantly in London, as much in London as in Scarnham. Gabriel Chestermarke certainly with, no doubt, Joseph in collusion. The probability is they run that money-lending office in Conduit Street under the name of Godwin Markham. They're within the law."

"What about the Moneylenders Act?" asked Easleby. "Compulsory registration, you know."

"It's this way," explained Starmidge. "The object of that Act was to enable a borrower to know for certain who it was that was lending him the money he borrowed. So registration was made compulsory. But, as in the case of many another Act of Parliament, Easleby, evasion is not only possible, but easy. A money-lender can register in a name which isn't his own if it's one which he generally uses in his business. So there you are! I've seen that name Godwin Markham advertised ever since I was a youngster, it's an old established business, well known. There's nothing to prevent Abraham Moses from styling himself Fitzwilliam Simpkins, if he's always done business as Fitzwilliam Simpkins see? And it's highly probable, as he's so much in town, Gabriel lives in town under the name of Godwin

Markham, double-life business, as you suggest. But you were going to suggest something else. What?"

"This," said Easleby. "You know Gabriel went to the stage-door of the Adalbert Theatre the other night. Go there officially and find out if he called there as Gabriel Chestermarke. That'll solve a lot."

"We'll both go!" assented Starmidge. "It's a good notion I hadn't thought of it. Whom shall we try to see?"

"Top man of all," counseled Easleby. "Lessee, manager, whatever he is. Our cards will manage it."

"I'm obliged to you, old man!" exclaimed Starmidge. "It's a bright idea! Of course, somebody there'll know who the man was that called last night...know his name, of course. And in that case..."

"Aye, but don't you anticipate too much, my lad!" interrupted Easleby. "There's no doubt Gandam traced your Gabriel Chestermarke to the stage-door of the Adalbert Theatre and lost him there. But, you know, for anything you know, Mr. Gabriel Chestermarke, banker, of Scarnham, may have had legitimate and proper business at that theatre. For anything you know, Gabriel Chestermarke may be owner of that theatre, ground-landlord...part-proprietor...financier. He may have a mortgage on it. All sorts of reasons occur to me as to why Gabriel Chestermarke may have called. He might be a personal friend of the manager's, or the principal actor's called to take them out to supper, on his arrival in town. So whoever we see there, you want to go guardedly, eh?"

"I'll tell you what," said Starmidge, "I'll leave it to you. I'll go with you, of course, but you manage it."

"Right, my lad!" assented Easleby. "All I shall want will be a copy of this morning's newspaper to lead up from."

One of the London morning journals had been making a great feature of the Scarnham affair from the moment Parkinson, on Starmidge's inspiration, had supplied the Press with its details, and it had that day printed an exhaustive résumé of the entire history of the case, brought up to the discovery of Frederick Hollis's body. Easleby bought a copy of this issue as soon as he and Starmidge returned to town, and carefully blue-penciled the cross-headed columns and the staring capitals above them. With the folded paper in his hand, and Starmidge at his heel, he repaired to the stage-door of the

Adalbert Theater at a quarter to eight, when the actors and actresses were beginning to pass in for their evening's work and thrust his head into the glass-fronted cage in which the stage door-keeper sat.

"A word with you, mister," whimpered Easleby. "A quiet word, you understand. Me and my friend here are from the Yard, New Scotland Yard, you know, and we've an inquiry to make. Our cards, do you see? I shall ask you to take them inside in a minute. But first, a word with you. Do you remember a gentleman coming here last night, late, who nodded to you and walked straight in? Little, stiffly built gentleman, very pale face, holds himself well up what?"

"I know him," answered the door-keeper, much impressed by the official cards which Easleby held before his nose. "Seen him here many a time, but I don't know his name. He's a friend of Mr. Castlemayne's, and he's the entry, do you see walks in as he likes."

"Ah, just so and who may Mr. Castlemayne be, now?" asked Easleby confidentially.

"Mr. Castlemayne?" repeated the door-keeper. "Why, he's the lessee, of course! The boss!"

"Ah, the boss, is he?" said Easleby. "Much obliged to you, sir. Well, now, then, just take these two cards to Mr. Castlemayne, will you, and ask him if he'll be good enough to see their owners for a few minutes on very important private business?"

The door-keeper departed up a dark passage, and Easleby pointed Starmidge to a playbill which hung, framed on the wall, behind them.

"There you are!" he said, indicating a line near the big capitals at the top. "Lessee and Manager, Mr. Leopold Castlemayne. That's our man. Fancy name, of course real name Tom Smith, or Jim Johnson, you know. But, Lord bless you, what's in a name? Haven't we got a case in point?"

"There's a good deal in what's in a name in our case, old man!" retorted Starmidge. "You're off it there!"

Easleby was about to combat this reply when a boy appeared, and intimated Mr. Castlemayne would see the gentlemen at once. And the two detectives followed up one passage and down another, and round corners and across saloons and foyers, until they were shown into a snug room, half office, half parlor, very comfortably furnished and ornamented, wherein, at a desk, and alone, sat a gentleman in evening dress, whose countenance, well-fed though it was, seemed to be just then clouded with suspicion and something that looked very like anxiety. He glanced up from the cards which lay before him to the two men who had sent them in, and silently pointed them to chairs near his own.

"Good-evening, sir," said Easleby, with a polite bow. "Sorry to interrupt you, Mr. Castlemayne, but you see our business from our cards, and we've called, sir, to ask if you can give us a bit of much-wanted information. I don't know, sir," continued Easleby, laying the blue-penciled newspaper on the lessee's desk, "if you've read in the papers any account of the affair which is here called the Scarnham Mystery!"

Mr. Leopold Castlemayne glanced at the columns to which Easleby pointed, rubbed his chin, and nodded.

"Yes...yes!" he said. "I have just seen the papers. Case of a strange disappearance, bank manager isn't it?"

"It's more than that, sir," replied Easleby. "It's a case of all sorts of things. Now you're wondering, Mr. Castlemayne, why we come to you? I'll explain. You'll see there, sir, the name blue-penciled—Gabriel Chestermarke. Mr. Gabriel Chestermarke is a banker at Scarnham. You don't happen to know him, Mr. Castlemayne?"

The two detectives watched the lessee narrowly as the question was put. And each knew instantly the prompt reply was a truthful one.

"Never heard of him in my life," said Mr. Castlemayne.

"Thank you, sir," said Easleby. "Just so! Well, sir, my friend here, Detective-Sergeant Starmidge has been down at Scarnham in charge of this case from the first, and he's formed some ideas about this Mr. Gabriel Chestermarke. Last night Gabriel Chestermarke travelled up to town from Ecclesborough, Mr. Starmidge arranged for him to be shadowed when he arrived at St. Pancras. A man of ours, not quite as experienced as he might be, you understand, sir did shadow him and lost him. He lost him here at your theater, Mr. Castlemayne."

"Ah!" said the lessee, half indifferently. "Got among the audience, I suppose?"

"No, sir," replied Easleby. "Mr. Gabriel Chestermarke,

sir, entered your stage-door at about eleven-thirty, walked straight in. But he never came out of that door so he must have left by another exit."

Mr. Leopold Castlemayne suddenly sat up very erect and rigid. His face flushed a little, his lips parted; he looked from one man to the other.

"Mr. Gabriel Chestermarke!" he said. "Entered my stage-door, eleven-thirty last night? Here! Describe him!"

Easleby glanced at Starmidge. And Starmidge, as if he were describing a picture, gave a full and accurate account of Mr. Gabriel Chestermarke's appearance from head to foot.

The lessee suddenly jumped from his chair, walked over to a door, opened it, and looked into an inner room. Evidently satisfied, he closed the door again, came back, seated himself, thrust his hands in his pockets, and looked at the detectives.

"All in confidence...strict confidence?" he said. "All right, then! I understand. I tell you, I don't know any Gabriel Chestermarke, banker, of Scarnham! The man you've described, the man who came here last night is Godwin Markham, the Conduit Street money-lender, damn him!"

Chapter 23

If Mr. Leopold Castlemayne's last word was expressive, his next actions were suggestive and significant. Returning to the door of the inner room, he turned the key in it; crossing to the door by which the detectives had been shown in, he locked that also; proceeding to a cupboard in an adjacent recess, he performed an unlocking process, after which he produced a decanter, a syphon, three glasses, and a box of cigars. He silently placed these luxuries on a desk before his visitors, and hospitably invited their attention.

"Yes!" he said presently, proceeding to help the two men to refreshment, and pressing the cigars upon them, "I've good reason to say that, gentlemen! Godwin Markham, indeed! I ought to know him! If I don't look out, that devil of a bloodsucker is going to ruin me...he is, so!"

Easleby gave Starmidge an almost imperceptible wink as he lighted a cigar. It was evident Mr. Leopold Castlemayne was not only willing to talk, but was uncommonly glad to have somebody to talk to. Indeed, his moody countenance began to clear as his tongue became unloosed; he was obviously at that stage when a man is thankful to give confidences to any fellow-creature.

"I've done business with gentlemen of your profession before," he went on, nodding to his visitors over the rim of his tumbler, "and I know you're to be trusted, naturally, you hear a good many queer things and queer secrets in your line of life. And as you come to me in confidence, I'll tell you a thing or two in confidence. It may help you, if you're certain the man you're wanting is the man who came here last night. Do you want him?"

"We...may..." replied Easleby. "We don't know yet. Mr. Starmidge here is much disposed to think we shall. But let's be clear, sir. We're all three agreed we're talking about the same man? Starmidge has accurately described a certain man who without doubt entered your stage-door about eleven-thirty last night..."

"And left, with me, by the box-office door, in the front street, a few minutes later," murmured the lessee. "That's how it was."

"Just so," agreed Easleby. "Now, Starmidge up to now has only known that man as Mr. Gabriel Chestermarke, senior partner in Chestermarke's Bank, at Scarnham, while you, up to now..."

"Have only known him as Godwin Markham, money-lender, financial agent, and so on, of Conduit Street," interrupted Castlemayne. "And known him a lot too much for my peace, I can tell you! Of course, we're talking of the same man! I can quite believe he runs a double show. I know he's a great deal away from town. It's very rarely he's to be found at Conduit Street, very, very rarely indeed, he's a clever manager there, who sees everybody and does everything. And I know he's quite two-thirds of his time away from his own house so, of course, he's got to put it in somewhere else."

"His own house!" said Starmidge, catching at an idea which presented itself. "You know where he lives in London, then, Mr. Castlemayne?"

"Do I know where my own mother lives!" exclaimed the lessee. "I should think I do! He's a neighbor of mine, lives close by me, up Primrose Hill way. Nice little bachelor establishment he has, Oakfield Villa. Spent many an evening there with him, Sunday evenings, of course. Oh, yes I know all about him as Godwin Markham. Bless me! So he's a country banker, is he? And mixed up in this affair, eh? Gosh! I hope you'll find out that he murdered his manager, and you'll be able to hang him. I'd treat the town to a free show if you could hang him in public on my stage, I would, indeed!"

"You were going to tell us something, sir?" suggested Easleby. "Something you thought might help us."

"I hope it will help you and me, too!" responded Castlemayne, who was obviously incensed and truculent. "Upon my honor, when I got your cards, I wondered if I'd been sleep-walking last night, and had gone and done for this man, I really did! It was all I could do to keep from punching his nose last night in the open street, and I left him feeling very bad indeed! It's this way, I dare say you know men like me, in this business, want a bit of financing when we start. All right! We do, like most other people. Now, when I thought of taking up the lease of this spot, a few years ago, I wanted money. I knew this man Markham as a neighbor, and I mentioned the matter to him, not knowing then he was the Markham of Conduit Street. He let me know who he was, then, and he offered to do things private, no need to go to his office, do you see? And he found me in necessary capital. And I dare say I signed papers without thoroughly understanding them. And, of course, when you get into the hands of a fellow like that, it's like putting your foot on a piece of butter in the street you're down before you know what's happened! But I ain't down yet, my boys!" concluded Mr. Castlemayne, drinking off the contents of his glass, and replenishing it. "And dang if I'm going to be, without a bit of a fight for it, that I ain't!"

"Putting some pressure on you, I suppose, sir?" suggested Easleby, who knew that their host would tell anything and everything if left to himself. "Wants his pound of flesh, no doubt?"

This Shakespearean allusion appeared to be lost on the lessee, but he evidently understood what pressure meant.

"Pressure!" he exclaimed. "Yah, there's nothing would suit that fellow better than to have one of his victims under one of those steam-hammers they have nowadays, and to bring it down on him till he'd crushed the last drop of blood out of his toes! Pressure! I'll tell you! This place didn't do well at first, everybody in town, in our line, anyway, knows that, but even in these days I paid him his interest regular down on the nail, mind, as prompt as the date came round.

But now things are different. I'm doing well in a bit I could pay my gentleman off though not just yet. But there's big money ahead, this house has caught on, got a reputation, become popular. And now what do you think my lord wants... what he's screwing me for? Turns out in one of those confounded papers I signed there's a clause, if I didn't repay him by a certain date I should surrender my lease to him! I no doubt signed it, not quite understanding, but dang if he didn't keep it dark till the date was expired! And now, when I've worked things up, not only as lessee, mind you, but as manager to success and big prospects, hanged if he doesn't want to collar my lease with all its fine possibilities, and put me into work for him at a blooming salary!"

"Dear me, sir!" exclaimed Easleby. "Now what might that exactly mean? We're not up in these matters, you know."

"Mean?" said the lessee. "It would mean this. I've paid that man as much in interest as the original loan was. He now wants my lease, all my interest, all my chances of reward, this lease is worth many a thousand a year now! If I surrender my lease peaceably without fuss, you understand, he'll wipe off my original debt to him and give me a blooming salary of twenty-five quid a week...me! Gosh! He ought to be burnt alive!"

"And if you don't?" asked Starmidge, deeply interested by this sidelight on financial dealings. "What then?"

"Then he relies on his damn paper and my signature to it, and turns me out!" replied the aggrieved one. "Thievery! That's what I call it. That's his blooming ultimatum, came in last night to tell me. I hope you'll catch him and hang him!"

The two detectives had long since realized Mr. Leopold Castlemayne's interest in the banker-money-lender was a purely personal one, based on his own unlucky dealings with him. But they wished for something outside that interest, and Starmidge, after a word or two of condolence, and another of advice to go to a shrewd and smart solicitor, asked a plain question.

"You say you've been on terms of...shall we call it neighborly intimacy with this man," he remarked. "Have you ever met his nephew?"

The lessee made a face expressive of deep scorn.

"Nephew!" he exclaimed. "Yah! Do you think a fellow like that would have a nephew? I don't believe he's any relations that's flesh and blood! I don't believe he ever had a mother! I believe he's one of these ghouls you read about in the story-books...what's he look like? A bloodsucker! That's what he is!"

Starmidge gave his host an accurate description of Joseph Chestermarke.

"Did you ever see a man like that at this Markham's house?" he asked.

"Never!" answered the lessee.

"Or at his office?" persisted Starmidge.

"No, don't know such a man! I've only been to the offices in Conduit Street a few times," said Castlemayne. "The chap you see there is a fellow called Stipp...Mr. James Stipp. A nice, smooth-tongued, mealy-mouthed chap you know. I say do you think you'll be able to fasten anything on to Markham, or Chestermarke, or whatever his name is?"

Easleby responded jocularly they certainly wouldn't if they sat there, and after solemnly assuring Mr. Leopold Castlemayne his confidence would be severely respected, he and Starmidge went away. Once outside they walked for a while in silence, each reflecting on what he had just heard.

"Well," remarked Starmidge at last, "we're certain on one point now, anyway. Godwin Markham, money-lender, of Conduit Street, is the same person as Gabriel Chestermarke, banker, of Scarnham. That's flat! And now that we've got to know that much, how much nearer am I to finding out the real thing I'm after?"

"Which is exactly what?" asked Easleby.

"I was called in," answered Starmidge, "to find out the secret of John Horbury's disappearance. It isn't my business to interfere with Gabriel Chestermarke or Godwin Markham in his money-lending affairs, nor to trace Lord Ellersdeane's missing jewels. My job is to find John Horbury, or to get to know what happened to him."

"And all this helps," answered Easleby. "Haven't you got anything?"

"Don't know that I have," admitted Starmidge. "Just now, anyway. I've had a dozen ideas, but they're a bit mixed at present. Have you...after what we've found out?"

"What sort of banking business is it the Chestermarke's carry on down there at Scarnham?" asked Easleby. "I suppose you'd get a general idea."

"Usual thing in a small country town," replied Starmidge. "Highly respectable, county family business, I should say, from what I saw and heard."

"All the squires, and the parsons, and the farmers, and better sort of tradesmen go to them, I suppose?" suggested Easleby. "And all the nice old ladies and that sort an extra-respectable connection, eh?"

"Just as I say regular country-town business," said Starmidge, half impatiently.

"Um!" remarked Easleby. "Now, if you were a highly respectable country-town banker, with a connection of that sort among very proper people, and if it so happened you were living a double life, and running a money-lending business in London, do you think you'd want your banking customers to know what you were after when you weren't banking!"

"What do you think he'd do?" asked Starmidge.

"I'm not quite sure," replied Easleby, with candor. "But I think I shall get there, all the same. Now, didn't you say from all the accounts supplied to you, this Mr. John Horbury was an eminently proper sort of person? Very well, supposing it suddenly came to his knowledge his employer or employers, for I expect both Chestermarke's are in at it, were notorious money-lenders in London, and they carried on this secret business in the greedy and grasping fashion, what do you suppose he'd do? Especially if he was, as you say Horbury was, a man of considerable means?"

"What do you think he'd do?" asked Starmidge.

"I think it's quite on the cards he'd chuck his job there and then," said Easleby, "and not only that, but he'd probably threaten exposure. Men of a very severe type of commercial religion would, my lad! I know them!"

"You're suggesting what?" inquired the younger detective.

"I'm suggesting on the night of Hollis's visit to Scarnham, Horbury, through Hollis, became acquainted with the Chestermarke secret," replied Easleby, "and he let the Chestermarkes know it. And in that case what would happen?"

Starmidge walked slowly on at his companion's side, thinking. He was trying to fit together a great many things; he felt as a child feels who is presented with a puzzle in many pieces and told to put them together.

"I know what you're after," he said suddenly. "You think the Chestermarke's murdered Horbury?"

"If you want it plain and straight," replied Easleby, "I do!"

"There's the other man, Hollis," suggested Starmidge.

"I should say they finished him as well," said Easleby. "Easy enough job, on the evidence. Supposing one of them took Hollis off, alone, across that moor you've told me about, and induced him to look into that old lead-mine? What easier than to push him into it? Meanwhile, the other could settle Horbury. Murder, my lad! That's what all this comes to. I've known men murdered for less than that."

Again Starmidge reflected in silence.

"There's only one thing puzzles me on that point," he said eventually. "It's not a puzzle, either...it" a doubt. Do you think the Chestermarke's or, we'll say Gabriel, as we're certain about him, do you think Gabriel would be so keen about keeping his secret as to go to that length? Do you think he's cultivated it as a secret, that it's been a really important secret?"

"We can soon solve that," answered Easleby. "At least tomorrow morning."

"How?" demanded Starmidge.

"By calling," said Easleby, "on Mr. Godwin Markham, in Conduit Street."

Chapter 24

Starmidge looked at his companion as if in doubt about Easleby's exact meaning.

"According to what the theater chap said just now," he remarked, "Markham is very rarely to be found in Conduit Street."

"Exactly," agreed Easleby. "That's why I want to go there."

Starmidge shook his head.

"Don't follow!" he said. "Make it clear."

Easleby tapped his fellow-detective's arm.

"You said just now, would Gabriel Chestermarke be so keen about keeping his secret as to go to any length in keeping it," he answered "Now I say we can solve that by calling at his office. His manager, as Castlemayne told us, is one Stipp...Mr. Stipp. I propose to see Mr. Stipp. You and I must be fools if, inside ten minutes, we can't find out if Stipp knows Godwin Markham is Gabriel Chestermarke! We will find out! And if we find out Stipp doesn't know, if we find Stipp is utterly unaware there is such a person as Gabriel Chestermarke, or, at any rate, he doesn't connect Gabriel Chestermarke with Godwin Markham why, then..."

He ended with a dry laugh, and waved his hand as if the matter were settled. But Starmidge had a love of precision, and liked matters to be put in plain words.

"Well and what then?" he demanded.

"What, then?" exclaimed Easleby. "Why, then we shall know, for a certainty, Gabriel Chestermarke is keen about his secret! If he keeps it from the man who does his business for him here in London, he'd go to any length to keep it safe if it was threatened by his manager at Scarnham. Is that clear, my lad?"

The two men in the course of their slow strolling away from the Adalbert Theater had come to the end of Shaftesbury

Avenue, and had drawn aside from the crowds during the last minute or two to exchange their confidences in private. Starmidge looked meditatively at the thronging multitudes of Piccadilly Circus, and watched them awhile before he answered his companion's last observation.

"I don't want to precipitate matters," he said at last. "I don't want an anti-climax. Suppose we found Markham or Chestermarke there? Or supposing he came in?"

"Excellent! In either case," replied Easleby. "Serve our purpose equally well. If he's there, you betray the greatest surprise at seeing him...you can act up to that. If he should come in, you're equally surprised see! We haven't gone there about any Chestermarke, you know, we aren't going to let it out there we know what we do know, not likely!"

"What have we gone there for then?" asked Starmidge.

"We've gone to say Mrs. Helen Lester, of Lowdale Court, near Chesham, has informed us, the police, she placed a certain sum of money in the hands of her friend, Mr. Frederick Hollis, for the purpose of clearing off a debt contracted by her son, Lieutenant Lester, with Mr. Godwin Markham. That Mr. Hollis had been found dead under strange circumstances at Scarnham, and we should be vastly obliged to Mr. Markham if he can give us any information or light on the matter, or hints about it," replied Easleby. "That, of course, is what we shall say and all that we shall say to Mr. James Stipp. If, however, we find Gabriel Chestermarke there well, then, we shall say nothing at first. We shall leave him to do the saying, it'll be his job to begin."

"All right," assented Starmidge, after a moment's reflection. "We'll try it! Meet you tomorrow morning, then corner of Conduit Street and New Bond Street...say at ten-thirty. Now I'm going home."

Starmidge, being a bachelor, tenanted a small flat in Westminster, within easy reach of headquarters. He repaired to it immediately on leaving Easleby, intent on spending a couple of hours in ease and comfort before retiring to bed. But he had scarcely put on his slippers, lighted his pipe, mixed a whisky-and-soda, and picked up a book, when a knock at his outer door sent him to open it and to find Gandam standing in the lobby. Gandam glanced at him with a smile which was half apologetic and half triumphant.

"I've been to the office after you, Mr. Starmidge," he said. "They gave me your address, so I came on here."

Starmidge saw the man was full of news, and he motioned him to enter and led him to his sitting-room.

"You've heard something, then?" he asked.

"Seen something, Mr. Starmidge," answered Gandam, taking the chair which Starmidge pointed to. "I'm afraid I didn't hear anything, I wish I had!"

Starmidge gave his visitor a drink and dropped into his own easy-chair again.

"Chestermarke, of course!" he suggested. "Well what!"

"I happened to catch sight of him this evening," replied Gandam. "Sheer accident it was, but there's no mistaking him. Half-past six I was coming along Piccadilly, and I saw him leaving the Camellia Club. He..."

"What sort of a club's that, now?" asked Starmidge.

"Social club, men about town, sporting men, actors, journalists, so on," replied Gandam. "I know a bit about it, had a case relating to it not so long ago. Well he went along Piccadilly, and, of course, I followed him. I wasn't going to lose sight of him after that set-back of last night, Mr. Starmidge! He crossed the Circus, and went into the Café Monico. I followed him in there. Do you know that downstairs saloon there?"

"I know it," assented Starmidge.

"He went straight down to it," continued Gandam. "And as I knew he didn't know me, I presently followed. When I'd got down he'd taken a seat at a table in a quiet corner, and the waiter was bringing him a glass of sherry. There was a bit of talk between them. Chestermarke seemed to be telling the waiter he was expecting somebody, and he'd wait a bit before giving an order. So I sat down in another corner and as I judged it was going to be a long job, I ordered a bit of dinner. Of course I kept an eye on him quietly. He read a newspaper, smoked a cigarette, and sipped his sherry. And at last, perhaps ten minutes after he'd got in a woman came down the stairs, looked round, and went straight over to where he was sitting."

"Describe her," said Starmidge.

"Tall, very good figure, very good-looking, well-dressed, but quietly," replied Gandam. "Had a veil on when she came in, but lifted it when she sat down by Chestermarke. What I should call a handsome woman, Mr. Starmidge and, I should say, about thirty-five to forty. Dark hair, dark eyes taking expression."

"Mrs. Carswell, for a fiver!" thought Starmidge. "Well?" he said aloud. "You say she went straight over to him?"

"Straight to him and began talking at once," answered Gandam. "It seemed to me it was what you might call an adjourned meeting. They began talking as if they were sort of taking up a conversation. But she did most of the talking. He ordered some dinner for both of them as soon as she came, she talked while they ate. Of course, being right across the room from them, I couldn't catch a word that was said, but she seemed to be explaining something to him the whole time, and I could see he was surprised more than once."

"It must have been something uncommonly surprising to make him show signs of surprise!" muttered Starmidge, who had a vivid recollection of Gabriel's granite countenance. "Yes, go on."

"They were there about three-quarters of an hour," continued Gandam. "Of course, I ate my dinner while they ate theirs, and I took good care not to let them see I was watching them. As soon as I saw signs of a move on their part, when she began putting on her gloves I paid my waiter and slipped out upstairs to the front entrance. I got a taxi-cab driver to pull up by the curb and wait for me, and told him who I was and what I was after, and if those two got into a cab he was to follow wherever they went, cautiously. Gave him a description of the man, you know. Then I hung round till they came out. They parted at once, she went off up Regent Street..."

"I wish you'd had another man with you!" exclaimed Starmidge. "I'd give a lot to get hold of that woman. She's probably the housekeeper who disappeared from the bank, you know."

"So I guessed, Mr. Starmidge, but what could I do?" said Gandam. "I couldn't follow both, and it was the man you'd put me on to. I decided, of course, for him. Well he tried to get my cab; when he found it was engaged, he walked on a bit to the corner of Shaftesbury Avenue and got one there. And, of course, we followed. A long follow, too! Right away up to the back of Regent's Park. You know those detached houses, foot of Primrose Hill? It's one of those, he was a cute chap, my driver, and he contrived to slow down and keep well behind, and yet to see where Chestermarke got out. The name of the house is Oakfield Villa, it's on the gateposts. Of course, I made sure. I sent my man off and then I hung round some time, passing and re-passing once or twice. And I saw Chestermarke in a front room, the blinds were not drawn and he was in a smoking-cap and jacket, so I reckoned he was safe for the night. But I can watch the house all night if you think it's necessary, you know, Mr. Starmidge."

"No!" answered Starmidge. "Not at all. But I'll tell you what, you be about there, first thing tomorrow morning. Can you hang about without attracting attention?"

"Easily!" replied Gandam. "Easiest thing in the world. Do you know where a little lodge stands, as you go into Primrose Hill, the St. John's Wood side? Well, his house is close by that. On the other side of the road there's a little path leading over a bridge into the Park, close by the corner of the Zoo, I can watch from that path. You can rely on me, Mr. Starmidge. I'll not lose sight of him this time."

Starmidge saw the man was deeply anxious to atone for his mistake of the previous night, and he nodded assent.

"All right," he said, "but take another man with you. Two are better than one in a job like that and Chestermarke might be meeting that woman again. Watch the house carefully tomorrow morning from first thing, follow him wherever he goes. If he should meet the woman, and they part after meeting, one of you follow her. And listen, I shall be at headquarters at twelve o'clock tomorrow. Contrive to telephone me there as to what you're doing. But don't lose him or her, if you see her again."

"One thing more," said Gandam, as he rose to go. "Supposing he goes off by train? Do I follow?"

"No," answered Starmidge after a moment's reflection, "but manage to find out where he goes."

He sat and thought a long time after his visitor had left, and his thoughts all centered on one fact: the undoubted fact Gabriel and Mrs. Carswell had met.

Chapter 25

The offices of Mr. Godwin Markham, at which the two detectives presented themselves soon after half-past ten next morning, were by no means extensive in size or palatial in appearance. They were situated in the second floor of a building in Conduit Street, and apparently consisted of no more than two rooms, which, if not exactly shabby, were somewhat well-worn as to furniture and fittings. It was evident, Mr. Godwin Markham's clerical staff was not extensive. There was a young man clerk, and a young woman clerk in the outer office.

The first was turning over a pile of circulars at the counter; the second, seated at a typewriter, was taking down a letter which was being dictated to her by a man who, still hatted and over coated, had evidently just arrived, and was leaning against the mantelpiece with his hands in his pockets. He was a very ordinary, plain-countenanced, sandy-haired, quite commercial-looking man, this, who might have been anything from a Stock Exchange clerk to a suburban house-agent. But there was a sudden alertness in his eye as he turned it on the visitors, which showed them he was well equipped in mental acuteness, and probably as alert as his features were commonplace. The circular-sorting young man looked up with indifference as Easleby approached the counter, and when the detective asked if Mr. Godwin Markham could be seen, turned silently and interrogatively to the man who leaned against the mantelpiece. He, interrupting his dictation, came forward again, narrowly but continually eyeing the two men.

"Mr. Markham is not in town, gentlemen," he said, in a quick, business-like fashion, which convinced Starmidge the speaker was not uttering any mere excuse. "He was here yesterday for an hour or two, but he will be away for some days now. Can I do anything for you? His manager."

Easleby handed over the two professional cards which he had in readiness, and leaned across the counter.

"A word or two in private," he whispered confidentially. "Business matter."

Starmidge, watching Mr. James Stipp's face closely as he looked at the cards, saw he was not the sort of man to be taken unawares. There was not the faintest flicker of an eyelid, not a motion of the lips, not the tiniest start of surprise, no show of unusual interest on the manager's part: he nodded, opened a door in the counter, and waved the two detectives towards the inner room.

"Be seated, gentlemen," he said, following them inside. "You'll excuse me a minute, important letter to get off I won't keep you long."

He closed the door upon them and Starmidge and Easleby glanced round before taking the chairs to which Mr. Stipp had pointed. There was little to see. A big, roomy desk, middle-Victorian in style, some heavy middle-Victorian chairs, a well-worn carpet and rug, a book-case filled with peerages, baronetages, county directories, Army lists, Navy lists, and other similar volumes of reference to high life, a map or two on the walls, a heavy safe in a corner, these things were all there was to look at. Except one thing which Starmidge was quick to see. Over the mantelpiece, with an almanac on one side of it, and an interest-table on the other, hung a somewhat faded photograph of Gabriel Chestermarke.

The younger detective tapped his companion's arm and silently indicated this grim counterfeit of the man in whose doings they were so keenly interested just then.

"That's the man!" he whispered. "Chestermarke! Gabriel!"

Easleby opened mouth and eyes and stared with eager interest.

"Egad!" he muttered. "That's lucky! Makes it all the easier. I'll lay you anything you like, my lad, this manager doesn't know anything, not a thing about the double identity business. We shall soon find out, leave it to me, at first, anyway. A few plain questions..."

Mr. Stipp came bustling in, closing the door behind him. He took off overcoat and hat, ran his fingers through his light hair, and, seating himself, glanced smilingly at his visitors.

"Well, gentlemen!" he demanded. "What can I do for

you now? Want to make some inquiries?"

"Just a few small inquiries, sir," replied Easleby. "I haven't the pleasure of knowing your name...Mr.?"

'Stipp's my name, sir," answered the manager promptly. "Stipp...James Stipp."

"Thank you, sir," said Easleby, with great politeness. "Well, Mr. Stipp, you see from our cards who we are. We've called on you...as representing Mr. Godwin Markham...on behalf informally, Mr. Stipp, of Mrs. Lester, of Lowdale Court, Chesham."

Mr. Stipp's face showed a little surprise at this announcement, and he glanced from one man to the other as if he were puzzled.

"Oh!" he said. "Dear me! Why...what has Mrs. Lester called you in for?"

Easleby, who had brought another marked newspaper with him, laid it on the manager's desk.

"You've no doubt read of this Scarnham affair, Mr. Stipp?" he asked, pointing to his own blue penciling. "Most people have, I think. Or perhaps it's escaped your notice."

"Hardly could!" answered Mr. Stipp, with a friendly smile. "Yes, I've read it. Most extraordinary! One of the most puzzling cases I ever did read. Are you in at it? But this call hasn't anything to do with that, surely? If it has...what?"

"This much," answered Easleby. "Mrs. Lester has told us, of course, her son, the young officer, is in debt to your governor. Well, last week, Mrs. Lester handed a certain sum of money to the Mr. Frederick Hollis who's been found dead at Scarnham, to be applied to the settlement of her son's liability in that respect."

Mr. Stipp showed undoubted surprise at this announcement. "She did!" he exclaimed. "Gave Mr. Hollis money, for that? Why! Mr. Hollis never told me of it!"

In the course of a long professional experience Easleby had learned to control his facial expression. Starmidge was gradually progressing towards perfection in that art. But each man was hard put to it to check an expression of astonishment. And Easleby showed some slight sign of perplexity when he replied.

"Mr. Hollis has called on you, then?" he said.

"Hollis was here last Friday afternoon," answered Mr.

Stipp. "Called on me at five o'clock just before I was leaving for the day. He never offered me any money! Glad if he had it's time young Lester paid up."

"What did Hollis come for, then, if that's a fair question?" asked Easleby.

"He came, I should say, to take a look at us, and find out who he'd got to deal with," replied the manager, smiling. "In plain language, to make an inquiry or two. He told me he'd been empowered by Mrs. Lester to deal with us, and he wanted the particulars of what we'd advanced to her son, and he got them from me. But he never made me any offer. He just found out what he wanted to know and went away."

"And, evidently, next day traveled to Scarnham," observed Easleby. "Now, Mr. Stipp, have you any idea whether his visit to Scarnham was in connection with the money affair of yours and young Lester's?"

Again the look of undoubted surprise; again the appearance of genuine perplexity.

"I?" exclaimed Mr. Stipp. "Not the least! Not the ghost of an idea! What could his visit to Scarnham have to do with us? Nothing that I know of, anyway."

"You don't think it rather remarkable Mr. Hollis should go down there the very day after he called on you?" asked Starmidge, putting in a question for the first time.

"Why should I?" asked Mr. Stipp. "What do I know about him and his arrangements? He never mentioned Scarnham to me."

Easleby laid a finger on the marked newspaper. "You see some names of Scarnham people there, Mr. Stipp?" he observed. "Those names, Horbury, Chestermarke. You don't happen to know them?"

"I don't know them," replied the manager, with obvious sincerity. "Banking people, all of them, aren't they? I might have heard their names, in a business way, sometime but I don't recall them at all."

"You said Mr. Markham was here yesterday," suggested Starmidge. "Did you tell him, you'll excuse my asking, but it's important did you tell him Hollis had called last Friday on behalf of Mrs. Lester?"

"I just mentioned it," replied Mr. Stipp. "He took no particular notice except to say what we claim from young

Lester will have to be paid."

"You don't know if he knew Hollis?" inquired Starmidge.

The manager shook his head in a fashion which seemed to indicate that Hollis's case was no particular business of either his or his principal's.

'I don't think he did," he answered. "Never said so, anyhow. But, I say! You'll excuse me, now what is it you're trying to get at? Do you think Hollis went to Scarnham on this business of young Lester's? And if you do, why?"

Easleby rose, and Starmidge followed his example.

"We don't know yet, exactly why Hollis went to Scarnham," said the elder detective. "We hoped you could help us. But, as you can't well, we're much obliged, Mr. Stipp. That your governor over the chimney-piece there?"

"Taken a few years ago," replied Mr. Stipp carelessly. "I say you don't know what Hollis was empowered to offer us, do you?"

The two detectives looked at each other; a quiet nod from Starmidge indicated he left it to Easleby to answer this question. And after a moment's reflection, Easleby spoke.

"Mr. Hollis was empowered to offer ten thousand pounds in full satisfaction, Mr. Stipp," he said. "And what's more a check for that amount was found on his dead body when it was discovered. Now, sir, you'll understand why we want to know who it was that he went to see at Scarnham!"

Both men were watching the money-lender's manager with redoubled attention. But it needed no very keen eye to see the surprise which Mr. Stipp had already shown at various stages of the interview was nothing to what he now felt. And in the midst of his astonishment the two detectives bade him good-day and left him, disregarding an entreaty to stop and tell him more.

"My lad," said Easleby, when he and Starmidge were out in the street again, "that chap has no more conception his master is Gabriel Chestermarke than we had twenty-four hours since. Gabriel Chestermarke and Godwin Markham are one and the same man. He's a clever chap, this Gabriel and now you can see how important it's been for him to keep his secret. What's next to be done? We ought to keep in touch with him from now."

"I'm expecting word from Gandam at noon at headquarters," answered Starmidge, who had already told Easleby of the visit of the previous night. "Let's ride down there and hear if any message has come in."

But as their taxi-cab turned out of Whitehall into New Scotland Yard they overtook Gandam, hurrying along. Starmidge stopped the cab and jumped out.

"Any news?" he asked sharply.

"He's off, Mr. Starmidge!" replied Gandam. "I've just come straight from watching him away. He left his house about nine-twenty, walked to the St. John's Wood Station, went down to Baker Street, and on to King's Cross Metropolitan. We followed him, of course. He walked across to St. Pancras, and left by the ten-thirty express."

"Did you manage to find out where he booked for!" demanded Starmidge.

"Ecclesborough," answered Gandam. "Heard him! I was close behind."

"He was alone, I suppose?" asked Starmidge.

"Alone all the time, Mr. Starmidge," assented Gandam. "Never saw a sign of the other party."

Starmidge rejoined Easleby. For the last twenty-four hours he had let his companion supervise matters, but now, having decided on a certain policy, he took affairs into his own hands.

"Now, then," he said, "he's off, back to Scarnham. A word or two at the office, Easleby, and I'm after him. And you'll come with me."

Chapter 26

At half-past seven in the evening Starmidge and Easleby stepped out of a London express at Ecclesborough, and walked out to the front of the station to get a taxi-cab for Scarnham. The newsboys were rushing across the station square with the latest editions of the evening papers, and Starmidge's quick ear caught the meaning of their unfamiliar North-country shouting's.

"Latest about the Scarnham mystery," he said, stopping a lad and taking a couple of papers from him. "Something about the adjourned inquest, of course that would be today. Now then what's this?"

He drew aside to a quiet corner of the station portico, and with his companion looking over his shoulder, read aloud a passage from the latest of the two papers.

"An important witness gave evidence this afternoon at the adjourned inquest held at Scarnham on the body of Mr. Frederick Hollis, solicitor, of London, who was recently found lying dead at the bottom of one of the old lead-mines in Ellersdeane Hollow. It will be remembered the circumstances of this discovery already familiar to our readers, allied with the mysterious disappearance of Mr. John Horbury, and the presumed theft of the Countess of Ellersdeane's jewels, seem to indicate an extraordinary crime, and opinion varies considerably in the Scarnham district as to whether Mr. Hollis, the reason of whose visit to Scarnham is still unexplained, fell into the old mine by accident, or whether he was thrown in.

At the beginning of the proceedings this afternoon, a shepherd named James Livesey, of Ellersdeane, employed by Mr. Marchant, farmer, of the same place, was immediately called. He stated in answer to questions put by the Coroner, on Monday morning last he had gone with his employer to an out-of-the-way part of Northumberland to buy new stock, and in consequence of his absence from home had not heard of the Scarnham affair until his return this morning, when, on Mr.

Marchant's advice, he had at once called on the Coroner's office to volunteer information. Livesey's evidence, in brief, was as follows: At nine o'clock last Saturday evening, he was walking home from Scarnham to Ellersdeane by a track which crosses the Hollow, and cuts into the high road between the town and the village at a point near the Warren, an isolated house which is the private residence of Mr. Gabriel Chestermarke, banker, of Scarnham. As he reached this point, he saw Mr. John Horbury, whom he knew very well by sight, accompanied by a stranger, come out of the Hollow by another path, cross the high road, and walk down the lane which leads to the Warren.

They were talking very earnestly, but Mr. Horbury saw him and said goodnight in answer to his own greeting. There was a strong moonlight at the time, and he saw the stranger's face clearly. He was quite sure the stranger was the dead man whose body had just been shown to him at the mortuary. Questioned further, Livesey positively adhered to all his statements. He was certain of the time; certain of the identity of the two gentlemen. He knew Mr. Horbury very well indeed; had known him for many years; Mr. Horbury had often talked to him when they met in the fields and lanes of the neighborhood. He had no doubt at all the dead man he had seen in the mortuary was the gentleman who was with Mr. Horbury on Saturday night.

He had noticed him particularly as the two gentlemen passed him, and had wondered who he was. The moon was very bright that night: he saw Mr. Hollis quite plainly: he would have known him again at any time. He was positive the two gentlemen entered the lane which led to Mr. Gabriel Chestermarke's house. They were evidently making a direct line for it when he first saw them, and they crossed the high road straight to its entrance. That lane led nowhere else than to the Warren, it was locally called the lane, but it was really a sort of carriage-drive to Mr. Chestermarke's front door, and there was a gate at the high-road entrance to it. He saw Mr. Horbury and his companion enter that gate; he heard it clash behind them.

Questioned by Mr. Polke, superintendent of police at Scarnham, Livesey said when he first saw the two gentlemen they were coming from the direction of Ellersdeane Tower.

There was a path right across the Hollow, from a point in front of the Warren, to the Tower, and then to the woods on the Scarnham side. That was the path the two gentlemen were on. He was absolutely certain about the time, for two reasons. Just before he saw Mr. Horbury and his companion, he heard the clock at Scarnham Parish Church strike nine, and after they had passed him he had gone on to the Green Archer public-house, and had noticed it was ten minutes past nine when he entered. Further questioned, he said he saw no one else on the Hollow but the two gentlemen.

At the conclusion of Livesey's evidence, the Coroner announced to the jury, having had the gist of the witness's testimony communicated to him earlier in the day, he had sent his officer to request Mr. Gabriel Chestermarke's attendance. The officer, however, had returned to say Mr. Chestermarke was away on business, and it was not known when he would be back at the bank. As it was highly important the jury should know at once if Mr. Horbury and Mr. Hollis called at the Warren on Saturday evening last, he, the Coroner, had sent for Mr. Chestermarke's butler, who would doubtless be able to give information on that point. They would adjourn for an hour until the witness attended."

"That's the end of it in that paper," remarked Starmidge. "Let's see if the other has any later news. Ah! Here we are! There is more in the stop press space of this one. Now then..."

He held the second newspaper half in front of himself, half in front of Easleby, and again rapidly read over the report.

"Scarnham...further adjournment. On the Coroner's inquiry being resumed at four o'clock, Thomas Beavers, butler to Mr. Chestermarke at the Warren, said so far as he knew, Mr. Horbury did not call on his master on Saturday evening last, nor did any gentleman call who answered the description of Mr. Hollis. It was impossible for anybody to call at the Warren, in the ordinary way, without his, the butler's, knowledge. As a matter of fact, the witness continued, Mr. Chestermarke was not at home during the greater part of that evening. Mr. Joseph Chestermarke had dined at the Warren at seven o'clock, and at half-past eight he and his uncle left the house together. Mr. Chestermarke did not return until eleven. Asked by Mr. Polke, superintendent of police, if he knew in which direction Mr. Gabriel and Mr. Joseph Chestermarke proceeded when they went away, the witness said a short time after they left the house, he, in drawing the curtains of the dining-room window, saw them walking in a side-path of the garden, apparently in close conversation. He saw neither of them after that until Mr. Gabriel Chestermarke returned home, alone, at the time he had mentioned. Later. The inquest was further adjourned at the close of this afternoon's proceedings. Before adjourning, the Coroner informed the jury he understood there were rumors in the town to the effect Mr. Hollis had been strangled before being thrown into the old lead-mine. He need hardly say there were not the slightest grounds for those rumors. But the medical men had some suspicion the unfortunate gentleman might have been poisoned, and he, the Coroner, thought it well to tell them a specialist was being sent down by the Home Office, who, with the Scarnham doctors, would perform an autopsy on his arrival. The result would be placed before the jury when these proceedings were resumed."

Starmidge dropped the paper and looked at Easleby with an expression of astonishment.

"Poison!" he exclaimed. "That's a new idea! Poisoned first and thrown into that old mine after? That's...but, there, what's the good of theorizing? Pick out the best of those cars, and let's get to Scarnham as quick as possible. Something's got to be done tonight."

Easleby made no immediate answer. But presently, when they were in a fast motor and leaving the Ecclesborough streets behind them, he shook his head, and spoke more gravely than was usual with him.

"The big question, my lad," he said, "is what to do? And there's another, what's been done and possibly, what's being done? It's my impression something's being done now, still going on!"

"I know one thing!" exclaimed Starmidge determinedly. "We'll confront Gabriel tonight with what we know. That's positive!"

"If we can find him," said Easleby. "You don't know! The coming down to Ecclesborough may have been all a blind. You can reach a lot of places from Ecclesborough and you can leave a train at more than one place between Ecclesborough and London."

"I telephoned Polke to keep an eye on him, anyway, if he

did arrive at either Scarnham or the Warren," answered Starmidge, still grimly determined. "And it's my impression he has come down to see that nephew of his. Easleby, they're both in at it. Both!"

Again the elder detective made no answer. He was obviously much impressed by the recent developments as related in the newspapers which they had just read, and was deep in thought about them and the possibilities which they suggested to him.

"Well!" he said at last, as the high roofs of Scarnham came in view, "we'll hear what Polke has to tell. Something may have happened since those inquest proceedings this afternoon."

But Polke, when they reached his office, had little to tell. Lord Ellersdeane, Betty Fosdyke, and Stephen Hollis were with him, evidently in consultation, and Starmidge at once saw Betty looked distressed and anxious in no ordinary degree. All turned eagerly on the two detectives. But Starmidge addressed himself straight to Polke with one direct inquiry.

"Seen him? Heard of him?" he asked.

"Not a word!" answered Polke. "Nor a sign! If he came down by that train you spoke of, he ought to have been in the town by four o'clock at the outside. But he's never been to the bank, and he certainly hadn't arrived at his house three-quarters of an hour ago. And since ten o'clock this morning the other's disappeared, too!"

"What Joseph?" exclaimed Starmidge.

"Just so!" replied Polke, with the expression of a man who feels things are getting too much for individual effort, "He was at the bank at eight o'clock this morning, one of my men saw him go in by the back way, orchard way, you know. The clerks say he went out that way again at ten, and he's never been seen since."

"His house!" said Starmidge. "Have you tried that?"

"Know nothing of him there. The old man and old woman said so, at any rate," answered Polke. "He seems to have cleared out. And now here's fresh bother, though I don't know if it's anything to do with this. Mr. Neale's missing, never been seen since six yesterday evening. Miss Fosdyke's anxious..."

"He was to see me at nine last night," said Betty. "No

one has seen him. His landlady says he never returned home last night. Do you think anything can have happened..."

"If anything's happened to Mr. Neale," interrupted Starmidge, "it's all of a piece with the rest of it. Now, superintendent!" he went on, turning to Polke, "never mind what news I've brought, we've got to find these two Chestermarkes at once! We must go, some of us, to the Warren, some to the Cornmarket. See here, Easleby and I will go on to the Cornmarket, now you get some of your men and follow. If we hear nothing there...then, the Warren. But quick!"

The two detectives hurried out of the police-station. Lord Ellersdeane and Betty, after a word or two with Polke, followed. Outside, Starmidge and Easleby paused a moment, consulting; the Earl stepped forward to speak to them.

"As regards Mr. Neale," he began, "Miss Fosdyke thinks you ought to know that..."

A sudden searching flash, as of lightning, glared across the open space in front, lighting up the tower of the old church, the high roofs of the ancient houses, and the drifting clouds above them. Then a crash as of terrible thunder shook the little town from end to end, and as it died away the street lamps went out, and the tinkle of falling glass sounded on the pavements of the Market Place. And in the second of dead silence which followed, a woman's voice, shrill, terrified, shrieked loudly, once, somewhere in the darkness.

Chapter 27

On the previous evening, Neale, who had spent most of the day with Betty, endeavoring to gain some further light on the disappearance of her uncle, had left her at eight o'clock in order to keep a business appointment. He was honorary treasurer of the Scarnham Cricket Club: the weekly meeting of the committee of which important institution was due that night at the Hope and Anchor Inn, an old tavern in the Cornmarket. Then Neale repaired, promising to rejoin Betty at nine o'clock.

There was little business to be done at the meeting. By a quarter to nine it was all over and Neale was going away. And as he walked down the long sanded passage which led from the committee-room to the front entrance of the inn, old Rob Walford, the landlord, came out of the bow-windowed bar-parlor, beckoned him, with a mystery suggesting air, to follow, and led him into a private room, the door of which he carefully closed. Walford, a shrewd-eyed, astute old fellow, well known in Scarnham for his business abilities and his penetration, chiefly into other people's affairs, looked at Neale with a mingled expression of meaning and inquiry.

"Mr. Neale!" he whispered, glancing round at the paneling of the old parlor in which they stood, as if he feared its ancient boards might conceal eavesdroppers, "I wanted a word with you, in private. How's this here affair going? Is anything being done? Is anything being found out? Is that detective chap any good? Him from London, I mean. Is there anything new since this morning?"

"Not to my knowledge, Mr. Walford," answered Neale, who knew well the old innkeeper was hand-in-glove with the Scarnham police, and invariably kept himself well primed with information about their doings. "I should think you know nearly everything just as much as I do, more, perhaps."

The landlord poked a stout forefinger into Neale's

waistcoat.

"Aye!" he said. "Aye, so I do! As to what you might call surface matter, Mr. Neale. But about the main thing, which, in my opinion, is the whereabouts of John Horbury? Does the young lady at the Scarnham Arms know anything more about her uncle? Do you? Does anybody? Is there anything behind, like; anything that hasn't come out on the top?"

"I don't know of anything," replied Neale. "I wish I did! Miss Fosdyke's very anxious indeed about her uncle. She'd give anything or do anything to get news of him. It's all rot, you know, to say he's run away. It's my impression he's never gone out of Scarnham or the neighborhood. But where he is, and whether dead or alive, is beyond my comprehension," he concluded, shaking his head. "If he's alive, why don't we hear something, or find out something?"

Walford gave his companion a quick glance out of his shrewd old eyes.

"He might be under such circumstances as wouldn't admit of that there, Mr. Neale," he said. "But come! I've got something to tell you, something I found out not half an hour ago. I was going on to tell Polke about it at once, but I remembered you were in the house at this cricket club meeting, so I thought you'd do instead, you can tell Polke. I'm in a bit of a hurry myself...you know it's Wymington Races tomorrow, and I'm off there tonight, at once, to meet a man I do a bit of business with in these matters, we make a book together, so I can't stop. But come this way."

He led Neale out into the long sanded passage, and down through the rear of the old house into a big stable-yard, enclosed by variously shaped buildings, more or less in an almost worn-out and dilapidated condition, whose roofs and gables showed picturesquely against the sky, faintly lighted by the waning moon. To one of these, a tower-like erection, considerably higher than the rest, the old landlord pointed.

"I suppose you know these back premises of mine partly overlook Joseph Chestermarke's garden?" he whispered. "They do, anyway you can see right over his garden and the back of his house, that is, in bits, for he's a fine lot of tall trees round his lawns. But there's a very fair view of that workshop he's built from the top story of this old dove-cot of mine, we use it as a store-house. Come up and mind these here broken steps there's no rail, you see, and you could easy fall over."

He led his companion up a flight of much-worn stone stairs which were built against the wall of the old dove-cot; through an open doorway twenty feet above; across a rickety floor; and up another stairway of wood, into a chamber in which was a latticed window, from which most of the glass and the woodwork had disappeared.

"Now, then," he said, taking Neale to this outlook, and pointing downwards. "There you are! You see what I mean?"

Neale looked out. Joseph's big garden lay beneath him. As Walford had said, much of it was obscured by trees, but there was a good prospect of one side of the laboratory from where Neale was standing. That side was furnished with a door and on the level of that door at the extreme end of the building was a window fitted with a light-colored blind. All the other windows, as in the case of the side which Neale had seen previously from the tree on the river-bank, were high up in the walls and fitted with red material. And from the curiously shaped smoke stack in the flat roof, the same differently tinted vapors which he had noticed on the same occasion were curling up above the elms and beeches.

"Now look here!" whispered the landlord. "Do you see that one window with the white blind and the light behind it? I came up here, maybe half an hour ago, to see if we were out of something that's kept here, and I chanced to look out on to Joseph's garden. Mr. Neale, there's a man in that room with the light-colored blind, I saw his shadow on the blind, pass and repass, you understand, twice, while I looked. And it's not Joseph Chestermarke!"

"Could you tell? Had you any idea whose shadow it was?" demanded Neale eagerly.

"No, he passed in a sort of slanting direction back and forward just once," answered Walford. "But his build was, I should say, about the like of John Horbury's. Mr. Neale, Horbury might be locked up there! He's a bad one, is Joe Chestermarke, oh, he's a rank bad one my lad, though most folk don't know it. You don't know what mayn't be happening, or what mayn't have happened in the place! But look here I can't stop. Me and Sam Barraclough's going off to Wymington now, in his motor he'll be waiting at this minute. You do what I say, stay here and watch a bit. And if you see anything, go to

Polke and insist on the police searching that place. That's my advice!"

"I shall do that, in any case, after what you've said," muttered Neale, who was staring at the lighted window. "But I'll watch here a bit. You've said nothing of this to anybody else?"

"No," replied the landlord. "As I said, I knew you were in the house. Well, I'm off, then. Shan't be back till late tomorrow night and I hope you'll have some news by then, Mr. Neale."

Walford went off across the creaking floor and down the stairs, and Neale leaned out of the dismantled window and stared into the garden beneath. Was it possible, he wondered, there was anything in the old fellow's suggestion? Possible the missing bank manager was really concealed in that mysterious laboratory, or workshop, or whatever the place was, into which Joseph never allowed any person to enter? And if he was there at all, was it with his consent, or against his will, or what? Was he being kept a prisoner or was he hiding?

In spite of his own knowledge of Horbury, and of Betty's assertions of her uncle's absolute innocence, Neale had all along been conscious of a vague, uneasy feeling, after all, there might be something of an unexplained nature in which the manager had been, or was concerned. It might have something to do with the missing jewels; it might be mixed up with Frederick Hollis's death; it might be Horbury and Joseph were jointly concerned in, but there he was at a loss, not knowing or being able to speculate on what they could be concerned in. Strange beyond belief it was, nevertheless, old Rob Walford should think the shadow he had seen to be the missing man's! Supposing...

The door of Joseph's laboratory suddenly opened, letting out a glare of light across the lawn in front. And Joseph came out, carrying a sort of sieve-like arrangement, full of glowing ashes. He went away to some distant part of the garden with his burden; came back, disappeared; re-appeared with more ashes; went again down the garden. And each time he left the door wide open. A sudden notion which he neglected to think over flashed into Neale's mind. He left the upper chamber of the old dove-cot, made his way down the stairs to the yard beneath, turned the corner of the buildings, and by the aid of some loose timber which lay piled against it, climbed to the top of Joseph's wall. A moment of hesitation, and then he quietly dropped to the other side, noiselessly, on the soft mold of the border.

From behind a screen of laurel bushes he looked out on the laboratory, at close quarters. Joseph was still coming and going with his sieve, now that Neale saw him at a few yards distance he saw the junior partner and amateur experimenter was evidently cleaning out his furnace. The place into which he threw the ashes was at the far end of the garden; at least three minutes was occupied in each journey. And yielding to a sudden impulse when Joseph made his next excursion and had his back fairly turned, Neale crossed the lawn in half a dozen agile and stealthy strides, and within a few seconds had slipped within the open door and behind it.

A moment later, and he knew he was trapped. Joseph came back and did not enter. Neale heard him fling the sieve on the gravel. Then the door was pulled to with a metallic bang, from without, and the same action which closed it also cut off the electric light.

Chapter 28

It needed no more than a moment's reflection to prove to Neale he had made a serious mistake in obeying that first impulse. Joseph had gone away, probably for the night. And there had been something in the metallic clang of that closing door, something in the sure and certain fashion in which it had closed into its frame, something in the utter silence which had followed the sudden extinction of the light, which made the captive feel he might beat upon door or wall as hard and as long as he pleased without attracting any attention.

This place into which he had come of his own free will was no ordinary place. Already he felt he was in a trap out of which it was not going to be easy to escape. He stood for a moment, heart thumping and pulses throbbing, to listen and to look. But he saw nothing beyond the faint indication of the waning moonlight outside the red-curtained, circular windows high above him, and a fainter speck of glowing cinder, left behind in the recently emptied furnace.

He heard nothing, either, save a very faint crackling of the expiring ashes in that furnace. Presently even that minute sound died down, the one speck of light went out, and the silence and gloom were intense. Neale now knew unless Joseph came back to his workshop he was doomed to spend the night in it and possibly part of the next day. He felt sure it was impossible to obtain release otherwise than by Joseph's coming. He could do nothing in all probability to release himself. No one in the town would have the remotest idea he was fastened up within those walls. The only man to whom such an idea could come on hearing he, was missing, was old Rob Walford and Walford, by that time, would be well on his way to Wymington, thirty miles off, and as he was to be there all night, and all next day, he would hear nothing until his return to Scarnham, twenty-four hours hence. No, he was caught. Joseph' had no idea of catching him, but he had caught him all the same. And now that he was safely caught, Neale began to wonder why he had slipped into that place. He had an elementary idea, of course, he had wanted to find out if anybody was concealed in the room which the landlord had pointed out. Certainly he had felt no fear about meeting Joseph. Yet, now that he was there he did not know what he should have done if Joseph had come in, as he expected he would, nor what he should, or could do now that he was in complete possession.

If he had been able to face Joseph, he would have demanded information, point-blank, about the shadow on the blind; he even had some misty notion about enforcing it, if need be. But he was now helpless. He could do no good; he could not tell Polke or anybody else what Walford had reported. And if he was to be left there all night, which seemed likely he had only gotten himself into a highly unpleasant situation. He moved at last, feeling about in the darkness. His hands encountered smooth, blank walls, on each side of the door. He dared not step forward lest he should run against machinery or meet with some cavity in the flooring.

And reflecting the small, insignificant gleam which it would make could scarcely be noticed from outside, he struck a match, and carefully holding it within the flap of his outstretched jacket, looked around him. A first quick glance gave him a general idea of his surroundings. Immediately in front of him was the furnace; a little to its side was a lathe; on one side of the place a long table stood, covered with a multitude of tools, chemical apparatus, and the like; on the other was a blank wall.

And in that blank wall, to which Neale chiefly directed his attention during the few seconds for which the match burned, was a door. The match went out; he dropped it on the floor and moved forward in the darkness to the door which he had just seen. That, of course, must open into the inner room to the outer window of which Walford had drawn his attention. He went on until his outstretched fingers touched the door. Then he cautiously struck another match and looked the door up and down. What he saw added to the mystery of the whole adventure. Neale had seen doors of that sort before, more than once, but they were the doors of very big safes or of strong rooms. Before the second match burned through he knew this particular door was of some metal...steel, most likely it was set into a framework of similar metal, and the room to which it afforded entrance was probably sound-proof. He struck a third match and a fourth. By their light he saw there was but one small keyhole to the door, and he judged from that was fitted with some patent mechanical lock. There was no way by which he could open it, of course, and though he stood for a long time listening with straining ears against it he could not detect the slightest sound from whatever chamber or recess lay behind it. If there really was a man in there, thought Neale, he must surely feel himself to be in a living tomb.

And after a time, taking the risk of being heard from outside the laboratory, he beat heavily upon the door with his fist. No response came: the silence all around him was more oppressive, if possible, than before. The expenditure of more matches enabled Neale to examine further into the conditions of what seemed likely to be his own prison for some hours. He was not sorry to see in one corner stood an old settee, furnished with rugs and cushions, if he was obliged to remain locked up all night, he would, at any rate, be able to get some rest. But beyond this, the furnace, a tall three-fold screen, evidently used to assist in the manipulation of draughts, and the lathe, table, and apparatus which he had already seen, there was nothing in the place.

There was no way of getting at the windows in the top of the high walls: even if he could have got at them they were too small for a man to squeeze through. And he was about to sit down on the settee and wait the probably slow and tedious course of events, when he caught sight of an object at the end of the table which startled him, and made him wonder more than anything he had seen up to that moment. That object was a big loaf of bread. He struck yet another match and looked at it more narrowly. It was one of those large loaves which bakers make for the use of families.

Close by it lay a knife: a nearer inspection showed Neale a slice had recently been cut from the loaf: he knew by the fact the crumb was still soft and fresh on the surface, in spite of the great heat of the place. It was scarcely likely Joseph would eat unbuttered bread during his experiments and labors, why, then, was the loaf there? Could it be this bread was the slice which had just been cut was, the ration given to somebody behind that door? This idea filled Neale with the first spice of fear which he had felt since entering the laboratory. The idea of a man being fastened up in a sound-proof chamber and fed on dry bread suggested possibilities which he did not and could not contemplate without a certain horror. And if there really was such a prisoner in that room, or cell, or whatever the place was, who could it be but John Horbury? And if it was John Horbury, how, under what circumstances, had he been brought there, why was he being kept there?

Neale sat down at last on the settee, and in the silence and darkness gave himself up to thoughts of a nature which he had never known in his life before. Here, at any rate, was adventure and of a decidedly unpleasant sort. He was not afraid for himself. He had a revolver in his hip-pocket, loaded. He had been carrying it since Tuesday, with some strange notion it might be wanted. Certainly he might have to go without food for perhaps many hours, but he suddenly remembered in the pocket of his Norfolk jacket he had a big box of first-rate chocolate, which he had bought on his way to the cricket club meeting, with a view of presenting it to Betty, later on. He could get through a day on that, he thought, if it were necessary as for the loaf of bread, something seemed to nauseate him at the mere thought of trying to swallow a mouthful of it. The rest of the evening went: the silence was never broken. Not a sound came from the mysterious chamber behind him. No step sounded on the gravel without: no hand unlocked the door from the garden. Now and then he heard the clock of the parish church strike the hours. At last he slept at first fitfully; later soundly and when he woke it was morning, and the sunlight was pouring in through the red-curtained windows high in the walls of his prison.

Chapter 29

Neale was instantly awake and on the alert. He sprang to his feet, shivering a little in spite of the rugs which he had wrapped about him before settling down. A slight current of cold air struck him as he rose. Looking in the direction from which it seemed to come, he saw one of the circular windows in the high wall above him was open, and a fresh north-east wind was blowing the curtain aside. The laboratory, hot and close enough when he had entered it the previous evening, was now cool. The morning breeze freshened and sharpened his wits. He pulled out his watch, which he had been careful to wind up before lying down.

Seven o'clock! In spite of his imprisonment and his unusual couch, he had slept to his accustomed hour of waking. Knowing Joseph might walk in upon him at any moment, Neale kept himself on the lookout, in readiness to adopt a determined attitude whenever he was discovered. By that time he had come to the conclusion whether force would be necessary or not in any meeting with Joseph, it would be no unwise thing to let that worthy see at once he had to deal with an armed man. He accordingly saw to it his revolver, already loaded, was easily get-at-able, and the flap of his hip-pocket unbuttoned: under the circumstances, he was not going to be slow in producing the revolver in suggestive, if not precisely menacing fashion. This done, he opened his box of chocolate, calculated its resources, and ate a modest quantity.

And while he ate, he looked about him. In the morning light everything in his surroundings showed clearly his cursory inspection of the night before had been productive of definite conclusions. There was no doubt whatever of the character of the mysterious door set so solidly and closely in its framework in the blank wall: the door of the strong room at Chestermarke's Bank was not more suggestive of security. He went over to the outer door when he had eaten his chocolate, and examined it at his leisure. That, in lesser degree, was set into the wall as strongly as the inner one. He saw no means of opening it from the inside: it was evidently secured by a patent mechanical lock of which Joseph presumably carried the one key. He turned from it to look more closely at a shelf of books and papers which projected from the wall above the table. Papers and books were all of a scientific nature, most of them relating to experimental chemistry, some to mechanics. He noticed there were several books on poisons; his glance fell from those books to various bottles and phials on the table, fashioned of dark-colored glass and three-cornered in shape, which he supposed to contain poisonous solutions.

So Joseph dabbled in toxicology, did he? Thought Neale, in that case, perhaps, there was something in the theory which had been gaining ground during the last twenty-four hours. Hollis had been poisoned first and thrown into the old lead-mine later on. And what of the somebody, Horbury or whoever it was, that lay behind that grim-looking door? Neale had never heard a sound during the time which had elapsed before he dropped asleep, never a faintest rustle since he had been awake again. Was it possible that a dead man lay there murdered? A cheerful chirping and twittering in the space behind him caused him to turn sharply away from the books and bottles. Then he saw he was no longer alone. Half a score sparrows, busy, bustling little bodies, had come in by the open window, and were strutting about amongst the grey ashes in front of the furnace.

Neale's glance suddenly fell on the loaf of bread, close at hand on the edge of the table, and on the knife which lay by it. Mechanically, without any other idea than feeding the sparrows and diverting himself by watching their antics, he picked up the knife, quietly cut off a half-slice of the loaf, and, crumbling it in his fingers, threw the crumbs on the floor. For a minute or two he watched his visitors fighting over this generous dole. Then he turned to the shelf again, to take down a book, the title of which had attracted him. Neale was an enthusiastic member of the Territorial Force, and had already gained his sergeant's stripes in the local battalion; he was accordingly deeply interested in all military matters…this book certainly related to those matters, though in a way with which he was happily as yet unfamiliar.

For its title was "On the Use of High Explosive in

Modern Warfare," and though Neale was no great reader, he was well enough versed in current affairs to know the name of the author, a foreign scientist of world-wide reputation. He opened the book as he stood there, and was soon absorbed in the preface; so absorbed indeed, it was some little time before he became aware the cheerful twittering behind him had ceased. It had made a welcome diversion, that innocent chirping of the little brown birds, and when it ceased, he missed it. He turned suddenly and dropped the book.

Seven or eight of the sparrows were already lying on the floor motionless. Some lay on their sides, some on their backs; all looked as if they were already dead. Two were still on their feet; at any other time Neale would have laughed to see the way in which they staggered about, for all the world as if they were drunk. And as he watched one collapsed; the other, after an ineffective effort to spread its wings, rolled to one side and dropped helplessly. And Neale made another turn to stare at the loaf of bread and to wonder what devilry lay in it.

Poison? Of course it was poison! And what of this man in that jealously guarded room, behind that steel door? Had he also eaten of the loaf? He turned to the sparrows again at last, stood staring at them as if they fascinated him, and eventually went over to the foot of the furnace and picked one up. Then he found, with something of a shock, the small thing was not dead. The little body was warm with life; he felt the steady, regular beating of the tiny heart. He laid the bird down gently, and picked up its companions, one by one, examining each. And each was warm, and the heart of each was beating. The sparrows were not dead but they were drugged and they were very fast asleep.

Neale now began to develop theories. If a mere tiny crumb of that loaf could put a sparrow, a remarkably vigorous and physically strong little bird to sleep within a minute or two, what effect would, say, a good thick slice of it produce upon a human being? Anyway, the probability was the captive in that room was lying in a heavily drugged condition, and that was the reason of his silence. He would wake and surely some sound, however faint, would come. He would wait, listening. The morning wore on, he waited, watched, listened.

None came, nothing had happened. He ate more of his chocolate. He read the book on explosives. It interested him deeply, so deeply that in spite of his anxiety, his hunger, his uncertainty as to what might happen, sooner or later, he became absorbed in it. And once more he was called from its pages by the sparrows. The sparrows were coming to life. After lying stupefied for some four or five hours they were showing signs of animation. One by one they were moving, staggering to their feet, beginning to chirp. And as he watched them, first one and then the other got the use of its wings; and, finally, with one consent, they flew off to the open window to disappear. Thereafter, Neale listened more keenly than ever for any sound from that mysterious room.

But no sound came. The afternoon passed wearily away; the light began to fail, and at last he had to confess to himself that the waiting, the being always on the alert, the enforced seclusion and detention, the desire for proper food and drink, especially the latter was becoming too much for him, and his nerves were beginning to suffer. Was Joseph never coming? Had he gone off somewhere? Possibly leaving a dead man behind, whose body was only a few yards away. There was no spark of comfort visible save one. Old Rob Walford would be home late that night from Wymington, sooner or later he would hear of Neale's disappearance and he would sharpen his naturally acute wits and come to the right conclusion. Yet, that might be as far off as tomorrow.

As the darkness came, Neale, now getting desperate for want of food, was suddenly startled by two sounds which, coming abruptly at almost the same time, made him literally jump. One, the first was a queer thump, thump, thump, which seemed to be both close at hand and yet a thousand miles away. The second was Joseph's voice in the garden outside heard clearly through the open window. He was bidding somebody to tell a cab driver to wait for him at the foot of the bridge. The next minute, Neale heard a key plunged into the outer door before it turned, following out a scheme which he had decided on during his long watch, had leaped behind the screen that stood near the furnace. Ere the door could open, he was safely hidden and in that second he heard the thumping repeated and knew it came from the inner room.

The electric light blazed up as Joseph strode in. He put the door to behind him without quite closing it, and walked into the middle of the laboratory, feeling in his waistcoat pocket for something as he advanced. And Neale, peering at him through the high screen, felt afraid of him for the first time in his life. For the junior partner had shaved off his beard and moustache, and the face which was thus clearly revealed, and on which the bright light shone vividly, was one of such mean and malevolent cruelty that the watcher felt himself turn sick with dread. Joseph went straight to the door in the far wall, unlocked it with a twist of the key which he had brought from his pocket, and walked in. The click of an electric light switch followed, and Neale stared hard and nervously into the hidden room. But he saw nothing but Joseph standing, hands planted on his sides, staring at something hidden by the door. Next instant Joseph spoke menacingly, sneeringly.

"So you're round again after one of your long sleeps, are you?" he said. "That's lucky! Now then, have you come to your senses?"

Neale thought his heart would burst as he waited for the unseen man's voice. But before he heard any voice he heard something which turned his blood cold with horror the clanking, plain, unmistakable, of a chain! Whoever was in there was chained...chained like a dog. And following on that metallic sound came a weary moan.

"Come on, now!" said Joseph. "None of that! Are you going to sign that paper? Speak, now!"

It seemed to Neale an age before an answer came. But it came at last and in Horbury's voice. But what a changed voice! Thin, weak, weary the voice of a man slowly being done to death.

"How long are you going to keep me here?" it asked. "How long..."

"Sign that paper on the table there, and you'll be out of this within twenty-four hours," replied Joseph. "And listen, you'll have good food and wine...wine within ten minutes. Come on, now!"

Further silence was followed by another moan, and at the sound of that, Neale, whose teeth had been clenched firmly for the last minute or two, slipped his hand round to the pocket in which the revolver lay.

"Don't be a damned fool!" said Joseph. "Sign and have done with it! There's the pen sign! You could have signed any time the last week and been free. Get it done damn you, I tell you, get it done! It's your last chance. I'm off tonight. If I leave you here, it's in your grave. Nobody'll ever come near this place for weeks you'll be dead...starved to death, long before that. Do you hear me? Come on, now sign!"

Neale half drew the revolver from his pocket. But, as he was about to step from behind the screen, a sudden step sounded on the gravel outside the outer door, and he shrank back, watching. The door opened was thrown back with some violence and at the same instant Joseph darted from the inner room, livid with anger, to confront Gabriel. The younger man had not expected to encounter the elder was instantly evident to Neale. Joseph drew back, step by step, watching his uncle, until his back was against the door through which he had just rushed. His hand went out behind him and pulled the door to, heavily. And as it closed he spoke and Neale knew there was fear in his voice.

"What...what is it?" he got out. "When did you come in here? Why..." Gabriel had come to a halt in the middle of the floor, and he was standing very still. His face was paler than ever, and his eyes burned in their deep-set sockets like live coals. And suddenly he lifted a forefinger and pointed it straight at his nephew.

"Thief!" he said, with a quietness which was startlingly impressive to the excited spectator. "Thief! Thief and liar and murderer, for anything I know! But you are found out. Scoundrel you stole those securities! You stole those jewels! Don't trifle, don't attempt to dispute! I know! You got the jewels last Saturday night, you took those securities at the sametime. You may have murdered that man Hollis for anything I know to the contrary, probably you did. But, no fencing with me! Now speak! Where are the jewels? Where are those securities? And where is Horbury! Answer without lying. You devil! I tell you I know...*know*! I have seen Mrs. Carswell!"

Gabriel had moved a little as he went on speaking moved nearer to his nephew, still pointing the incriminating and accusing finger at him. And Joseph had moved, too backward. He was watching his uncle with a queer expression.

Neale saw the tip of his tongue emerge from his lips, as if the lips had become dry, and he wanted to moisten them. And suddenly his face changed, and Neale, closely watching him, saw his hand go quickly to his breast pocket, and caught the gleam of a revolver. Neale was a cricketer of reputation and experience. On a felt-covered stand close by him lay a couple of heavy spherical objects, fashioned of some shining-surfaced metal and about the size of a cricket ball, which he had previously noticed and handled in looking round. He snatched one of them up now, and flung it hard and straight at Joseph, intending to stun him. But for once in a way he missed his mark; the missile crashed against the wall behind. And then came a great flash, and the roar of all the world going to pieces, and a mighty lifting and up heaving and he saw and felt and knew no more.

Chapter 30

The four people standing beneath the portico of the police-station remained as if spell-bound for a full moment after the sudden flash and the sudden roar. Betty unconsciously clutched at Lord Ellersdeane's arm. Lord Ellersdeane spoke, wonderingly.

"Thunder?" he exclaimed. "Strange!"

Easleby turned sharply from Starmidge, who, holding by one of the pillars, was staring towards the quarter of the Market-Place, from whence the scream of dire fear had come.

"That's no thunder, my lord!" he said. "That's an explosion and a terrible one, too! Are there any gasworks close at hand? It was like..."

Polke came rushing out of the lobby behind them, followed by some of his men. And at the same instant people began running along the pavements, calling to each other.

"Did you hear that?" cried the superintendent excitedly. "An explosion! Which direction?"

Starmidge suddenly started, as if from a reverie. He put up his hand and wiped something from his cheek, and held the hand out to a shaft of light which came from the open door behind them. A smear of blood lay across his open palm.

"A splinter of falling glass," he said quietly. "Come on, all of you! That was an explosion and I guess where! Get help, Polke come on to the Cornmarket! Get the firemen out."

He set off running towards the end of the Market-Place, followed by Easleby, and at a slower pace by Lord Ellersdeane and Betty. Crowds were beginning to run in the same direction. Very soon the two detectives found it difficult to thread a way through them. But within a few minutes they were in the Cornmarket, and Starmidge, seizing his companion's arm, dragged him round the corner of Joseph's house to the high garden wall which ran down the slope to the river bank. And as they turned the corner, he pointed.

"As I thought!" he muttered. "It's Joseph Chestermarke's workshop! Something's happened. Look there!"

The wall, a good ten feet high on that side, was blown to pieces, and lay, a mass of fallen masonry, on the green sward by the roadside. Through the gap thus made, Starmidge plunged into the garden to be brought up at once by the twisted and interlaced boughs of the trees which had been lopped off as though by some giant ax, and then instantaneously transformed into a cunningly interwoven fence. The air was still thick with fine dust, and the atmosphere was charged with a curious, acid odor, which made eyes and nostrils smart.

"No ordinary burst up, this!" muttered Starmidge, as he and Easleby forced their way through branches and obstacles to the open lawn. "My God! Look at it! Blown to pieces!"

The two men stood for a moment staring at the scene before them, as it was revealed in the faint light of a waning moon. Neither had ever seen the effect of high explosives before, and they remained transfixed with utter astonishment at what they saw. Never, until then, had either believed it possible that such ruin could be wrought by such means. The laboratory was a mass of shapeless wreckage.

It seemed as if the roof had been blown into the sky, only to collapse again on the shattered walls. The masonry and woodwork lay all over lawns and gardens, and a midst the surrounding bushes and trees. In the middle of it yawned a black, deep cavity, from the heart of which curled a wisp of yellowish smoke. Between these ruins and the house a beech tree of considerable size had been completely uprooted, and had crashed down on the lower windows of the house, part of the wall and roof of which had been wrecked. And on the opposite side of the garden a great gap had been made in the smaller trees, and the shrubberies beneath them by the falling in of Rob Walford's old dove-cot, the ancient walls and timber roof of which had completely collapsed under the force of the explosion. Over the actual area of the wreckage everything was still as death, save for a faint crackling where some loose wood was just catching fire. Starmidge began to make his way towards it.

"The thing is," he said mechanically, "the thing is, the

thing is...yes, is...was there anybody here...anybody here! We must have lights."

And just then as he came to where the burst of flame was growing bigger, and Polke with a body of firemen and constables came hurrying through a gap in the lower wall, he caught sight of a man's face, turned up to the half-light. Easleby saw it at the same time, together they went nearer. And Starmidge bent down and found himself looking at Gabriel.

"Him!" he whispered. "Then he came here!"

"He's gone, anyway," muttered Easleby. "Dead as can be!" He lifted himself erect and called to Polke who was making his way towards them. "Bring a lantern!" he said. "There's a dead man here!"

"And keep the crowd out," called Starmidge. "Keep everybody out while we look round."

But at that moment he caught sight of Betty, with Lord Ellersdeane in close attendance, had made her way into the garden and was clambering towards him. Starmidge stepped back to her.

"Hadn't you better go back?" he urged. "There'll be unpleasant sights. Do go back amongst the trees, anyway. We've found one dead man already, and there'll probably be..."

"No!" she said firmly. "I won't! Not until I know who's here. Because I think...I'm afraid Mr. Neale may be here. I must...I will stay! I'm not afraid. Whose body have you found?"

"Gabriel Chestermarke's," replied Starmidge quietly. "Dead! And whoever's here, Miss Fosdyke, I don't see how he can possibly be alive. Do go back and let us search."

But Betty turned away and began to search, climbing from one mass of wreckage to another. Presently an exclamation from her brought the others hurriedly to her side. She pointed between two slabs of stone.

"There!" she whispered. "A man's face!"

Starmidge turned to Lord Ellersdeane.

"Get her away...aside anywhere for a minute!" he muttered. "Let's see what condition he's in, anyway. The other was blown to pieces."

Lord Ellersdeane took a firm grip of Betty's arm and turned her round.

"That was not Mr. Neale?" he asked.

"No!" she said faintly. "No!"

"Then leave them to deal with that, and let us look elsewhere," he said. "Come after all, you don't know he would be here."

"Where else should he be?" she answered. "I'm sure he's here, somewhere. Help me!"

She turned away with him in another direction, and the two detectives, with some of the firemen helping them, got to work on the place which she had pointed out. Presently Polke directed the light of a bullseye on the dead face beneath them. He broke into an exclamation of amazement.

"Who's this?" he demanded. "Look!"

One of the firemen bent closer, and suddenly glanced up at the superintendent.

"It's young Chestermarke, sir," he said. "He must have shaved his beard off. But...it's him!"

They took out what was to be found of Joseph at that particular spot, and went on to search for the rest of him, and for anything else. And eventually they came across Neale, unconscious, but alive. His partial protection by the projecting iron walls of the furnace had saved him. He had evidently been carried back with them when the explosion occurred and wedged between them and the outer wall of the laboratory. He came round to find a doctor administering restoratives to him on one side, and Betty kneeling at the other. And suddenly he remembered, and made a great shift to speak.

"All right!" he muttered at length. "Bit knocked out, that's all! But Horbury! Horbury's somewhere! Get at him!"

They found the missing bank manager at last, he, too, had been saved by the thick wall which stood between him and the explosion. He was alive and conscious when they had dug down to him and his rescuers stared from him to each other when they saw the broken links of a steel chain were still securely manacled about his waist.

Chapter 31

It was not until a week later Neale, with a bandaged head and one arm in a sling, and Betty, inexpressibly thankful the recent terrible catastrophe had at any rate brought relief in its train, were allowed to visit Horbury for their first interview of more than a few minutes duration. Neale had made a quick recovery; beyond the fracture of a small bone in his arm, some cuts on his head, and a general shock to his system, he was little the worse for his experience. But the elder victim had suffered more severely; he had suffered, too, from a week's ill-treatment and starvation. Nevertheless, he managed an approving smile when the two young people were brought to his bedside, and he looked at them afterwards in a narrow and scrutinizing fashion, which made Betty redden and grow somewhat conscious.

"Not more than three-quarters of an hour at most, the nurse said," she remarked, as they sat down at the bedside. "So if you have anything to say, Uncle John, you must get it said within that."

"One can say a lot within three-quarters of an hour, my dear," answered the invalid. "There is something I wanted to say," he went on, glancing at Neale. "I suppose there has been an inquest on the two Chestermarkes?"

"Adjourned until you're all right," replied Neale. "You and I, of course, are the two important witnesses. You, principally. You know everything, I only came in at the end."

"I suppose there are and have been all sorts of rumors?" said Horbury. "I don't see how anybody but myself could know all that happened in this horrible business. Hollis, for instance, have they come to any conclusion about his death?"

"None!" replied Neale. "All that's known is he was found at the bottom of one of the old lead mines. We," he added, nodding at Betty, "were there when he was taken out."

Horbury's face clouded.

"And I," he said, shaking his head, "was there when...

but I'll tell you two all about it. I should like to go over it all again before the inquest is resumed. Not that I've forgotten it," he went on, with a shudder. "I will never do that! It's all like a bad dream. You remember the Saturday night when all this began, Neale? If I had any idea of what was to happen during the next week....! That night, between half-past five and six o'clock, I was rung up on the telephone.

Greatly to my surprise I found the caller to be Frederick Hollis, an old schoolmate of mine, whom I had only seen once. I'll tell you when later since we were at school together. Hollis said he had come down specially from London to see me. He was at the Station Hotel, about to have some food, and would like to meet me later. He said he had reasons for not coming to the Bank House; he wished to meet me in some quiet place about the town. I told him to walk along the river-side at half-past seven, and I would meet him. And after I had dined I went out through my garden and orchard and met him coming along. I took him over the foot-bridge into the woods.

Hollis told me an extraordinary story, yet one which did not surprise me as much as you might think. I knew he was a solicitor in London. He said only a few days before this interview a lady friend of his had privately asked his advice. She was a Mrs. Lester, the widow of a man, an old friend of Hollis's who in his time made a very big fortune.

They had an only son, a lad who went into the Army, and into a crack cavalry regiment. The father made his son a handsome, but not sufficient allowance, the son, finding it impossible to get it increased, had recourse, after he was of age, to a London money-lender, named Godwin Markham, of Conduit Street, from whom, in course of time, he borrowed some seven or eight thousand pounds. Old Lester died, instead of leaving a handsome fortune to the son, he left every penny he had to his wife. The lad was pressed for repayment. Markham claimed some fifteen or sixteen thousand. Young Lester was obliged to tell his mother. She urged him to make terms for cash. Markham would not abate a penny of his claim. So Mrs. Lester called in Frederick Hollis and asked his advice. At his suggestion she gave him a check for ten thousand pounds: he was to see Markham and endeavor to get a settlement for that sum. The day before he came down to Scarnham, Friday Hollis did two things. He got young Lester to come up to town and tell him the exact particulars of his financial dealings with Godwin Markham. Primed with these, and knowing the demand was extortionate, he went, alone, to Markham's office in Conduit Street. Markham was away, but Hollis saw the manager, a man named Stipp. He saw something more, too. On Stipp's mantelpiece he saw a portrait which he recognized immediately as one of Gabriel Chestermarke. Now, you want to know how Hollis knew Gabriel Chestermarke.

In this way: I told you just now Hollis and I had only met once since our school-days. Some few years ago I think the year before you came into the bank, Neale, Hollis came up North on a holiday. He was a bit of an archaeologist; he was looking round the old towns, and he took Scarnham in his itinerary. Knowing an old schoolmate of his was manager at Chestermarke's Bank in Scarnham, he called in to see me. He and I lunched together at the Scarnham Arms. I showed him round the town a bit, after bank hours. And as we were standing in the upper-room window of the Arms, Gabriel Chestermarke came out of the bank and stood talking to some person in the Market-Place for a while.

I drew Hollis's attention to him, and asked, if he had ever seen a more remarkable and striking countenance? He answered it was one which, once seen, would not readily be forgotten. And he had not forgotten it once he saw the portrait at Markham's office he knew very well it was extremely unlikely so noticeable a man as Gabriel Chestermarke could have a double. Now, Hollis was a sharp fellow. He immediately began to suspect things. He talked awhile with Stipp, and contrived to find out the portrait over the mantelpiece was of Godwin Markham. He also found out Mr. Godwin Markham was rarely to be found at his office, there was no such thing as daily, or even weekly attendance there by him. And after mutual desires the Lester affair should be satisfactorily settled, but without telling Stipp anything about the ten thousand pounds, he left the office with a promise to call a few days later. Next day, certain of what he had discovered, Hollis came down to see me, and told me all that I have just told you. It did not surprise me as much as you would think. I knew for a great many years Gabriel had spent practically half his time in London.

I had always felt sure he had a finger in some business there, and I naturally concluded he had some sort of a *pied-à-terre* in London as well. One fact had always struck me as peculiar, he never allowed letters to be sent on to him from Scarnham to London. Anything that required his personal attention had to await his return. So when I heard all that Hollis had to tell, I was not so greatly astonished. In fact, the one thing that immediately occupied my thoughts was Joseph also concerned in the Godwin Markham money-lending business? He, too, was constantly away in London or believed to be so. He, too, never had letters sent on to him. Taking everything into consideration, I came to the conclusion Joseph was in all probability his uncle's partner in the Conduit Street concern, just as he was in the bank at home.

Hollis and I walked about the paths in the wood for some time, discussing this affair. I asked at last what he proposed to do. He inquired if I thought the Chestermarke's would be keen about preserving their secret. I replied in my opinion, seeing they were highly respectable country-town bankers, chiefly doing business with ultra-respectable folk, they would be very sorry indeed to have it come out they were also money-lenders in London, and evidently very extortionate ones. Hollis then said that was his own opinion, and it would influence the line he proposed to take. He said he had a check in his pocket, already made out for ten thousand pounds, and only requiring filling up with the names of payee and drawer. He would like to see Gabriel, tell him what he had discovered, offer him the check in full satisfaction of young Lester's liabilities to the Markham concern, and hint plainly if his offer of it was not accepted, he would take steps which would show Gabriel Chestermarke and Godwin Markham were one and the same person.

Now, I had no objection to this. I had not told you of it, Neale, but I had already determined to resign my position as manager at Chestermarke's. I had grown tired of it. I was going to resign as soon as I returned from my holiday. So I assented to Hollis's proposal, and offered to accompany him to the Warren. I don't mind admitting I was a little, perhaps a good deal eager to see how Gabriel would behave when he discovered his double dealing was found out and known to me. We therefore set off across Ellersdeane Hollow. I have been told while lying here some of you found the pipe which you, Betty, gave me last Christmas, lying near the old tower quite right. I lost it there that night, as I was showing Hollis the view, in the moonlight, from the top of the crags. I meant to pick it up as we returned, but what happened put it completely out of my mind. Hollis and I crossed the moor and the high road and went into the little lane, or carriage-drive, which leads to the Warren. Half-way down it we met Joseph.

He was coming away from the Warren from the garden. He, of course, wanted to know if we were going to see his uncle. I told him my companion, Mr. Frederick Hollis, a London solicitor, had come specially from town to see Gabriel Chestermarke, and being an old friend of mine, he had first come to see me. Joseph therefore said we were too late to find his uncle at home. Gabriel, he went on, had been suffering terribly from insomnia, and, by his doctor's advice, he was trying the effect of a long solitary walk every night before going to bed, and he had just started out over the moor at the back of his house. Turning to Hollis, he asked if he could do anything, was his visit about banking business?

Now I determined to settle at once the question as to Joseph's participation in the affairs of the Conduit Street concern. Before Hollis could reply, I spoke. I said, 'Mr. Hollis wishes to see your uncle on the affairs of Lieutenant Lester and the Godwin Markham loans.' I watched Joseph closely. The moonlight was full on his face. He started a little. And he gave me a swift, queer look which was gone as quickly as it came, it meant 'So you know!' Then he answered in quite an assured, off-hand manner, 'Oh, I know all about that, of course! I can deal with it as well as my uncle could. Come back across the moor to my house we'll have a drink, and a cigar, and talk it over with Mr. Hollis.'

I nudged Hollis's arm, and we turned back with Joseph towards Scarnham, crossing the Hollow in another direction, by a track which leads straight from a point exactly opposite the Warren to the foot of Scarnham Bridge, near the wall of Joseph's house. It is not a very long way, half an hour's sharp walk. We did not begin talking business as a matter of fact, Hollis began talking about the curious nature of that patch of moorland and about the old lead-mines. And when we were nearly half-way, the affair happened which, I suppose, led to all that has happened since. It gave Joseph an opening. Having lost my pipe, and being now going in a different direction from that necessary to recover it, I had nothing to smoke. Joseph offered me a cigar. He opened his case. I was taking a cigar from it when Hollis stepped aside to one of the old shafts which stood close by, and resting his hands on the parapet leaned over the coping, either to look down or to drop something down. Before we had grasped what he was doing, certainly before either of us could cry out and warn him, the parapet completely collapsed before him and he disappeared into the mine! He was gone in a second with just one scream.

And after that we heard nothing. We hurried to the place and got as near as we dared. Joseph dropped on his hands and knees, and peered over and listened. There was not a sound except the occasional dropping of loosened pebbles. And we both knew in that drop of seventy or eighty feet, Hollis must certainly have met his death. We hastened away to the town to summon assistance.

I don't think we had any very clear ideas, except to tell the police, and to see if we could get one of the fire brigade men to go down. I was in a dreadful state about the affair. I felt as though some blame attached to me. By the time we reached the bridge I felt like fainting. And Joseph suggested we should go in through his garden door to his workshop he had some brandy there, he said it would revive me. He took me in, up the garden, and into the workshop. I dropped down on a couch he had there, feeling very ill. He went to a side table, mixed something which looked and tasted like brandy and soda, brought it to me, and bade me drink it right off. I did so and within I should say a minute, I knew nothing more.

The next I knew I awoke in pitch darkness, feeling very ill. It was some little time before I could gather my wits together. Then I remembered what had happened. I felt about, I was lying on what appeared to be a couch or small bed, covered with rugs. But there was something strange apart from the darkness and the silence. Then I discovered I was chained...chained round my waist, and the chain had other chains attached to it. I felt along one of them, then along the other, they terminated in rings in a wall.

I can't tell you what I felt until daylight came, I knew however, I was at Joseph' perhaps at Gabriel's mercy. I had discovered their secret. Hollis was out of the way, but what were they going to do with me? Oddly enough, though I had always had a secret dislike of Gabriel, and even some sort of fear of him, believing him to be a cruel and implacable man, it was Joseph that I now feared. It was he who had drugged and trapped me without a doubt. Why? Then I remembered something else. I had told Joseph, but not Gabriel about my temporary custody of Lady Ellersdeane's jewels, and he knew where they were safely deposited at the bank, in a certain small safe in the strong room, of which he had a duplicate key. I found myself when the light came in a small room, or cell, in which was a bed, a table, a chair, a dressing-table, evidently a retreat for Joseph when he was working in his laboratory at night. But I soon saw it was also a strong room. I could hear nothing, the silence was terrible. And eventually so was my hunger. I could rise, I could even pace about a little, but there was no food there and no water.

I don't know how long it was, nor when it was, Joseph came. But when he came, he brought his true character with him. I could not have believed any human being could be so callous, so brutal, so coldly indifferent to another's sufferings. I thought as I listened to him of all I had heard about that ancestor of his who had killed a man in cold blood in the old house at the bank and I knew Joseph would kill me with no more compunction, and no less, than he would show in crushing a beetle that crossed his path.

His cruelty came out in his frankness. He told me plainly he had me in his power. Nobody knew where I was, nobody could get to know. His uncle knew nothing of the Hollis affair, no one knew. No one would be told. His uncle, moreover, believed I had run away with convertible securities and Lady Ellersdeane's jewels, he, would take care that he and everybody should continue to think so. And then he told me cynically he had helped himself to the missing securities and to the jewels as well. The event of Saturday night, he said, had just given him the chance he wanted, and in a few days he would be out of this country and in another, where his great talent as a chemist and an inventor would be valued and put to grand use. But he was not going empty-handed, not he! He was going with as much as ever he could rake together. And it was on that first occasion he told me what he wanted of me. You know, Neale, I am trustee for two or three families in this town. Joseph knew I held certain securities, deposited in a private safe of mine at the bank which could be converted into cash in, say, London, at an hour's notice. He had already helped himself to them, and had prepared a document which only needed my signature to enable him to deal with them. That signature would have put nearly a quarter of a million into his pocket.

He used every endeavor to make me sign the paper which he brought. He said if I would sign, he would leave an ample supply of the best food and drink within my reach, and I should be released within thirty-six hours, by which time he would be out of England. When I steadily refused he had recourse to cruelty. Twice he beat me severely with a dog-whip; another time he assaulted me with hands and feet, like a madman. And then, when he found physical violence was no good, he told me he would slowly starve me to death. But he was doing that all along. The first three days I had nothing but a little soup and dry bread, the remaining part of the time, nothing but dry bread. And during the last two days, I knew there was something in that bread which sent me off into long, continued periods of absolute unconsciousness. And I was glad! That's all. You know the rest better than I do. I don't know yet how that explosion came about. He had been in to me only a few minutes before it happened, badgering me again to sign that authority. And I felt myself weakening. Flesh and blood were alike at their end of endurance. Then it came! And as I say, that's all, but there's one thing I wanted to ask you. Have those jewels been found?"

"Yes!" replied Neale. "They were found all safe in a suit-case in Joseph's house, along with a lot of other valuables, money, securities, and so on. He was evidently about to be off; in fact, the luggage was already, and so was a cab which he'd ordered, and in which he was presumably going to Ellersdeane."

"And another thing," said Horbury, turning from one to the other, "I heard this morning you'd left the Bank, Neale. What are you going to do? What has happened?"

Betty looked at Neale warning, stooped over the invalid, kissed him, rose and took Neale's unwounded arm.

"No more talk today, Uncle John!" she commanded.

"Wait until tomorrow. Then if you're very good we shall perhaps tell you what is going to happen to...both of us!"

The End

Printed in Great Britain
by Amazon